THE WORLD'S CLASSICS

JOURNEY TO THE CENTRE
OF THE EARTH

JULES VERNE was born in Nantes in 1828, the eldest
of five children of a prosperous family claiming French,
Celtic, and Scottish ancestry. His early years were
happy apart from an unfulfilled passion for his cousin
Caroline. Literature always attracted him and while
taking a law degree in Paris he wrote a large number of
plays. His first book, however, about a journey to
Scotland, was not published during his lifetime. But
in 1862, *Cinq semaines en ballon* was accepted by
the publisher Hetzel, becoming an immediate success
worldwide—to be followed by *Journey to the Centre
of the Earth*, *Twenty Thousand Leagues under the Sea*,
Around the World in Eighty Days, and sixty other
volumes, covering the whole world (and below and
beyond). Verne himself travelled over three continents,
but suddenly sold his yacht in 1886, and shortly afterwards was shot at and permanently wounded by an
unbalanced nephew. Eight of the books appeared after
his death in 1905—but were in fact written partly by
his son, Michel.

DR WILLIAM BUTCHER is a lecturer in French. He
has studied at Warwick, Lancaster, London, and the
École Normale Supérieure, and has taught languages
and pure mathematics in Malaysia and France. As well
as numerous articles on French literature and natural
language processing, he has published *Mississippi Madness: Canoeing the Mississippi-Missouri* (1990) (in collaboration), *Verne's Journey to the Centre of the Self:
Space and Time in the 'Voyages extraordinaires'*
(1990), and a critical edition of Verne's *Humbug*
(1991). He is at present working on *Around the World
in Eighty Days* for the World's Classics.

THE WORLD'S CLASSICS

JULES VERNE

Journey to the
Centre of the Earth

Translated with an Introduction and Notes by
WILLIAM BUTCHER

Oxford   New York
OXFORD UNIVERSITY PRESS

Oxford University Press, Walton Street, Oxford OX2 6DP
Oxford New York
Athens Auckland Bangkok Bombay
Calcutta Cape Town Dar es Salaam Delhi
Florence Hong Kong Istanbul Karachi
Kuala Lumpur Madras Madrid Melbourne
Mexico City Nairobi Paris Singapore
Taipei Tokyo Toronto

and associated companies in
Berlin Ibadan

Oxford is a trade mark of Oxford University Press

British Library Cataloguing in Publication Data
Data available

Library of Congress Cataloging in Publication Data
Verne, Jules, 1828-1905.
[Voyage au centre de la terre. English]
Journey to the centre of the earth / Jules Verne: translated and with an
introduction and notes by William Butcher.
p. cm.—(World's classics)
Translation of: Voyage au centre de la terre.
Includes bibliographical references.
I. Butcher, William, 1951-   . II. Title. III. Title: Journey to
the centre of the earth. IV. Series.
PQ2469.V75E5 1992 843'.8—dc20 91-46759
ISBN 0-19-282900-9

5 7 9 10 8 6 4

Printed in Great Britain by
BPC Paperbacks Ltd
Aylesbury, Bucks

CONTENTS

CONTENTS

INTRODUCTION

IN France, Jules Verne is not the same person as in Britain. South of the Channel, Verne is recognized as an authentic, nineteenth-century writer with a proper set of Collected Works. Since the 1960s, any surprise, condescension, or irony at reading or studying the *Voyages extraordinaires* has disappeared, even among those who never actually buy any books. Balzac, Stendhal, Verne, Zola: the odd man out, the least integrated into Gallic national culture, is the Italianate Stendhal.

But in the English-speaking countries it is rare to meet adults who will admit to liking Verne. He is a children's author, a writer of science fiction, a poor stylist, at best responsible for films starring James Mason. His works may be fiction, but certainly don't count as literature. He is short-trousered, not really French, and has nothing to say about the 'human condition'.

One reason for such a disparity must be the generally atrocious English 'translations'. The overwhelming majority of books by 'Djools' Verne are leaden or wooden, and possibly infringe the Trade Descriptions Act. They have lost up to half their contents, but have gained instead some wonderful howlers. There is no equivalent here to Baudelaire's Poe or to Scott Moncrieff's Proust, with their textual 'thickness' and their sense of overall belonging.

Journey to the Centre of the Earth itself has been translated more than ten times, but the most recent dates from the 1960s. The best-known version is still the atrocious 1872 one, which rebaptizes Axel as Harry and Lidenbrock as Hardwigg, makes them both Scottish, and finishes each paragraph with at least one totally invented sentence.

But this novel hardly deserves such treatment. It was the first unqualified critical success of Verne's—and the first to be completed under the close monitoring of his publisher and mentor Hetzel. *Journey to the Centre of the Earth* is, above all, a brilliant piece of writing. It is an unparalleled entertainment, but one that also stands comparison with other literary works of the nineteenth century.

The plot can be quickly summarized: Professor Lidenbrock and his nephew Axel discover a document in a twelfth-century Icelandic book which, when deciphered, records the claim of a certain Arne Saknussemm to have gone down into the crater of Snæfells and reached the centre of the Earth. Lidenbrock decides to try this for himself and, dragging Axel away from his fiancée Gräuben, travels to Reykjavik and across Iceland. With the help of the stoical Hans, they find the crater and travel down through the geological layers of the past, experiencing various adventures. A long way down, they discover a huge cavern containing a large sea—plus various biological specimens, some dead and some very much alive. After trying to cross the sea, they discover a path down again, marked with Saknussemm's runic initials. But it is now blocked. They attempt to blow up the obstacle, while sheltering on their raft, but instead carry part of the sea down with them into the bowels of the Earth. They then start rising again; and end up riding a volcanic eruption, which throws them out on the slopes of Stromboli.

Journey to the Centre of the Earth prefigures many of the ideas of *Twenty Thousand Leagues under the Sea*, *Around the World in Eighty Days*, and *From the Earth to the Moon*. The mood is light-hearted—although hardly optimistic, for it contains tragic, obsessive, and sometimes morbid elements. There is even a love-element, of sorts. In this novel, more than elsewhere, Verne seems to let himself go, while at the same time drawing inspiration from many different sources. Before examining these systematically, it is useful to look at Verne's life and the *Extraordinary Journeys* as a whole.

Jules-Gabriel Verne was born in 1828, on an island in central Nantes in western France. His father had a successful law practice, and wrote occasional amateur verses. His mother's maiden name was Allotte de la Fuÿe, derived from a Scottish Allott who had emigrated in the fifteenth century to join Louis XI's Scottish Guard of archers and eventually been ennobled.

There have been over a dozen biographies of Verne, most notably by his niece Marguerite Allotte de la Fuÿe and his grandson Jean Jules-Verne. The former, however, is embellished and bowdlerized; and even the latter is a mixture of family legends and manuscript sources often readily accessible, including over 1,000 letters from Verne to his parents and publisher. About a dozen interviews are also known to exist, mostly with British and American journalists, plus a brief autobiographical piece, 'Memories of Childhood and Youth'. Lastly there is *Backwards into Britain*, a lightly fictionalized account of his visit to England and Scotland in 1859 with his friend Hignard.

A no doubt apocryphal story has Jules running away to sea at the age of 11 to fetch coral on the *Coralie* for his cousin Caroline. Her rejection of him, several years later, certainly seems to have left its mark on him. But otherwise his schooldays were unexceptional—apart from a passion for messing about on makeshift rafts on the River Loire with his brother Paul.

In 1847 Jules arrived in Paris to study law. For the next ten years, he lived in a succession of single rooms, sometimes with barely enough to eat. He devoted himself during this period to writing plays, at which he was moderately successful: of the total of approximately twenty-nine, seven had been performed or published by 1863, at least one of them with the help of Dumas *père*. In 1856 he met Honorine de Viane, a widow with two daughters, and married her a few months later.

The journey to Britain (his first outside France) had a major impact on him, especially Edinburgh and the Highlands. Although his visit was carefully written up (making it the first book Verne wrote), *Voyage en Angleterre et en Ecosse* was rejected by Hetzel—and lay hidden until 1989, when it was published and hailed as a brilliant piece of travel writing, and a vital document for understanding Verne. It was published in English in 1992.

In 1851–5, Verne published five short stories, in which

many of the themes and structures of his novels are already visible. Each one concerns the difficulty of getting things going (like Verne's own career). All are set in foreign parts, all are influenced by late Romanticism, and all finish more or less tragically.

In 1862, Hetzel accepted a book entitled *Five Weeks in a Balloon*. Within months, it had become a huge success, and led to a series of contracts for the next forty years. The principal aims of the collected works, at least according to Hetzel's immodest announcement, was 'to sum up all the geographical, geological, physical and astronomical knowledge amassed by modern science, and to rewrite the history of the universe'. At the age of 37, Verne acquired some security, even if the contracts were far from generous (the plays adapted from the novels proved much more lucrative). Starting in 1864 with *Journey to the Centre of the Earth*, one or two books duly appeared each year, eventually totalling sixty-three novels and eighteen short stories.

Verne continued to travel. In 1861 he had visited Norway and Denmark, again with Hignard, and in 1867 he sailed to America on the liner the *Great Eastern*. He also bought three yachts of successively greater size, on which he went back to Scotland and Scandinavia and visited North Africa. In 1872 the family moved permanently to Amiens. In 1886, for reasons which remain unknown, Verne sold his yacht and gave up travelling.

In 1861 his only child, Michel, had been born. He proved unruly, and was at one stage forcibly packed off to India as an apprentice pilot. In 1883, he eloped with a 16-year-old girl—but eventually divorced his first wife and re-married. He tried his hand at many careers, including scientific journalism and fiction-writing, one of his short stories being published in 1889 under his father's name.

After Verne's death in 1905, eight novels and three short stories were published in the series of *Extraordinary Journeys*. These works are subtly different from the previous ones; Michel publicly declared that he had prepared some of them for publication, but denied doing anything more. Only in 1978 was it proved, on the basis of the manuscripts, that he had made considerable changes, including writing whole chapters. Two-thirds of *The Survivors of the 'Jonathan'*, for instance, are his, including the many philosophico-political passages; plus perhaps even more of the masterpiece 'The Eternal Adam', set 20,000 years in the future.

The *Journeys* are characterized by simplicity, most evidently in their language, where clarity of thought and a flowing style produce ease of comprehension. Like the Parables or Aesop's Fables, though, there are layers of implicit meanings that often work against the surface level, making Verne an 'underground revolutionary'. Again, the subject matter ostensibly avoids what many have thought to be the primary aim of the novel, namely an account of psychological processes, especially relationships between men and women. In the best-known works, the depiction of society at large in its sociological, political, and historical aspects is not very much in evidence either; and nor is the transmission of pure ideas. Verne's works are concerned with physical, material existence, or, more simply, the interaction between people and things. Virtually all of them are situated in a definite time and place, often far away, with the journey a central element.

Genre fiction has a poor reputation. By placing writer *x* in genre *y*, the assumption is sometimes that he or she deals with matters tangential to personal experience and hence to the real aims of literature. But such an assumption would seem to be based on a double misapprehension. Direct personal experience does not exist as such; and there is no simple recounting in literature (or in life). Experience can only be talked about in relation to specific concerns, which normally implies some genre or another. To call Defoe an adventure writer, Swift a travel writer, the Brontës writers of sentimental fiction, or Shakespeare a crime and historical writer, may be true— but will shock, because we are accustomed to viewing great literature as transcending any particular pigeon-hole. In other words, a mistaken view holds literature to be genre-free and genre fiction to be literature-free.

In Verne's case, if a genre classification really is necessary, he falls into that of travel and adventure. But in no case can he be considered a science fiction writer. One good reason is that only about a third of the *Extraordinary Journeys* really involve any science; and another, that despite his futuristic reputation the events recounted nearly always happen just before the present. What is more, the science is not generally innovative or designed to change society. A significant number of the works do depend on a novel form of transport, whether underground, under water, or in the air or beyond. But Verne prefers 'intermediate technology'. His first vehicle is the balloon, invented long before he was writing, and which he in fact considered too high-tech, but the only way to get across Africa in 1862. His next vehicles are foot- and raft-power in *Journey to the Centre of the Earth* and sailing-ship and dog-sled in the greatly underestimated *Adventures of Captain Hatteras*. Even *Twenty Thousand Leagues under the Sea* is more about the ocean than submarines, more about Nemo than nuclear propulsion. *Around the World in Eighty Days* goes out of its way to avoid any technological extrapolation, reverting to elephants or wind-sled each time the railway fails.

The real thrust of Verne's works, their *raison d'être*, is to explore the globe. All the *Extraordinary Journeys in the Known and Unknown Worlds* (as Hetzel baptized them in 1866) deal with an 'elsewhere'. Even *Backwards into Britain* is a voyage of discovery: Verne describes his excitement at the idea of a myth-laden Caledonia, where every hill and street is redolent with memories—an excitement specifically literary and historical. True, he prefers the ship to Liverpool to be propeller-driven; and the scene where the train hurtles along the Scottish crags is most striking. But such enthusiasm at poetry in motion hardly makes him science fiction.

Verne's imagination works instead on an unusual sensitivity to the physical world, with the dimensions of space representing a constant interest (rarely 'outer space', but frequently 'inner'). Modern criticism has found a very wide variety of innovative elements in his treatment of the globe. The 'world-view' conveyed includes, in brief summary: an anthropomorphization of the Earth and a mechanization of the human, with the biological often acting as a go-between; an attempt at sensual 'totalization', an exhaustive knowledge (in the biblical sense) of the world; a constant scepticism; the undermining by juxtaposition, humour, and irony of any dogmatic view of existence; a metaphorization of everyday objects and ideas, which are then often re-metaphorized or even de-metaphorized; a distinctive rhythm, made up of repetitions, silences, minor and major keys, counterpoint, and slow movements leading up to explosive crescendos; and an innovative narrative technique, whether in the use of tense, person, point of view, voice, or structure.

Reading Verne nearly a century after his death, the abiding impression is that of a distinctive voice and a personal vision: of literary works that remain (or have become?) startlingly modern.

One problem for a detailed analysis of Verne is the sheer volume of his production. Nevertheless, his non-posthumous works have often been divided into three periods. The first dozen novels are self-confident in tone and structure. The second period deals with less 'prestigious' territories, and increasingly with social, political, and historical issues, in novels like *Mathias Sandorf* (1885), set in the Mediterranean, or *North against South* (1887), about the American Civil War. The final period often comes back to ideas treated in the first, but in ironic, derisory, or negative fashion: *Le Sphinx des glaces* (1897), for instance, designed to be a sequel to Poe's *Narrative of Arthur Gordon Pym of Nantucket*, or

Master of the World (1904), which makes the rebel Robur of *The Clipper of the Clouds* (1886) into a misanthropic destroyer.

Verne's imagination is fired by 'one-offs', by unique events. The Dark Continent, the poles, the interior of the Earth, the dark side of the moon, and the bottom of the ocean were unexplored when he began writing. In each case a central point then represented a maximum of exoticism, an *ultima Thule*, further-than-which-it-was-not-possible-to-go. But each could only be done once. Even from the beginning, as a consequence, Verne's travellers seem torn between a hasty extravagance and a thrifty reluctance: one eye on the efforts of real-life explorers and of the author's competitors in the fiction business, the other on spinning the series out for as long as possible. Then, once all the possibilities *have* been exhausted, all corners of the universe visited, the works 'have nowhere to go'.

Such a view of the plots has more than an element of truth. But it must be conjugated with the real nature of invention in the *Journeys*. The travelling carries much more weight than the arriving. A constantly expressed fear is that of a 'fiasco' on arrival in port; and hence a perpetual strategy, that of the most roundabout route— the 'heroic' method, as Lidenbrock puts it. Verne's writing is essentially about maximizing the potential of the blank areas on or off the maps, those non-historical, non-geographical, and sometimes non-spatial domains where his imagination can be given full rein. In the later works his inventiveness turns back on itself and becomes in some ways more creative. One's reaction to the different phases of the *Journeys* is therefore ultimately a matter of individual taste.

But in any case one of the aims of exploring the universe is in reality the search for traces of the past, much more attractive to Verne than any conceivable future. And clearly the exploration of the history of an individual, a species, or a world can be pursued almost indefinitely. Paradoxically, only the past is open-ended.

The three-way division is not therefore clear-cut, and the transitions are particularly evasive. The 'follow-up' to *Journey to the Centre of the Earth*, *The Child of the Cavern* (1877), is perhaps the last novel where some 'transcendent' discovery seems probable, where access to a life-giving mystery is at stake; but throughout the 1870s a mixture of anguished and good-humoured works appeared, from *Around the World in Eighty Days* (1872) via *The Boy Captain* (1879) to *The Tribulations of a Chinese Gentleman* (1879). The first one is a journey-to-end-all-journeys, an effortless summmum of all possible worldly travel—but is itself a repetition, as *Captain Grant's Children* (1865–7) had already gone round the world. *The Mysterious Island* (1874–5) is another culmination or cul-de-sac, for it is situated in the finite space of a small desert island.

It would be tempting, therefore, to say that 1875 must be approximately when 'something happened'. However, this would be to ignore the extraordinary *The Chancellor*, probably written in 1870. It was influenced by the notorious events on the Raft of the *Méduse*, when over three-quarters of the people who abandoned ship in shallow waters off the west coast of Africa failed to survive. Perhaps also echoing the Franco-Prussian War of 1870–1, Verne's novel is a horrific story of man's inhumanity to man, complete with murder and several varieties of cannibalism. It contains no science whatsoever; and precious little optimism. It is also a landmark in the history of French literature, being the first narrative novel to be written in the present tense—a clear sign of the breaking down of the old order.

Any tidy schema of Verne's works is thus difficult to sustain. Two of the rare constants are the pessimism, incipient even in the early fiction, and the retreat into the past.

This is where *Journey to the Centre of the Earth* comes in, both as the second of the *Journeys* to be published and because of its theme of descent into the most distant past.

We know very little about its inception. There are no surviving manuscripts or proofs, and virtually the only reference in the contemporary correspondence occurs in a letter of 12 August 1864. Since it is not mentioned in the contract of 1 January 1864, it was probably written between these two dates (the action of the novel itself runs up to March 1864 and beyond). At the time of writing, Verne was probably correcting the proofs of *The Adventures of Captain Hatteras* (hence the similarities: in each a liquid Ariadne's thread leads to an electric, illuminated sea, representing a return to paradise, but one protected by a volcanic fire).

One of the strands common to all the early books is Scotland. Verne's urge to go ever further north, abruptly curtailed after only three days in the Highlands in *Backwards into Britain*, re-emerges in both the *Journey* and *Hatteras*, each expedition being made to pass close to Scotland at least once. All three books confront the untamed wilderness, which for classically educated French people was northern barbarianism. In all three the harshness of life fits in with a reductionism, a *misérabilisme*, even a masochistic streak. All feature protagonists who structure their existence in terms of how far they have travelled. The bare Romantic landscapes in all three are suited to admiring the patterns of nature: an obsessively repeated phrase is 'criss-crossing meanders'. Linearity and networks, sensual curves and brutal straight lines, nature and artifice: this phrase, first used in describing railways in Liverpool, is perhaps emblematic of Verne's view of existence.

The publishing history of the *Journey* indicates another concern, for this novel is unique among Verne's in undergoing changes after publication in book form. Most of chapters 37–9 were added in the first large-octavo edition (1867). The reason for the insertion was undoubtedly developments in 1865 establishing prehistory as a major field of study. If the 1864 edition featured ancient seamonsters, the new pages go much further. They present the perfectly preserved body of a human being amongst remains dating from the Quaternary Era—and, what is more, a white human being. But they also feature a living herd of mastodons, together with an equally living herdsman: a 12-foot giant carrying a giant club. Although his existence is subsequently called into doubt, these chapters go well beyond the limits of plausibility Verne normally set himself.

Both in the new section and in the *Journey* as a whole, Verne drew from a wide range of sources, constructing a veritable meeting-place for the most varied literary and scientific authors.

There may be some slight influence from Dante's *Inferno*, the Icelandic legends about Hamlet (one of Shakespeare's sources), Chateaubriand (for some of the Romantic language), and Baudelaire ('To plunge to the chasm's bottom, Heaven or Hell, what difference?'). But the text often indicates more direct influences. Most obvious are Virgil's *Et quacumque viam dederit fortuna sequamur* (ch. 11), *facilis descensus Averni* (ch. 18), and *Immanis pecoris custos, immanior ipse!* (ch. 39) (see Explanatory Notes for translations). If the ascription is explicit in the first two cases, it may not have been needed in the third for readers brought up on the classics. More generally, the word *Averni* ('the Underworld') may indicate a source of inspiration in medieval ideas of an underground Hell.

An explicit reference is made to E. T. A. Hoffmann's character 'who lost his shadow' (ch. 29), an important feature in the underground cavern being the lack of shadows. But Hoffmann's *Mines of Falun* also enthusiastically describes underground passages walled with mineral riches and sparkling crystals of strange-sounding substances, with striking similarities to Verne's descriptions.

Verne quotes 'a British captain' (ch. 30) who thought that the Earth was 'a vast hollow sphere, inside which the air was kept luminous by reason of the great pressure, while two heavenly bodies, Pluto and Proserpina, traced their mysterious orbits'. The Captain (of infantry) John

Cleve Symmes was a real-life figure, in fact an American, and almost certainly the author of *Symzonia* (1820, under the pseudonym 'Captain Adam Seaborn'). 'Captain Synnes' is quoted in *Captain Hatteras* (ch. 24) as believing that access to the centre of the Earth was very slightly shorter via the Poles—and as having suggested such an expedition to the equally real-life scientists and explorers Davy, Humboldt, and Arago!

Edgar Allan Poe is perhaps the most important literary influence on the *Journey*. Verne published a long study of his works in April 1864, analysing in particular 'The Gold Bug' and *Arthur Gordon Pym*. The borrowings from Poe in the *Journey* include the word-puzzle and its solution, the leper scene, the mummified body, the fear of cataracts, the vertigo produced by 'high places' and the accompanying suicidal temptation—plus possibly the hurricane, the battle between the sea-monsters, and the 'bone-graveyard'.

The *Journey* also shares material with Dumas's *Isaac Laquédem* (1853). These include a retracing of man's past, an underground descent that leads to gigantic monsters and shady forests, a discovery of animal bones, volcanoes described with a similar vocabulary of 'bowels', 'mouths', and 'strata', the idea of air becoming denser than mercury, a hollow globe with two planets lighting it, lessons in geology and palaeontology, including 'zoophytes', hints at evolution, and so on. Some sort of connection between the two would therefore seem indisputable.

There are also disturbing similarities with George Sand's 'Laura: Voyage dans le cristal' (1864). This tale presents a young mineralogist, Alexis, who is in love with his cousin and dreams that he is visiting the inside of a 'geode'—a hollow stone covered in crystal—then that he is going to the North Pole, from where he explores the interior of the Earth. Significant parallels include a fall into a chasm, an uncle with a speech impediment and a quick temper, the increasing decisiveness of the hero, the lack of heat in the centre, difficult descents, and an encounter with pre-historic animals. Sand subsequently noted in her diary the uncanny resemblance. Both authors were published by

Hetzel, were close friends of his, and had read Figuier, an expert on volcanoes. Both had also read Charles Edmond, a friend of Sand's and the source of much of the voyage and the travel across Iceland in the *Journey*. But Verne's and Sand's works were published within weeks of each other, so a mystery remains as to how the similarities came about.

Verne was in addition sued for plagiarism by a Léon Delmas. Under the pseudonym René de Pont-Jest, he had published a short story called 'La Tête de Mimers' in the *Revue contemporaine* of September 1863. The hero is similarly German; the document causing the journey is found in an old book; it is written in runic characters; and it is a shadow that indicates where to look. The affair dragged on until a court case in 1877, which Verne won: but the similarities remain disturbing.

Among more scientific works which contributed to the *Journey* are those of Élie de Beaumont and Charles Sainte-Claire Deville, a friend of Verne's who had visited the crater of Stromboli as a specialist in seismic phenomena, particularly intermittent volcanoes. Boitard's *Paris avant les hommes* (1863) and Louis Figuier's *La Terre avant le déluge* (1863) have also been suggested for the prehistoric aspect; plus Ludvig Holberg's *Nicolai Klimii Iter Subterraneum, novam telluris theoriam . . .* (Copenhagen, 1741—translated as *Nicolas Klimius dans le monde souterrain*, 1741). This was subsequently republished in the same series as the anonymous *Relation of a Journey from the North Pole to the South Pole via the Centre of the World* (1721)—and certainly influenced Poe's 'A Descent into the Maelstrom'. Poe also seems to have drawn from it for the cataract ending of *Arthur Gordon Pym*.

What is common to many of the sources, in sum, is the medieval belief, not entirely dismissed in the nineteenth century, that the centre of the Earth could be reached via huge openings at the poles. Poe acts as a clearing-house for many of them; but Verne also seems to have drawn directly from a wide variety of literary and scientific

sources, although he then reworked them into a coherent
tale of his own.

The *Journey* has had in turn an influence on later
writers. It has been explicitly borrowed from by the
French writers Auguste Villiers de l'Isle Adam, Alfred
Jarry, and Boris Vian, but seems also to have influenced
Mark Twain (in *Tom Sawyer*), Arthur Conan Doyle (in
The Lost World), possibly the playwright Paul Claudel—
and the surrealist painter André Delvaux, obsessively.
Much of the work of the contemporary French writer
Michel Tournier is a homage to Verne, with one section
of his key novel *The Meteors* constituting a sustained
pastiche of the *Journey*—like all good pastiches, a re-
spectful and sophisticated dissection and an exaggeration
of some of the absurder sides to the tale.

Journey to the Centre of the Earth is unusual in its degree
of escape from contemporary (and indeed historical) reality. Verne is here in his element. He delights in the feel of
subterranean existence, with imagination, even dreams,
playing an important role. His writing is *volcanic*.

But only three-fifths of the *Journey* actually takes place
underground. Also, the 'to' of the title is misleading, for it
is not clear whether one can even reach the centre. Verne
works round the question of whether a great heat exists
without ever answering it. Saknussemm claimed to have
been there (although not necessarily to have come back);
but, as Axel points out, reliable ways of measuring depth
underground had not been invented at the time. *But*, as
Lidenbrock had remarked just before, one is weightless at
the centre, so . . .

The whole story contains in fact many more mysteries,
implausibilities, and ambivalences than Verne's positivistic
reputation allows. Quite apart from the doubt attached to
the scene of the mastodons and the giant herdsman, riding
an eruption on a raft of wood, even if fossilized, can
legitimately raise eyebrows. Even the route is not clear:
the tunnel discovered in the great cavern probably starts

from the *other* side of the Lidenbrock Sea, but the narrator repeatedly affirms the opposite.

Again, man's past is riddled with unsolved problems. Did man arrive relatively late in the scheme of things, as had generally been recognized by mid-nineteenth century? Did the human bodies discovered in the interior actually live there; and does this then re-establish man at the beginnings (*a*) down there and/or (*b*) up here? If so, what sort of man: the most highly evolved, comparable to modern Europeans, in the racist views current at the time; or a giant, a relative of the first man; or else some intermediate being?

Verne apparently dislikes all theories of evolution, for mainly humanistic but still partly religious reasons. But this is not the essential point: he raises questions, provides ambiguous signs, and then plays Axel off against Lidenbrock, modern science against old-fashioned natural philosophy. Ultimately he argues in this book that any overall conception can be destroyed by a single new find. It is things that count, not theories.

If the *Journey* itself leaves any certainties, they may not last. Probably at about this time, Verne wrote 'Humbug', in which a giant human skeleton is dug up in the United States, thus radically transforming evolutionary theories—but is then shown to be a hoax. Another short story, 'The Eternal Adam' (1910), suggests that civilizations inevitably expand and then go into terminal decline, so that any number have perhaps lived and died. Consequently man may have simply 'evolved' from his own degenerate forefathers—he may always have existed. But then again, what the story *shows*, as distinct from tells, is perhaps the opposite, that humanity may transmit wisdom down through the generations, so that it is not necessarily stuck in an eternal cycle after all. But in any case most or all of the story was written by Michel Verne. On the other hand, his ideas were very much drawn from his father's . . .

One should not, therefore, seek positive views on evolution in the *Journeys*. The attention paid to the question covers up gaps in knowledge rather than fills them in. Our interest, over a century on, lies more in *how* it is done than in the answers to the questions themselves.

One method Verne uses to sustain interest is to set Lidenbrock's erudition against Axel's *naïveté* and ignorance, providing a role-model for the reader. Dialogue is often employed, with Axel's simple questions sometimes, however, not having simple answers, thus allowing him to confound his uncle. Verne popularizes knowledge by means of models and comparisons, with frequent appeals to instinct and common sense. The personality clashes of the scholarly world, and particularly the drives of the individual scholars, further reduce the abstraction. In accordance with the contemporary usage—and that of the eighteenth century, which often models Verne's conceptions—a relatively homely language is used, of 'elastic', 'cracks', 'bones', or 'monsters'—with, however, learned words like 'Japhetic', 'Devonian', or 'subliming' thrown in for effect.

One apparently scientific example central to the novel is the time–space equivalence: by going down into the Earth, the heroes go back through the layers of past time. They leave the nineteenth century, pass through the successive geological ages, and become 'prehistoric' or 'fossilized'. Even the adverbs like 'soon' or 'after a while' play the game. The result is phrases like 'Creation had made obvious progress since the day before': in other words, Verne is playing on the reversing of time and the absurdity of interpreting Genesis literally. This time–space equivalence is, once again, a literary device: the plot and the narrative voice structure the science, rather than the other way round.

Another learned-looking device in the *Journey* is the large number of figures. Quite often they are erroneous—although not as frequently as the foreign words. Again, lists are frequently in evidence. Mostly composed of nouns, they incorporate material from varied sources, although Verne invariably adapts them to his own ends. The style is emphasized as much as the content, by means of careful selection, by placing in context, by emphasizing the immediate and dramatic features; but above all by using euphony, alliteration, analogy, and metaphorization.

Science thus becomes consistently subordinate to wider conceptions. Any body of organized knowledge is ultimately for Verne just a sub-genre of creative writing: the only all-embracing discourse that he allows. A few of the early reviewers misread Verne and assumed he was a scientist—but the more perceptive emphasized the plausibility and the quality of the writing. His science and knowledge are really just vehicles for highly personal conceptions of the world. As a literary endeavour, the work contains human truth: it examines all conventional wisdoms, producing more problems than solutions. It is made up of myths, metaphors, and a fair amount of mayhem.

Most of the ideas are mediated via the characters. Although the characterization is hardly conventional, it is quite sophisticated. The verbal and other foibles of the contrasting but complementary couple Lidenbrock—Axel make for a more complex relationship than many in Verne's works. Both characters employ the full resources of plays on words, repartee, interchange of position, understatement, exaggeration, and the taking of logical positions to absurd extremes.

The opening description of Lidenbrock in terms of his tics and eccentricities reveals the volcanic forces within him. He is an obsessive, a driven man, so much in a hurry that he crams double helpings into his mouth and pulls at plants and pushes at trains to make them go faster. The linear drive of his watchword 'Forward!' compels him on and then down, refusing all deviations or retreats, making him into 'the man of the perpendiculars'. Not that the portrait is entirely unsympathetic: the professor's heart is in the right place, if slightly difficult to find. He is energetic, courageous, competent, knowledgeable, and bears no malice—he is simply a little excitable, absent-minded, and narrow-sighted.

We often view his nephew from the outside, from an ironical distance, for Axel-the-narrator knows things that Axel-the-character does not. He is at first passive, lacking in character. His main impulse is to stay at home with Gräuben, and his main virtues are scepticism and self-knowledge, those of an unimpassioned observer. From the beginning, however, he also embodies spontaneity and hence true discovery and creativity. With time, a role-reversal occurs and many of the professor's characteristics and functions are transferred to him, including the passionate subjectivity. He is thus initiated into the adult world, making the partnership more or less equal. It is significant that Lidenbrock writes relatively dry scientific works, but Axel, even if he writes at his uncle's bidding, produces the more creative book that we end up holding in our hands.

Hans provides the perfect foil, governed by phlegm, rationality, cerebrality, and efficiency. The main barrier to understanding him is that he has no common language with Axel, so communication is virtually limited to nouns. Although an admirable and generous person, he demonstrates few human feelings; and although highly ingenious, he is uncreative. As a northerner and a hunter (and therefore a destroyer, albeit a pacific one), he lacks that vital spark: even direct application of ball-lightning cannot bring this perfect being to life. In sum, he is one of Verne's psychological limiting cases, an experiment in extremes. The great ancestor Saknussemm, in contrast, seems to embody many different traits: a northerner but achieving more than the nineteenth-century heroes combined; a writer of sorts; a misunderstood genius; and the explorer who unfairly benefits from getting there first, destroying the patch for ever after.

Verne's humour is applied to any pretension or artificiality in the characters, most simply by means of a juxtaposition with the hard facts—and with the hidden intentions of the person concerned. Networks of desire are thus revealed, particularly where the libido is involved. From the correspondence, we know that Verne had an unbridled sexual imagination. But since it cannot operate openly here, it is clothed in humour.

There is also a striking recurrent vocabulary of phrases like 'instinctive', 'automatic', and 'without thinking'. Even though the noun itself 'the unconscious' (*l'inconscient*) does not seem to have been used before the 1890s, Verne is clearly demonstrating an awareness of the underlying concept. In the chapters added in 1867, he mentions a William Carpenter, an expert on dredging the ocean depths and author of *Zoology ... and Chief Forms of Fossil Remains* (1857, reissued 1866) and *The Unconscious Action of the Brain* (1866–71). A man of such varied, and Vernian, interests may easily be the source of the innovative psychological terminology of the depths in the *Journey*.

Considerable energy is in fact both repressed and displayed by Axel and Lidenbrock—and by the author. The whole book is charged. Electricity acts as a convenient metaphor for sexual energy; horses have a field day; and hands play an important role throughout the book. So do reinforced staves, pens, knives, telescopes, trees, giant mushrooms, thick pillars, verticality in general, tubes, pockets, leather wallets, purses, and the goatskin bottle ('outre' from 'uterus'). The Earth itself is a blatant sexual object, with a rich vocabulary to describe the twin firm white peaks, pointed waves seething with fire, mouths wide open, gaping orifices, cavities, bays, fjords, gashes, and slits; but also the thrusting (and blocking) of the most varied penetrations, glows, eruptions, effusions, and discharges, as well as repeated instances of falling and sinking.

But Verne's originality may lie equally in his linking of these fixations with others: most bodily functions are also obsessively present in the Earth's bowels, including sweating, trembling, eating, digesting, elimination of waste matter, and pregnancy and childbirth. The sex is only part of a general view of the world as a reflection of the observer's own consciousness—and unconscious. Freud himself said that writers had most of the ideas before the scientists; whatever the truth of this, in the *Journey* we can certainly detect pre-Freudian views on the role of dreams and the libido in the subconscious mind.

How does the *Journey to the Centre of the Earth* fit in with the literary movements of the period? The question has not really been answered to date. One reason is the very variety of his production, extending over seventy years, making him the contemporary of both Charlotte Brontë and James Joyce. Equally important, Verne is *sui generis*.

One influence on the *Journeys* is undoubtedly the contemporary theatre, Verne's lifelong love. His attention to dialogue and care for timing and suspense, especially in the 'set scenes' and the ending, doubtless derive from this. But the novel is also under the spell of the Romantic literary movement. A brief list of features might include: a sense of melancholy, personal *angst*, or existential doubt; a tendency to flee society and search for consolation in nature; a 'poetic' use of language, particularly the use of adjectives, the imperfect tense, and long sentences; a search for the transcendental or absolute, values outside 'this world'; a fixation on time and the transitory nature of existence, producing an obsession with decay and death; and a retreat into the past, a search for the origins of the individual and the species. The sum of these tendencies means that the *Journey* cannot be excluded from the general orbit of late Romanticism.

But Verne is simultaneously a Realist. The *Journey* encompasses scepticism and reductionism, but also shares with Realism a preference for male characters (and virtues), a reluctance to indulge in unsubstantiated psychologism, a tendency to short, sharp, sometimes verbless sentences. The paradox, though, is that so much Realism in the externals leads to the opposite of realism in the mood: Verne's positivistic aspects culminate in the wildest longings and imaginings. The short sentences then highlight the long ones; the nouns, the adjectives. Opposites not only attract in Verne, but produce a pole-reversal, an inversion of signs—as most of the conditions of surface existence are inverted underground. The *Journey* proves that the most down-to-earth Realism can, despite the labels in the histories of literature, lead to the most high-blown Romanticism.

In a chronological course on literature, *Journey to the Centre of the Earth* falls between Stendhal's *Charterhouse of Parma* and Flaubert's *Sentimental Education*, between Dickens and Disraeli—and yet somehow appears more modern than these works. To describe it, the most appropriate terms may be those associated with the twentieth century. Verne participates in the Modernist movement, if by Modernism we mean an obsession with speed, with machines, a de-humanization, and an abstraction. In purely literary terms, the *Journey* must be considered modern because of its anticipation of the twentieth century's use of self-awareness or 'self-consciousness' at all levels: the creation of self-reflecting structures, devices turned back on themselves, symbols that symbolize their own existence, a text that exposes itself, lays bare its own innards.

The word 'Averni', as one example, contains the letters *v*, *e*, *r*, *n*. 'Might he not have inserted his name at some point in the manuscript?' (ch. 3). The novel is generated by the personal anagram, not once but repeatedly. Thus the text-within-the-text word-puzzle that starts everything off is 'à l'ENVERs' ('backwards'); the compass that determines all movements underground is 'RENVErsée' ('reversed'); at the centre is a vast 'caVERNE'; within it movements are governed by the helm ('gouVERNail'); and the girl at the centre of the quest is 'ViRlaNdaisE' ('from Virland'). The author lays bare his own building-blocks, which in turn refer to their own reversal of the letters constituting the novel. Verne plays hide-and-seek, blatantly concealing himself at the centre of his text.

Another example of the textual self-reference is the

change of narration in chapters 32–5, where Axel's 'ship's log' replaces the after-the-event narration. One of the functions of this 'journal' is to transcribe indications of time and weather, and so to convey the monotony of a sea-journey, where there is no landscape to observe (a paradox in the interior of the Earth). Another is to add to the suspense, for by definition the narrator–character cannot know what is going to happen. The 'ship's log' also enables convenient gaps to be inserted in the story when Axel is unconscious. But it is above all a stylistic experiment.

Axel's account is in the present tense: despite appearances, however, it is not really a 'log-book', 'journal', or 'diary', but a complex narration. In fact Axel gives no general indication *when* he is writing, except the contradictory 'daily . . . as it were at the dictation of events' (ch. 32). French commentators have assumed that the events are meant to be transcribed instantaneously—and so have argued that writing notes in a darkening storm is implausible. In fact the lengthy dream and the extended conversations can much less easily have been written down at the time. But in any case Axel sometimes self-referentially *reports* his own *writing*, whether of a note to Hans or of his own 'ship's log'—and the writing must precede the writing of the writing! The present tense, then, is very far from indicating either an authentic diary or a simultaneity of events and narration.

One consequence is on the description of the sea-monsters. By using the present tense, the problem of whether we are in past or present time is avoided. The nineteenth century has become authentically prehistoric. There are also further surprising consequences on notions of self-reference and intentionality. Thus in the traditional mode of narration there is a distinction between *j'allais* ('I was going to') and *j'allai* ('I moved to . . .'), between subjective intention and objective action. But in Verne's present, the two are collapsed down to *je vais* (both 'I am going to' and 'I move to . . .'). In sum, the pretence of a naive transcription cannot be sustained. There is a temporal distance between the events and the text. The transparency and self-referentiality of the present tense, the equivalence between doing and reporting, the short-circuiting of the normal process of narration, are only apparent. There is a narrator lurking in the shadows. The keeper of the 'log-book' is just a character in his own story after all.

The reader who expects *Journey to the Centre of the Earth* to be simple is therefore in for a surprise. This novel might be described as a virtuoso exercise in 'eversion': the complex topological process of turning a body inside out. Things are not what they seem. Verne takes a perverse pleasure in creating as many trails as possible—and diversions to throw the pursuants off. It is almost as if he foresaw a scholarly edition of the *Journey*, with the full apparatus of introduction and endnotes attempting to explain what is going on. Not bad for a short-trousered writer without style or substance!

I would like to thank Angela Brown and Katy Randle for their help with the preparation of the manuscript.

ortal distance between the events and the text. The transparency and self-referentiality of the present tense, the
equivalence between doing and reporting, the short-
circuiting of the normal process of narration, are only
apparent. There is a narrator figuring in the shadows. The
keeper of the 'log-book' is here a character in his own
story after all.

The reader who expects Journey to the Centre of the Earth
to be simple is therefore in for a surprise. This novel might
be described as a virtuoso exercise in 'eversion': the complex topological process of turning a body inside out.
Things are not what they seem. Verne takes a perverse
pleasure in creating as many trails as possible—and diversions to throw the pursuers off in as almost as if he
foresaw a scholarly edition of the journey, with the full
apparatus of introduction and endnotes attempting to
explain what is going on. Nor for bed for a short onward
water without style or substance.

I would like to thank Angela Brown and Kay Randles for
their help with the preparation of the manuscript.

NOTE ON THE TRANSLATION

THE text used for the present edition is based on the 1867 one used in modern French editions (Livre de Poche, Garnier-Flammarion, Rencontre, Hachette). The first edition (18mo) appeared on 25 November 1864, and was unillustrated. As was usual, the illustrations were added only with the first large-octavo edition (1867) (the seventh edition). But *Journey to the Centre of the Earth* is unique in that Verne used this opportunity to add a new section, chapters 37–9 (pp. 177–87 in the present text). What is also very unusual is that the novel was not published first in serial form (Hetzel only launched the *Magasin d'éducation et de récréation* in 1864).

The present translation is an entirely new one, benefiting from the most recent scholarship on Verne. It aims to be faithful to the original (including the absence of chapter titles and the retention of the mock-learned footnotes). The use of phrases like 'he said' and 'he replied', of exclamation marks, and of semicolons in ternary sentences has, however, been slightly reduced.

In the early works Verne uses pre-Revolutionary measures like *pieds*, *lignes* (one-twelfth of an inch), *lieues*, and *toises* ('fathoms'). Throughout this edition, British feet (about 7 per cent smaller than the French ones), miles (about 10 per cent larger), and so on will be used. A few of Verne's figures have consequently had to be slightly adjusted.

Foreign-language words and names are erratic in the *Voyages extraordinaires*, sometimes even internally inconsistent. These have normally been corrected (for instance 'Snæfells' for 'Sneffels'). Some of Verne's learned terms do not seem authentic, whether through error or deliberate mystification. In such cases an Anglicized equivalent is given, but usually an endnote indicates its absence from the dictionaries.

A recurrent problem in translating Verne is his delight in reactivating fixed expressions, by subtly altering them or by implying a literal meaning. In such cases, the aim has been to retain the ambiguity or else find a happy medium between the two possible senses.

In this edition, unlike previous English translations, the present tense has been retained throughout the 'log-book' section (chs. 32–5).

SELECT BIBLIOGRAPHY

AMONGST the modern French editions, Livre de Poche, with forty-four of the seventy-odd volumes, has been the usual reference edition. In 1988, however, Hachette completed publication of the *Voyages extraordinaires* at a very reasonable price. Michel de l'Ormeraie and Rencontre (reprinted by Edito-Service) are the only other complete editions since the original Hetzel one.

The only British scholarly books on Verne to date are: Andrew Martin's *The Mask of the Prophet: The Extraordinary Fictions of Jules Verne* (Oxford University Press, 1990) and William Butcher's *Verne's Journey to the Centre of the Self: Space and Time in the 'Voyages extraordinaires'* (Macmillan, 1990). Arthur B. Evans's *Jules Verne Rediscovered: Didacticism and the Scientific Novel* (New York, Greenwood Press, 1988) is also worth consulting.

Among the French critics, François Raymond and Daniel Compère's *Le Développement des études sur Jules Verne* (Minard (Archives des Lettres Modernes), 1976) is still the most readable introduction to 'Vernian Studies'. There are many stimulating collections of articles, notably: *L'Herne: Jules Verne*, ed. P. A. Touttain (L'Herne, 1974), *Colloque de Cerisy: Jules Verne et les sciences humaines*, ed. François Raymond and Simone Vierne (Union générale d'éditions, 1979), the six volumes of the Minard (Lettres Modernes) series on Verne, especially *Machines et imaginaire* (1980) and *Texte, image, spectacle* (1983), and *Modernités de Jules Verne*, ed. Jean Bessière (Presses Universitaires de France, 1988).

The following volumes are also useful: Jean Chesneaux, *Une Lecture politique de Jules Verne* (Maspero, 1971, 1982), translated as *The Political and Social Ideas of Jules Verne* (Thames and Hudson, 1972), Simone Vierne, *Jules Verne* (Balland (Phares), 1986), Alain Froidefond, *Voyages au centre de l'horloge: Essai sur un texte-genèse, 'Maître Zacharius'* (Minard, 1988), and Olivier Dumas, *Jules Verne* (Lyon, La Manufacture, 1988).

The best biography is Jean Jules-Verne, *Jules Verne* (Hachette, 1973), translated and adapted by Roger Greaves as *Jules Verne: A Biography* (MacDonald and Jane's, 1976). But there are also Charles-Noël Martin, *La vie et l'œuvre de Jules Verne* (Michel de l'Ormeraie, 1978) and Marc Soriano, *Jules Verne (le cas Verne)* (Julliard, 1978).

Studies specifically on *Journey to the Centre of the Earth* (and which provided some of the material on which the Introduction to this volume is based) include the well-organized Daniel Compère, *Un Voyage imaginaire de Jules Verne: Voyage au centre de la Terre* (Minard (Archives Jules Verne), 1977), Christian Chelebourg, 'Le Paradis des fossiles', pp. 213–27, in *Modernités de Jules Verne*, and Andrew Martin, *The Knowledge of Ignorance: From Genesis to Jules Verne* (Cambridge University Press, 1985), pp. 137–41 and *passim* plus the relevant sections of Butcher, Jules-Verne, Vierne and of the L'Herne, Minard (Lettres Modernes), and Presses Universitaires de France volumes.

[All places of publication are London or Paris unless otherwise indicated.]

A CHRONOLOGY OF
JULES VERNE

1828   8 February: birth of Jules Verne, on the Ile Feydeau in Nantes, to Pierre Verne, a lawyer and son and grandson of lawyers, and Sophie, née Allotte de la Fuÿe, from a military line.

1829   Birth of brother, Paul, later a naval officer, but who retired in 1859 and became a stockbroker; followed by those of sisters Anna (1836), Mathilde (1839), and Marie (1842).

1834–8   Goes to school: the teacher, Mme Sambain, is the widow of a sea-captain, whose return she is still waiting for.

1838–41   Collège Saint-Stanislas. Performs well in geography, translation from Greek and Latin, and singing.

1841–6   Goes to Petit Séminaire, then to Lycée Royal de Nantes. Above average; probably won a prize in geography. Passes *baccalauréat* without difficulty. Writes short pieces in prose.

1847   Studies law in Paris: at this time his cousin, Caroline Tronson, with whom he has been unhappily in love for several years, is getting engaged. Writes a play called *Alexandre VI*.

1848   June: revolution in Paris. Verne is present at the July disturbances. He continues his law studies, sharing a room at 24 Rue de l'Ancienne-Comédie. His uncle Châteaubourg introduces him into literary *salons*. Meets writers Alexandre Dumas *père* and *fils*. Writes plays probably including *La Conspiration des poudres*.

1849   Passes law degree. Father allows him to stay on in Paris. Writes more plays.

1850   12 June: his one-act comedy *Les Pailles rompues* runs for twelve nights at Dumas's Théâtre Historique, and is published.

1851   Publishes short stories 'Les Premiers navires de la Marine mexicaine' and 'Un Voyage en ballon'.

1852–5 Becomes secretary at Théâtre Lyrique. Publishes 'Martin Paz', 'Maître Zacharius', 'Un Hivernage dans les glaces', and the play *Les Châteaux en Californie* in collaboration with Pitre-Chevalier. His operette *Le Colin-maillard*, written with Michel Carré, is performed to music by Hignard.

1856   20 May: goes to a wedding in Amiens, and meets a young widow with two children, Honorine de Viane.

1857   10 January: marries Honorine, becomes a stock-broker in Paris, and moves house several times.

1859–60 Visits Scotland with Hignard. Writes *Voyage en Angleterre et en Ecosse*.

1861   Goes to Norway and Denmark with Hignard.
        3 August: birth of only child, Michel.

1863   31 January: *Cinq semaines en ballon* appears, three months after first submission to publisher Jules Hetzel, and is immediate success.

1864   Publication of 'Edgar Poe et ses œuvres', *Voyages et aventures du capitaine Hatteras* and *Voyage au centre de la Terre*. (All dates are those of beginning of first publication, usually in serial form.) Gives up his unsuccessful stockbroker practice, and moves to Auteuil.

1865   *De la Terre à la Lune* and *Les Enfants du capitaine Grant*. Death of Mme Estelle Duchêne of Asnières, close friend of Verne's.

1867   16 March: goes with brother Paul to Liverpool, thence on *Great Eastern* to United States.

1868   Buys a boat, *Saint-Michel*. Visits London.

1869   Rents a house in Amiens. *Vingt mille lieues sous les mers* and *Autour de la Lune*.

1870   Outbreak of Franco-Prussian War: Verne is coast-guard at Le Crotoy (Somme).

1871   3 November: father dies.

1872   Moves to 44 Boulevard Longueville, Amiens; be-comes member of Académie d'Amiens. *Le Tour du monde en quatre-vingts jours*.

1874　　*Le Docteur Ox*, *L'Ile mystérieuse* and *Le Chancellor*. Begins collaboration with Adolphe d'Ennery on stage adaptation of novels (*Le Tour du monde en 80 jours*, performed 1874, *Les Enfants du capitaine Grant*, 1878, *Michel Strogoff*, 1880: all highly successful).

1876–7　*Michel Strogoff*, *Hector Servadac* and *Les Indes noires*. Buys second, then third boat, *Saint-Michel II* and *III*. Gives huge fancy-dress ball. Wife very seriously ill, but recovers.

1878　　June–August: sails to Lisbon and Algiers.

1879–80　*Les Cinq cents millions de la Bégum*, *Les Tribulations d'un Chinois en Chine*, and *La Maison à vapeur*. Michel, who had caused problems throughout his childhood, marries an actress, despite the opposition of his father. Verne sails to Norway, Ireland, and Scotland, including Edinburgh and probably the Hebrides.

1881　　*La Jangada*. Sails to Rotterdam and Copenhagen.

1882　　October: moves to a larger house at 2 Rue Charles-Dubois, Amiens. *Le Rayon vert*.

1883–4　Michel abducts a minor, Jeanne. Has two children by her within eleven months. Divorces, and marries her. *Kéraban-le-têtu*.

　　　　Verne leaves with wife for grand tour of Mediterranean, but cuts it short. On the way back, is probably received in private audience by Pope Leon XIII.

1885　　8 March: another large fancy-dress ball. *Mathias Sandorf*.

1886　　*Robur-le-conquérant*.
　　　　15 February: sells *Saint-Michel III*.
　　　　9 March: his nephew Gaston, mentally ill, asks for money to travel to England. Verne refuses, and the nephew fires at him twice, making him lame for life.
　　　　17 March: Hetzel dies.

1887　　15 February: mother dies.

1888　　Is elected local councillor on a Republican list. For next fifteen years attends council meetings, administrates theatre and fairs, opens Municipal Circus (1889), and gives public talks.

1889   *Sans dessus dessous* and 'In the Year 2889' (published in New York: signed Jules Verne but written by Michel, and then either translated or revised by an English-speaker).

1890   Stomach problems.

1892   *Le Château des Carpathes.* Pays debts for Michel.

1895   *L'Ile à hélice,* apparently the first novel written in a European language in the present tense and the third person.

1896–7 *Face au drapeau* and *Le Sphinx des glaces.* Sued by chemist Turpin, inventor of melinite, who recognizes himself in the former novel. Successfully defended by Raymond Poincaré, future President of France. Health deteriorates.
        27 August: brother dies.

1899   Dreyfus Affair: Verne is anti-Dreyfusard, but approves of the case being reviewed.

1900   Moves back into 44 Boulevard Longueville. Sight weakens (cataract).

1901   *Le Village aérien.*

1904   *Maître du monde.*

1905   17 March: falls seriously ill with diabetes.
        24 March: dies, and is subsequently buried in Amiens.

1905–14 On his death, *L'Invasion de la mer* and *Le Phare du bout du monde* are in the process of publication. Michel takes responsibility for the remaining manuscripts, and publishes *Le Volcan d'or* (1906), *L'Agence Thompson and Co.* (1907), *La Chasse au météore* (1908), *Le Pilote du Danube* (1908), *Les Naufragés du 'Jonathan'* (1909), *Le Secret de Wilhelm Storitz* (1910), *Hier et demain* (short stories, including 'L'Éternel Adam') (1910), and *L'Étonnante aventure de la mission Barsac* (1914). In 1978, it is proved that Michel in fact wrote considerable sections of these works, and in 1985–9 the original (i.e. Jules's) versions of most of them are published.

Journey to the Centre of the Earth

1

ON 24 May 1863, a Sunday, my uncle, Professor Lidenbrock,* came rushing back towards his little house at No. 19 Königstrasse, one of the oldest streets in the historic part of Hamburg.

Martha the maid must have thought she was running very late, for dinner had hardly begun to simmer on the kitchen range.

'H'm,' I said to myself. 'If my uncle is hungry, he'll shout out his annoyance, for he is the most impatient of men.'

'Professor Lidenbrock here already!' Martha exclaimed in amazement, slightly opening the dining-room door.

'Yes, indeed. But dinner has every right not to be cooked, for it's not two o'clock yet. It's only just struck the half-hour on St Michael's.'

'Then why has Professor Lidenbrock come back?'

'Presumably he will tell us.'

'Here he is: I'm off, Master Axel.* You *will* make him see reason, won't you?'

And the good Martha disappeared back into her culinary laboratory.

I remained alone. But to make the worst-tempered of professors see reason did not seem possible, given my slightly indecisive character. So I was getting ready for a prudent retreat to my little bedroom at the top of the house, when the front-door groaned on its hinges. Large feet made the wooden staircase creak, and the master of the house came through the dining-room and burst into his study.

On his hurried way through, though, he had thrown his nutcracker-head cane in the corner, his broad hat brushed up the wrong way on the table, and the ringing words to his nephew:

'Axel, I'm here!'

I hadn't had time to move before the professor shouted again, in a most impatient voice:

'We-ell? Are you not here yet?'

I rushed into my formidable master's study.

Otto Lidenbrock was not a bad man, I will gladly concede. But unless changes happen to him, which is highly unlikely, he will die a terrible eccentric.

He was a professor at the Johanneum,* and gave a course on mineralogy, during which he normally got angry at least once or twice. Not that he was worried whether his students were assiduous at his lectures, or whether they paid attention, or whether they were successful later: he hardly bothered about these details. He lectured 'subjectively', to use the expression from German philosophy, for himself and not for others. He was a learned egoist and a selfish scholar, a well of science whose handle groaned whenever someone wanted to draw something out of it: in a word, a miser.

In Germany there are one or two professors like this.

Unfortunately my uncle suffered from a slight pronunciation problem, if not in private at least when speaking in public: a regrettable handicap for an orator. Thus, during his demonstrations at the Johanneum, often the professor would stop short. He would struggle with a recalcitrant word which his mouth refused to pronounce, one of those words which resist, swell up, and end up coming out in the unscientific form of a swear-word. Then he would get very angry.

Now, in mineralogy, there are many learned words, half-Greek, half-Latin, and always difficult to pronounce, many unpolished terms that would scorch a poet's lips. I do not wish to criticize this science. Far from it. But when one is in the presence of rhombohedral crystallizations, retinasphalt resins, ghelenites, fangasites,* lead molybdates, manganese tungstates, zircon titanites, the most agile tongue is allowed to get tied in knots.

The townspeople knew about this pardonable disability of my uncle's, and took unfair advantage. They watched out for the difficult sections, and he got furious, and they laughed; which is not in good taste, even for Germans. And if there was always a healthy attendance at Lidenbrock's lectures, how many followed them regularly simply in order to enjoy the professor's terrible outbursts!

But despite all this, my uncle was an authentic scholar— I cannot emphasize this too much. Although he sometimes broke his samples by handling them too roughly, he combined the geologist's talent with the mineralogist's eye. With his mallet, his steel spike, his magnetic needle, his blowlamp, and his flask of nitric acid, he was highly gifted. From the fracture, appearance, resistance, melting point, sound, smell, and taste of any given mineral, he could put it without hesitation into any one of the 600 classifications recognized by modern science.

Lidenbrock's name was accordingly very much honoured in the gymnasiums and learned societies. Sir Humphry Davy, Humboldt, and Captains Franklin and Sabine* made sure they visited him on their way through Hamburg. Messrs Becquerel, Ebelmen, Brewster, Dumas, Milne-Edwards, and Sainte-Claire Deville* liked to consult him on the most stimulating questions in chemistry. That science owed him some wonderful discoveries. In 1853 there had appeared in Leipzig a *Treatise on Transcendental Crystallography* by Professor O. Lidenbrock, printed in large-folio pages with plates—but without covering its costs.

Add to that that my uncle was the curator of the mineralogical museum of Mr Struve, the Russian ambassador, which was a valuable collection much esteemed throughout Europe.

Such was the character calling for me so impatiently. Imagine a tall, thin man, with an iron constitution and youthful blond hair that made him look a good ten years younger than his fifty. His big eyes darted incessantly around behind imposing glasses; his nose, long and thin, was like a sharpened blade; unkind people even claimed it was magnetized, and picked up iron filings. Absolute slander: it only picked up snuff, but in rather large quantities to tell the truth.

If I add that my uncle took mathematical strides of exactly three feet, and that, while walking, he firmly clenched his fists—the sign of an impetuous temperament—then you will know him well enough not to wish to spend too much time in his company.

He lived in his little house on Königstrasse, a half-wood, half-brick construction with a crenellated gable-end. It looked out on to one of the winding canals that criss-cross in the centre of the oldest part of Hamburg, fortunately unharmed by the fire of 1842.

The old house leaned a little, it is true, it pushed its stomach out at the passers-by, and it wore its roof over one ear, like the cap of a Tugendbund* student. The harmony of its lines could have been better, then; but, all things considered, it held up well thanks to an old elm, vigorously embedded in the façade, and which, each springtime, used to push its flowering blossoms through the latticed windows.

My uncle was not poor, not for a German professor. The house was entirely his, both building and contents. The latter consisted of his goddaughter Gräuben, a seventeen-year-old girl from Virland,* and Martha and myself. In my dual capacity as nephew and orphan, I had become the laboratory assistant for his experiments.

I will admit that I devoured geological science with great relish; I had mineralogist's blood in my veins, and never felt bored in the company of my precious pebbles.

In sum, life could be happy in this miniature house in Königstrasse, despite its owner's impatience; for, while setting about it in rather a rough manner, he did not love me any the less. But the man had never learned to wait, he was permanently in a hurry.

When, in April, he planted heads of mignonette or morning glory in the china pots in his living-room, he would go and pull their leaves each morning to make them grow faster.

With such an eccentric, the only thing to do was to obey. I accordingly hurried into his study.

2

THIS study was a real museum. Specimens of the whole mineral order could be found here, labelled with the most perfect care, following the three great divisions into inflammable, metallic, and lithoidal minerals.

How well I knew them, these trinkets of mineralogical science; how many times, instead of wasting my time with boys of my own age, I had enjoyed dusting these graphites, these anthracites, these coals, these lignites, and these peats. The bitumens, the resins, the organic salts which had to be preserved from the least speck of dust. The metals, from iron to gold, whose relative value didn't count beside the absolute equality of scientific specimens. And all those stones, which would have been enough to rebuild the whole house in Königstrasse, even with a fine extra room, which would have suited me down to a T.

But when I went into the study, I was scarcely thinking about such wonders. My uncle formed the sole focus of my thoughts. He was buried in his large armchair covered with Utrecht velvet, holding a tome in both hands and studying it with the deepest admiration.

'What a book, what a book!' he kept saying.

This exclamation reminded me that Professor Lidenbrock was a fanatical book collector in his spare time. But a volume had no value in his eyes unless it was unfindable or, at the very least, unreadable.

'Well?' he said. 'Do you not see? It's a priceless gem I discovered this morning while poking around in the shop of Hevelius the Jew.'

'Magnificent,' I replied, with forced enthusiasm.

What was the point of making such a fuss about an old quarto book whose spine and covers seemed to be made out of coarse vellum, a yellowish book from which hung a faded tassel?

The professor's exclamations of admiration didn't stop, however.

'Look,' he said, addressing both the questions and the replies to himself, 'isn't it beautiful? Yes, it's wonderful, and what a binding! Does the book open easily? Yes, it stays open at any page whatsoever. But does it close well? Yes, because the cover and leaves form a unified whole, without separating or gaping anywhere. And this spine, which does not have a single break after seven hundred years of existence. Oh, it's a binding to have made Bozérian,* Closs, or Purgold proud!'

While speaking, my uncle alternately opened and closed the old book. The only thing I could do was ask him about its contents, though they didn't interest me a single bit.

'And what's the title of this marvellous volume?' I asked with too eager an enthusiasm to be genuine.

'This work', replied my uncle getting excited, 'is the *Heimskringla* of Snorre Turleson,* the famous twelfth-century Icelandic author. It is the chronicle of the Norwegian princes who ruled over Iceland.'

'Really,' I exclaimed as well as I could. 'It's presumably a German translation?'

'What!' the professor replied animatedly. 'A translation! What would I be doing with your translation? Who's bothered about your translation? This is the original work, in Icelandic: that magnificent language, both simple and rich, containing the most diverse grammatical combinations as well as numerous variations in the words.'

'Like German?' I slipped in, fortuitously.

'Yes,' replied my uncle shrugging his shoulders, 'not to mention that Icelandic has three genders, like Greek, and declensions of proper nouns, like Latin.'

'Ah,' I said, my indifference a little shaken, 'and are the characters in this book handsome?'

'Characters? Who's speaking of characters, benighted Axel! You did say "characters", did you not? Oh, so you are taking this for a printed book. Ignoramus, this is a manuscript, and a runic* manuscript at that.'

'Runic?'

'Yes. Are you now going to ask me to explain this word as well?'

'There is certainly no need,' I replied in the tone of a man wounded in his pride.

But my uncle continued all the more, and told me things, despite my opposition, that I wasn't specially interested in knowing.

'Runes', he said, 'were handwritten characters formerly used in Iceland and, according to the tradition, were invented by Odin himself. But look, irreverent boy, admire these forms which sprang from a god's imagination.'

I swear that, having no other reply to give, I was going to prostrate myself, the sort of response that necessarily pleases gods and kings, because it has the advantage of never embarrassing them—when an incident happened to set the course of the conversation off on a different path.

This was the appearance of a filthy parchment, which slid out of the book and fell to earth.

My uncle rushed to pick up this knick-knack with an eagerness easy to understand. An old document locked up in an old book since time immemorial could not fail to have a signal value in his eyes.

'But what is it?' he exclaimed.

At the same time he carefully spread the parchment out on his desk. It was five inches long and three inches wide, with horizontal lines of mumbo-jumbo-style characters written on it.

The following is the exact facsimile. It is important that these bizarre forms be known, because they were to lead Professor Lidenbrock and his nephew to undertake the strangest expedition the nineteenth century has ever known:

The professor examined the series of characters for a few moments. Then he said, lifting up his glasses:

'They're runes—the forms are absolutely identical to those in Snorre Turleson's manuscript. But what can it all mean?'

As runes seemed to me to be an invention by scholars to mystify the poor rest-of-the-world, I wasn't displeased to see that my uncle didn't understand anything. At least, that seemed to be the case from his hands, which had begun to shake terribly.

'And yet it *is* Old Icelandic!' he muttered through clenched teeth.

And Professor Lidenbrock surely knew what he was talking about, for he was reputed to be a genuine polyglot: not that he spoke fluently the 2,000 languages and 4,000 dialects employed on the surface of this globe, but he did know his fair share.

Faced with such a difficulty, he was just about to give in to all the impulsiveness of his character, and I could foresee a violent scene, when two o'clock sounded on the wall-clock over the mantelpiece.

Martha immediately opened the study door.

'The soup is served.'

'The devil take your soup,' shouted my uncle. 'And the person who made it. And those who will drink it.'

Martha fled. I followed close behind and, without knowing quite how, found myself sitting at my usual place in the dining-room.

I waited for a few moments: the professor didn't come. It was the first time, to my knowledge, that he was missing the ceremony of luncheon. And what a lunch, moreover! Parsley soup, ham omelette with sorrel and nutmeg, loin of veal with plum sauce; with, for pudding, prawns in sugar;* the whole lot being washed down with a good Moselle.

That was what an old bit of paper was going to cost my uncle. By George, in my capacity as devoted nephew, I considered it my duty to eat for both him and me; which I did, very conscientiously.

'I've never known such a thing,' said Martha. 'Professor Lidenbrock not at table.'

'It's unbelievable.'

'It portends some serious happening,' said the old servant, shaking her head.

In my opinion, it portended nothing at all, except for a terrible scene when my uncle found his lunch already eaten.

I was just on the last prawn when a resounding voice called me from the delights of pudding. I was in the study in a single bound.

3

'IT's quite obviously runic,' said the professor, knitting his brows. 'But there is a secret and I am going to discover it. If not...'

A violent gesture completed his thought.

'Sit down', he added, indicating the table with his fist, 'and write.'

In a moment I was ready.

'Now I'm going to dictate the letter in our alphabet corresponding to each of the Icelandic characters. We will see what that gives. But, by God, be careful not to make a mistake.'

The dictation began. I concentrated as hard as I could. Each letter was spelled out one after the other, to form the incomprehensible succession of words that follows:

mm.rnlls	esreuel	seecJde
sgtssmf	unteief	niedrke
kt,samn	atrateS	Saodrrn
emtnael	nuaect	rrilSa
Atvaar	.nscrc	ieaabs
ccdrmi	eeutul	frantu
dt,iac	oseibo	KediiY

When this work was finished, my uncle eagerly snatched up the sheet on which I had been writing, and examined it for a long time with great care.

'What does it mean?' he kept automatically repeating.

I swear I couldn't have told him anything. In any case he wasn't asking me and continued speaking to himself:

'This is what we call a cipher, in which the meaning is hidden in letters which have deliberately been mixed up, and which, if properly laid out, would form an intelligible sentence. When I think that there is perhaps here the explanation or indication of a great discovery!'

For my part, I thought there was absolutely nothing here, but kept my opinions carefully to myself.

The professor then took the book and the parchment and compared them with each other.

'The two documents are not in the same hand. The cipher is posterior to the book for I can see an immediate and irrefutable proof: the first letter is a double *m** that would be sought in vain in Turleson's book, for it was added to the Icelandic alphabet only in the fourteenth century. So therefore, at least two hundred years elapsed between the manuscript and the document.'

That, I must admit, seemed quite logical.

'I am therefore led to think', said my uncle, 'that one of the owners of the book must have written out the mysterious characters. But who the devil was this owner? Might he not have inserted his name at some point in the manuscript?'

My uncle lifted his glasses up, took a strong magnifying glass, and carefully worked his way over the first few pages of the book. On the back of the second one, the half-title page, he discovered a sort of stain,* which to the naked eye looked like an ink-blot. However, looking closer, it was possible to distinguish a few half-erased characters. My uncle realized that this was the interesting part, so he concentrated on the blemish, and with the help of his big magnifying glass he ended up distinguishing the following symbols, runic characters which he spelled out without hesitation:

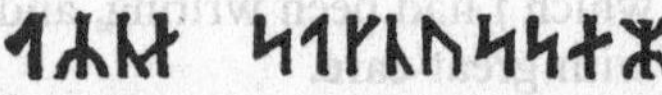

'Arne Saknussemm!'* he cried in a triumphant voice. 'But that *is* a name to conjure with, and an Icelandic one at that: the name of a scholar of the sixteenth century, a celebrated alchemist.'

I looked at my uncle with a certain admiration.

'Those alchemists, Avicenna, Bacon, Lull, Paracelsus,* were the veritable, nay the only, scholars of their time. They made discoveries at which we can reasonably be astonished. Why might this Saknussemm not have hidden some surprising invention in the incomprehensible cryptogram? That must be the case—that *is* the case.'

The professor's imagination caught fire at his assumption.

'Perhaps it is,' I dared to reply. 'But what would be the point of a scholar hiding a marvellous discovery in such a way?'

'Why? Why? How should I know? Galileo—did he not act in this way for Saturn? In any case, we shall soon see. I shall have the secret of this document, and will neither eat nor sleep until I have discovered it.'

'Uh-oh,' I thought.

'Nor will you, Axel!'

'My God,' I thought to myself. 'What luck I ate for two!'

'First of all, we must find out the language of this cipher: it cannot be difficult.'

At his words, I looked up quickly. My uncle continued his soliloquy:

'Nothing could be easier. There are 132 letters in the document, of which 79 are consonants and 53 vowels. Now the southern languages conform approximately to this ratio, while the northern tongues are infinitely richer in consonants: it is therefore a language of the south.'

These conclusions were highly convincing.

'But what language is it?'

It was there that I expected to find a scholar, but discovered instead a deep analyst.

'This Saknussemm', he said, 'was an educated man.

Now, when he was not writing in his mother tongue, he must naturally have chosen the language customarily used amongst educated people of the sixteenth century—I refer to Latin. If I am proved wrong, I can try Spanish, French, Italian, Greek, or Hebrew. But the scholars of the sixteenth century generally wrote in Latin. I have therefore the right to say, a priori, that this *is* Latin.'

I almost jumped off my chair. My memories as a Latinist protested at the claim that this baroque series of words could belong to the sweet language of Virgil.

'Yes, Latin,' repeated my uncle, 'but Latin scrambled up.'

What relief, I thought. If you can unscramble it again, you're a genius, Uncle.

'Let's have a proper look at it,' he said, again picking up the sheet on which I had written. 'This is a series of 132 letters, presented in apparent disorder. There are words where the consonants are encountered on their own, like the first one, "mm.rnlls"; others in contrast where the vowels are abundant, for example the fifth word, "unteief", or the second-but-last one, "oseibo". Now the arrangement is clearly not deliberate. It is given *mathematically* by the unknown formula governing the succession of the letters. It seems certain to me that the original sentence must have been written normally, then jumbled up following a rule we have yet to discover. The person who got access to the key of the cipher would be able to read it fluently: but what is this key? Axel, do you have the key?'

To his question I replied nothing, and for a good reason. I was gazing at a charming portrait on the wall: one of Gräuben. My uncle's ward was then in Altona,* staying at one of her relatives'. Her absence made me very sad, because, I can admit it now, the pretty little Virland girl and the professor's nephew loved each other with all Germanic patience and calm. We had got engaged without my uncle knowing—he was too much of a geologist to understand such feelings. Gräuben was a charming girl, blonde with blue eyes, of a slightly serious character; but she did not love me any the less for all that. For my part, I adored her—if, that is, the word exists in the Teutonic language. As a result of all this, the picture of my little Virland girl immediately switched me from the world of reality to that of daydreams, that of memories.

I was watching the faithful companion of my work and pleasure. Each day she helped me organize my uncle's precious stones, and labelled them with me. Miss Gräuben was a very fine mineralogist. She would have borne comparison with more than one scholar, for she loved getting to the bottom of the driest scientific questions. How many charming hours we had spent studying together; and how often I had been jealous of the fate of the unfeeling stones that she had manipulated with her graceful hands!

Then, when the time for recreation had come, the two of us would go out. We used to walk through the bushy paths of the Alster* and head together for the old tar-covered mill which looked so fine at the far end of the lake. On the way we would chat while holding hands. I would tell her things and she would laugh heartily at them. In this way we would arrive on the banks of the Elbe; then, having said goodnight to the swans gliding around amongst the great white water-lilies, we would come back by steam-ferry to the quayside.

I was just at this point in my daydream when my uncle, hitting the table with his fist, brought me violently back to reality.

'Let's see,' he said. 'In order to mix up the letters of a sentence, it seems to me that the first idea to come into one's mind ought to be to write the words vertically instead of horizontally.'

'Clever . . .' I thought.

'We must see what it produces. Axel, write any sentence at all on this scrap of paper; but, instead of writing the letters one after the other, put them in vertical columns made up of groups of fives or sixes.'

I understood what was required and immediately wrote from top to bottom:

I y y l u
l o l e b
o u i G e
v , t r n
e m t ä .

'Good,' said the professor without reading it. 'Now write these words in a horizontal line.'

I did so and obtained the following sentence:

Iyylu loleb ouiGe v,trn emtä.

'Perfect,' said my uncle, tearing the paper out of my hands. 'This is beginning to look like the old document: the vowels and the consonants are both grouped together in the same confusion. There are even capitals in the middle of the words, and commas as well, just as in Saknussemm's parchment.'

I couldn't help thinking that these remarks were highly ingenious.

'Now,' said my uncle again, addressing me directly, 'in order to read the sentence that you have just written and which I do not know, all I have to do is take the first letter of each successive word, then the second letter, then the third, and so on.'

And my uncle, to his great amazement and even more to mine, read out:

I love you, my little Gräuben.

'H'm,' said the professor.

Yes, without being aware of it, awkwardly in love, I had written out this compromising sentence.

'Oh, so you're in love with Gräuben, are you?' said my uncle in an authentic guardian's tone.

'Yes . . . No . . .' I spluttered.

'So you do love Gräuben,' he said mechanically. 'Well, let's apply my procedure to the document in question.'

My uncle had returned to his engrossing ideas and had already forgotten my risky words: I say 'risky' because the scholar's mind could never understand the matters of the heart. But fortunately, the vital question of the document took precedence.

Just before performing his critical experiment, Professor Lidenbrock's eyes were throwing sparks out through his glasses. His hands trembled as he picked the old parchment up again. He was profoundly excited. Finally he coughed loudly, and in a solemn voice, calling out successively the first letter of each word, then the second, he dictated the following series to me:

> mmessunkaSenrA.icefdoK.segnittamurtn
> ecertserrette,rotaivsadua,ednecsedsadne
> lacartniiiluJsiratracSarbmutabiledmek
> meretarcsilucoYsleffenSnI

When he had finished I will admit that I was excited. These letters, called out one after another, had not produced any meaning in my mind. I was therefore waiting for the professor to produce pompously from his mouth a sentence of Latin majesty.

But who could have foreseen it?—a violent blow from his fist shook the table. The ink spurted; the pen jumped from my hands.

'That's not it!' shouted my uncle. 'It makes no sense.'

Then, crossing the study like a cannonball and going downstairs like an avalanche, he threw himself into Königstrasse and shot off at a rate of knots.

4

'HAS he gone out?' shouted Martha, running up at the slam of the front door, which had just shaken the house to its very foundations.

'Yes, completely gone!'

'But what about his lunch?'

'He's not having any!'

'And his dinner?'

'No dinner either!'

Clasping her hands: 'Pardon?'

'Yes, Martha, he's given up food, and so has the entire household. Uncle Lidenbrock has put us all on a strict diet until he's deciphered a piece of old mumbo-jumbo that is totally undecipherable!'

'Goodness, we'll all die of starvation!'

I didn't dare admit that with such an uncompromising individual as my uncle, this fate seemed nigh-on certain.

The old servant went back into the kitchen, looking very worried, and muttering.

Alone again, I thought of going to tell Gräuben everything. But how could I get out of the house? The professor might come back at any moment. What if he summonsed me? Or if he wanted to start work again on that word-puzzle which even old Oedipus couldn't have solved?* And if I wasn't there when he called for me, what might happen then?

It was safest to stay put. As it happened, a mineralogist from Besançon had just sent us a collection of siliceous geodes that needed sorting out. I set to work. I classified these hollow stones with their little crystals moving inside, I prepared labels, I arranged them in the presentation cases.

But this activity didn't require all my concentration. The problem of the old document wouldn't stop disturbing me in a most peculiar fashion. My head was swirling and I felt vaguely anxious. I had the feeling that something terrible was about to happen.

An hour later, my geodes were stacked in neat little rows. I fell into the massive Utrecht armchair, my arms lolling over the sides and my head leaning back. I lit my pipe, the one with the long curved stem and the bowl carved into a casually reclining water-nymph; and then had great fun watching it burn, slowly converting my nymphette into an unalloyed negress. From time to time I listened out for steps hammering up the stairs. But none came. Where could my uncle be at this moment? I imagined him running around under the splendid trees on the Altona road, waving his arms, firing at the walls with his walking-stick, flattening the grass at a stroke, beheading the thistles, disturbing the lonely storks from their sleep.

Would he come back triumphant or discouraged? Who would win, him or the secret? I was wondering about such matters, and without thinking picked up the sheet of paper on which I had written the incomprehensible sequence of letters. I repeated to myself:

'What can it possibly mean?'

I tried to group the letters into words. I couldn't! Whether you put them into twos, threes, fives, or sixes, nothing came out that made sense. The 14th, 15th, and 16th letters did produce the English word *ice*. The 84th, 85th, and 86th ones gave *sir*. In the middle of the document, in the third line,* I spotted the Latin words *rota*, *mutabile*, *ira*, *nec*, and *atra*.

'It's amazing! These last few words seem to confirm my uncle's view about the language of the document! In the fourth line I can even see *luco*, which means "sacred wood". It's true that the third line also includes *tabiled*, that sounds completely Hebrew to me, and the last one, *mer*, *arc*, and *mère*, pure and unadulterated French.'

It was enough to drive you out of your mind. Four different languages in the same preposterous sentence! What possible connection could there be between *ice*, *sir*, *anger*, *cruel*, *sacred wood*, *changeable*, *mother*, *bow*, and *sea*? Only the first and last were easily linked: in a document written in Iceland, it was hardly surprising that there should be a 'sea of ice'. But putting the rest of the puzzle back together was another matter entirely.

I was struggling with an insoluble problem; my brain started overheating, my eyes blinking at the sheet. The 132 letters seemed to dance around me, like those silver drops which float above your head when there is a sudden rush of blood to it.

I was having a sort of hallucination; I was suffocating; I needed some fresh air. Absent-mindedly I fanned myself with the piece of paper, with the back and the front passing alternately before my eyes.

Imagine my surprise when I thought I caught sight of

perfectly intelligible words during a quick turn of the sheet, just as the other side came into view: Latin words like *craterem* and *terrestre*!

Suddenly my mind sparked; through the fleeting glimpses I had caught sight of the truth; I had discovered how the code worked. To understand the document, you didn't even need to read it through the paper. Far from it. In its original form, exactly as it had been spelled out to me, it could easily be decoded. The professor's ingenious attempts were all finally paying off. He had been right about the way the letters were arranged and right about the language the document was written in. A mere 'nothing'* had stopped him reading the Latin sentence from beginning to end, and this self-same 'nothing' had just fallen into my lap by pure chance.

You can imagine how excited I felt. My eyes went out of focus and I couldn't see anything. I had spread the piece of paper out on the table. All I had to do now to possess the secret was to glance at it.

At last I managed to calm down. I forced myself to walk round the room twice to settle my nerves; then came back and immersed myself again in the huge armchair.

I drew a large supply of air into my lungs, and shouted: 'Read on!'

I bent over the table. I placed my finger on each successive letter and, without stopping, without slowing down at all, read the whole message out loud.

What amazement, what terror entered my soul! At first it was like being hit by a blow you didn't expect. What, had the things I had just discovered really happened? A man had been daring enough to penetrate . . .

'No!' I cried indignantly. 'No! I'm not going to tell my uncle. It would be terrible if he got to know about such a journey. He'd just want to have a go himself. Nothing would stop a geologist of such determination. He would leave anyway, against all obstacles, whatever the cost. And he'd take me with him, and we wouldn't come back. Never. Not no-how!'

I was in an awful state, one difficult to describe.

'No, no, NO! It won't happen like that!' I said firmly.

'And since I am able to prevent any such idea crossing the mind of the dictator who governs my life, I *will* do so. By turning this document in every direction, he might accidentally discover the code. I'm going to destroy it.'

The fire hadn't quite gone out. I picked up the sheet of paper, together with Saknussemm's parchment. My trembling hand was just about to throw the whole lot on to the coals and thus destroy the dangerous secret— when the study door opened. My uncle came in.

5

I HAD barely had time to put the wretched document back on the desk.

Professor Lidenbrock seemed preoccupied. His obsessive idea clearly hadn't given him a moment's rest. He had obviously pondered the question during his walk, considered it, called on every resource of his imagination. And he had plainly come back to try out some new combination.

Sure enough, he sat down in his armchair and, pen in hand, began to write out formulae that looked like algebraic calculations.

I watched his frantic hand: not a single movement was lost on me. Was some surprising new result suddenly going to spring forth? I was afraid it would, irrationally, since the correct combination, the only one, had already been discovered—and so any other line of exploration was doomed to failure.

For three long hours, my uncle worked without a word, without looking up—rubbing out, starting again, crossing out, setting to for the umpteenth time.

I knew full well that if he managed to put the letters into every single order possible, then the right sentence would come out. But I also knew that a mere 20 letters can form 2,432,902,008,176,640,000 combinations. In fact there were 132 letters in the sentence; and these 132 letters produced a total number of sentences that had at least 133 digits,* one that is virtually impossible to enumerate and goes completely beyond the bounds of imagination.

I therefore felt reassured about the heroic way of solving the problem.

But time passed; night came; the street noises died down; my uncle, still bent over his work, didn't see anything, didn't notice Martha half-opening the door. He heard nothing, not even the voice of the faithful servant:

'Will Sir be dining tonight?'

Martha had to go away again without a response. As for myself, after fighting it for some time, an irresistible drowsiness came over me, and I fell asleep on the end of the sofa, while my Uncle Lidenbrock continued his adding up, his taking away, and his crossing out.

When I woke again the following morning, the inexorable worker was still at it. His eyes were red, his face pale, his hair tousled by a feverish hand, and his cheekbones glowed purple. All were signs of a terrible struggle with the impossible, showing what tiredness of mind and what exertions of the brain must have filled the long hours.

I was genuinely sorry for him. In spite of the reproaches I probably had the right to make, I felt considerable pity. The poor man was so possessed by his idea that he had quite forgotten to be angry. His whole energy was concentrated on a single point, and since it could not escape through its normal outlet, it was to be feared that it might simply explode at any moment now.

With a single act I could undo the iron hoop wrapped tight round his brain—with just one word. I did nothing.

But I had a kind heart. Why did I not speak out in such circumstances? For my uncle's own sake.

No, no, I repeated, no. I'm not going to say anything. He would only want to go there, I know him, nothing would stop him. He has a volcanic imagination and he would risk his life to do what no geologist has ever done before. I will not say anything; I will keep this secret given to me by chance. To let it out would be tantamount to killing Professor Lidenbrock. Let him guess if he can. I don't want to feel responsible one day for having sent him to his death!

Once my mind was made up, I crossed my arms and waited. But I hadn't reckoned with something that happened a few hours later.

When Martha tried to go out to the market, she found the door locked. The big key was not in the keyhole. Who had taken it out? Obviously my uncle, when he had come back from his hasty excursion the day before.

Was it on purpose? Or through absent-mindedness? Did he want us to feel real hunger pains? That seemed to be going a bit far. Why should Martha and I suffer because of a situation that had nothing whatsoever to do with us? But apparently this *was* the case, and I recalled a frightening precedent. A few years before, when my uncle had been working on his grand mineral classification, he had remained 48 hours without eating, and his whole household had had to follow his scientific diet. As a result, I acquired stomach cramps that were not much fun for a boy of a fairly ravenous nature.

It now seemed that breakfast was going to go the same way as dinner the day before. Nevertheless I resolved to be heroic and not to give in to the demands of hunger. Martha took it very seriously: she was inconsolable, the poor woman. As for myself, being unable to leave the house upset me more, with good reason, as I am sure you will understand.

My uncle was still working; his mind was lost in a world of combinations; he lived far from the Earth and truly beyond worldly needs.

At about twelve o'clock, though, hunger began to cause me serious problems. Martha, very innocently, had devoured the supplies in the larder the day before, and so there was nothing left in the whole house. I held on, however. I considered it a matter of honour.

Two o'clock chimed. The situation was becoming ridiculous, intolerable even. My eyes began to look very big. I started to tell myself that I was exaggerating the importance of the document; that in any case my uncle wouldn't believe what it said; that he would regard it as a mere practical joke; that if the worst came to the worst he could be restrained against his will if he wanted to attempt the expedition; and that he might easily find the code himself, in which case all my efforts at abstinence would have been in vain.

These all seemed excellent reasons to me, although I would have indignantly rejected them the day before. I even considered it a terrible mistake to have waited so long; and I made up my mind to reveal all.

I was therefore looking for a way into the subject, one that wasn't too sudden, when, without warning, the professor stood up, put his hat on, and got ready to go out.

What, leave the house, and shut us in again? Never!

'Uncle?'

He didn't appear to have heard.

'*Uncle Lidenbrock!*' I repeated, raising my voice.

'Huh?' he said, like someone abruptly woken up.

'What about the key?'

'What key? The door?'

'No,' I cried. 'The key to the document!'

The professor scrutinized me over his glasses; he must have noticed something unusual in my face, for he firmly grabbed me by the arm while still carefully inspecting me, although unable to utter a word. All the same, never was a question asked more clearly.

I moved my head up and down.

He shook his, with a sort of pity, as if dealing with a lunatic.

I made a more positive sign.

His eyes shone brighter; his hand became threatening.

Given the situation, this silent conversation would have absorbed the most indifferent spectator. I had in fact really reached the point of not daring to say anything, such was my fear of my uncle suffocating me when he first began to joyfully embrace me. But he became so insistent that I just had to speak.

'Yes, the code . . . Purely by chance . . .'

'What are you saying?' he cried with an intensity that cannot be described.

'Look,' I said, giving him the paper with my writing on. 'Read.'

'But it doesn't make sense!' he replied, screwing it up.

'No sense, when you begin at the beginning, but . . .'

I hadn't finished before the professor produced a shout, more than a shout, an actual roar! A revelation had just occurred in his brain. His face was transmogrified.

'Oh, clever old Saknussemm!' he bellowed. 'So you wrote your message backwards?'

And throwing himself on the sheet of paper, his eyes unfocused, his voice trembling, he spelled the whole document out, working his way from the last letter back to the first.*

This was what he read:

In Snæfells Yoculis craterem kem delibat umbra Scartaris Julii intra calendas descende, audas viator, et terrestre centrum attinges. Kod feci. Arne Saknussemm.

Which, when translated from the dog-Latin, reads as follows:

Go down into the crater of Snæfells Yocul which the shadow of Scartaris caresses before the calends* of July, O audacious traveller, and you will reach the centre of the Earth. I did it. Arne Saknussemm.

As he read, my uncle jumped as if drawing current from a Leyden jar.* His courage, his joy, his certainty, knew no bounds. He walked up and down; he held his head in both hands; he moved the chairs around; he piled the books up; unbelievably, he juggled with his precious geodes; he threw a punch here, a blow there. At last his nerves calmed down and, like a man exhausted after discharging too much fluid, he flopped back in his armchair.

'So what time is it?' he asked after a few moments' silence.

'Three o'clock.'

'H'm, lunch has gone down quickly. I'm dying of hunger. To table. And then after that . . .'

'After?'

'You can pack my trunk.'

'?'

'And yours too!' concluded the merciless professor, striding into the dining-room.

6

THESE last words sent a shiver through my whole body. I kept my self-control though. I even resolved to put on a brave face. Only scientific arguments could stop Professor Lidenbrock now. And there was no lack of arguments, and good ones, against such a journey being possible. Go to the centre of the Earth? What madness! But I kept my reasoning for a more suitable moment, and instead gave my full attention to the meal.

There would be little point in reproducing here my uncle's curses when he saw the cleared-away table. Things were duly explained to him, and Martha freed again. Running to the market, she managed so well that an hour later my hunger was satisfied, and I could begin to be aware of the situation once more.

During the meal, my uncle had been almost cheerful: there escaped from him some of those scholars' jokes that never become really dangerous. After the last course, he beckoned me into his study.

I obeyed. He sat at one side of his desk, with me at the other.

'Axel,' he said in a voice that was almost kindly, 'you are a highly gifted boy; you were of great assistance to me when I was worn out by my efforts and about to give up looking for the combination. Where would I have ended up? No-one can guess. I will never forget that, my boy, and you will have your fair share of the fame we are going to acheive.'

Now's my chance! I thought. He's in a good mood: the moment to discuss the aforementioned fame.

'. . . above all,' my uncle continued, 'total secrecy must

be maintained, do you hear? In the scientific world, there is no shortage of people jealous of me, and many of them would dearly love to tackle this journey. But they will have no inkling of it until we get back.'

'Do you really believe there'd be so many takers?'

'Most definitely! Who would think twice about gaining such celebrity? If people knew of the document, a whole army of geologists would rush to follow in Arne Saknussemm's footsteps!'

'That's where I'm not totally convinced, Uncle, for nothing proves that the manuscript is genuine.'

'What! And the book we discovered it in?'

'All right, I accept that this Saknussemm wrote the message, but does it necessarily follow that he actually carried out the journey? Couldn't the old parchment just be a practical joke?'

I half-regretted this last idea, admittedly a bit daring. The professor's thick eyebrows frowned, and I was afraid that the rest of the conversation might not go as I wished. But fortunately it didn't turn out like that. A sort of smile played over my stern questioner's lips, as he replied:

'That is what we are going to find out.'

'H'm!' I said, a little annoyed. 'Allow me first to exhaust all possible objections concerning the document.'

'Speak, my boy, give yourself full rein. I grant you every freedom to express your opinion. You are no longer my nephew, but my colleague. Pray proceed.'

'Well, I will first ask you what Yocul, Snæfells, and Scartaris mean, since I have never even heard of them.'

'That's easy. As it happens, I received a map not very long ago from my friend August Petermann of Leipzig.* It couldn't have arrived at a better time. Take down the third atlas on the second section in the big bookcase, series Z, shelf 4.'

I got up and, thanks to the precise instructions, quickly found the required atlas. My uncle opened it:

'This is Handerson's, one of the best maps of Iceland, and it may easily provide us with solutions to all your problems.'

I leant over the map.

'See this island of volcanoes,' said the professor, 'and notice that they all bear the name "jökull". This means "glacier" in Icelandic and, at that northerly latitude, most of the eruptions reach the light of day through the layers of ice. Hence this name "jökull" applied to all the fire-producing peaks of the island.'

'Fine. But what about Snæfells?'

I hoped there would be no answer to this question. I was wrong.

'Follow me along the western coast of Iceland. Do you see Reykjavik, the capital? Yes. Good. Work your way up along the countless fjords of these shorelines eaten by the sea, and stop a little before the line of 65° N. What do you see?'

'A peninsula rather like a bare bone, with an enormous kneecap at the end.'

'Not an inappropriate comparison, my dear boy. Now, do you see anything on the kneecap?'

'Yes, a mountain that looks as if it's sprouted in the middle of the sea.'

'Good. That's Snæfells.'

'Snæfells?'

'The one and only. A 5,000-foot-high mountain, one of the most remarkable on the island—and definitely the most famous in the whole world, if its crater leads to the centre of the globe.'

'But it's quite impossible!' I said, raising my shoulders in protest at such a conjecture.

'Impossible?' said Professor Lidenbrock severely. 'And why should that be?'

'Because this crater is obviously blocked up with lava and scorching rocks, and so . . .'

'And supposing it is an extinct crater?'

'Extinct?'

'Yes. There are now only about 300 volcanoes in activity on the surface of the Earth—but the number of extinct ones is much greater. Snæfells falls into this latter category, and in historical times has only had a single eruption, the

1219 one. Since then its rumblings have gradually died down, and it is no longer considered an active volcano.'

I had no reply at all for these categorical statements, so fell back on the other mysteries hidden in the document.

'But what does the word "Scartaris" mean, and what have the calends of July got to do with anything?'

My uncle concentrated for a few seconds. My hope came back for a moment, but only for a moment, for soon he replied to me as follows:

'What you call a mystery is crystal-clear for me. It proves with what care and ingenuity Saknussemm wished to indicate his discovery. Snæfells is composed of several craters; it was therefore necessary to pinpoint which is the one that leads to the centre of the globe. What did our scholarly Icelander do? Our Icelandic scholar observed that as the calends of July approached, that is towards the end of June, one of the mountain peaks, called Scartaris, cast its shadow as far as the opening of the relevant crater, and he noted this fact in his document. Could he have found a more precise indication, and—once we are on the summit of Snæfells—can there be a moment's hesitation as to the path to follow?'

Decidedly my uncle had an answer for everything. I saw full well that he was unassailable on the words of the ancient parchment. So I stopped pressing him on that subject and, since the most important thing was to convince him, turned to the scientific objections, in my view much more serious.

'All right, I am forced to accept that Saknussemm's message is clear and can leave no doubt in one's mind. I even grant that the document looks perfectly authentic. So this scholar went to the bottom of Snæfells; he saw the shadow of Scartaris lingering on the edge of the crater just before the calends of July; he probably even heard the people of his time recounting legends that this crater led to the centre of the Earth. But as to whether he went down there himself, whether he carried out the journey and came back, whether he even undertook it: no, a hundred times NO!'

'And the reason?' asked my uncle in a singularly mocking tone.

'Because all the scientific theories demonstrate that such an undertaking is impossible!'

'All the theories say that?' replied the professor, putting on a good-natured appearance. 'Oh the nasty theories. They're going to get terribly in our way, the poor theories!'

I could see that he was making fun of me, but continued regardless:

'Yes, it is well known that the temperature increases by approximately one degree centigrade for every 70 feet you go below the surface of the globe. Now, assuming that this ratio remains constant, and given that the radius of the Earth is about 4,000 miles,* the temperature at the centre will be well over 200,000°. The substances at the Earth's core exist therefore as white-hot gases, for even metals like gold or platinum, even the hardest rocks, cannot resist such a temperature. My question whether it is possible to travel in such an environment is consequently a reasonable one!'

'So, Axel, it is the heat that bothers you?'

'Certainly. If we were to attain a depth of only 25 miles, we would have reached the limit of the Earth's crust, for the temperature would already be more than 1,400°.'

'And you are afraid of melting?'

'I leave the question for you to decide,' I replied sharply.

'*Here* is what I decide,' said Professor Lidenbrock, assuming an important air. 'It is that neither you nor anyone else knows for certain what happens in the Earth's interior, given that scarcely a 12,000th part of its radius is known. It is that science is eminently perfectible, and that each existing theory is constantly replaced by a new one. Was it not believed before Fourier* that the temperature of interplanetary space went down indefinitely, and is it not known now that the greatest cold in the ether does not go beyond 40 or 50° below zero? Why should it not be the same for the internal heat? Why at a certain depth should it not encounter a limit that cannot be crossed, instead of reaching the point where the most obdurate minerals liquefy?'

Since my uncle placed the question on the terrain of hypotheses, I had no reply to make.

'Well, Axel, I can tell you that real scientists, amongst them Poisson,* have proved that if a temperature of 200,000° actually existed inside the globe, the white-hot gases produced by the fusion of the solids would acquire such force that the Earth's crust could not resist and would explode like the walls of a boiler under steam-pressure.'

'Poisson's opinion, Uncle, that's all.'

'Agreed, but it is also the opinion of other distinguished geologists that the interior of the globe is not formed of gas, nor of water, nor of the heaviest rocks that we know. The reason is that, if it were, the Earth would only weigh half as much as it does.'

'Oh, you can prove anything you want with figures!'

'And can you, my boy, with facts? Is it not true that the number of volcanoes has considerably decreased since the first days of the world? And if there is indeed heat in the centre, can one not deduce that it is also tending to diminish?'

'Uncle, if you're entering the realm of suppositions, there is nothing more I can say.'

'And *I* have to say that my opinion is shared by highly competent figures. Do you remember a visit that the famous British chemist Sir Humphry Davy paid me in 1825?'*

'Hardly, as I only came into the world nineteen years later.'

'Well, Sir Humphry came to see me as he was passing through Hamburg. Amongst other things, we had a long discussion about the hypothesis that the innermost core of the Earth was liquid. We both agreed that a molten state could not exist, for a reason to which science has never found a response.'

'What reason is that?' I said, slightly stunned.

'Because the liquid mass would be subject, like the

ocean, to the moon's attraction, thus producing internal tides twice a day which would push up at the Earth's crust and cause regular earthquakes!'

'But it is none the less obvious that the surface of the globe was once exposed to combustion, and one can suppose that the outer crust cooled down first while the heat retreated to the centre.'

'Not so. The Earth heated up through combustion on its surface, not from any other cause. The surface was composed of a great quantity of metals such as potassium and sodium, which have the property of catching fire as soon as they are in contact with air and water. These metals started to burn when the water-vapour in the atmosphere fell to the ground as rain. Little by little, as the water worked its way into the cracks in the Earth's crust, it produced further fires, explosion, and eruptions. Hence the large number of volcanoes during the first days of the world.'*

'What an ingenious hypothesis!' I cried, rather in spite of myself.

'Which Sir Humphry brought to my notice by means of a highly simple experiment on this very spot. He constructed a ball made mainly of the metals I have just mentioned, and which perfectly represented our globe. When a fine dew was dropped on to its surface, it blistered, oxidized, and produced a tiny mountain. A crater opened at the summit; an eruption took place; and it transmitted so much warmth to the whole ball that it became too hot to hold.'

To tell the truth, I was beginning to be disturbed by the professor's arguments. What didn't help either was that he was presenting them with his usual verve and enthusiasm.

'You see, Axel, the state of the central core has produced various hypotheses amongst geologists; nothing is less proven than the idea of an internal heat. In my view it does not exist, could not possibly exist. In any case we shall see for ourselves and, like Arne Saknussemm, discover where we stand on this important question.'

'Yes, we shall!' I shouted, won over by his excitement.

'We'll see for ourselves, provided, that is, anything at all can be seen down there!'

'And why not? Can we not count on electrical phenomena to light the way and even on the atmosphere, which the pressure may make more and more luminous as the centre approaches?'

'Yes. *Yes!* It's possible after all.'

'It is certain,' retorted my uncle in triumph. 'But it must be kept quiet, do you hear? All this must be maintained totally secret, so that no-one else has the idea of discovering the centre of the Earth before us.'

7

OUR memorable session ended here. The discussion had given me a fever. I left my uncle's study as if in a trance; there was not enough air to calm me down in all the streets of Hamburg put together. So I made for the banks of the Elbe, near the steamboat service connecting the town with the Harburg Railway Line.

Was I really convinced by what I'd just been told? Hadn't I been won over by Professor Lidenbrock's forceful manner? Could I take seriously his decision to go to the core of the terrestrial mass? Had I just heard the senseless speculations of a lunatic or the scientific analyses of a great genius? In all this, where did the truth end and illusion begin?

I drifted amongst a thousand contradictory hypotheses, without being able to seize hold of any of them.

However, I did remember being convinced, although my enthusiasm was now beginning to wane: I would in fact have preferred to set off immediately so as not to have time to think. Yes, I would easily have been able to pack my cases at that very moment.

Yet I have to confess that an hour later my excitement had subsided; my nerves grew less tense and, from the deep chasms of the Earth, I slowly came back to the surface.

'It's all preposterous!' I shouted. 'Completely devoid of common sense. It's not the sort of proposal to put to a sensible boy. None of all that exists. I didn't sleep properly. I must have had a bad dream.'

I had meanwhile walked along the banks of the Elbe and reached the other side of town. I had worked my way along the port and arrived at the Altona road. Inspiration had guided me, a justified intuition, for soon I caught sight of my little Gräuben walking nimbly back to Hamburg.

'Gräuben!' I shouted from afar.

The girl stopped, a little flustered I imagine to hear her name called out on the public highway. Ten strides took me to her side.

'Axel!' she said in surprise. 'Oh, so you came to meet me—you can't deny it!'

But when she looked at me, Gräuben could not avoid noticing my worried, upset appearance.

'What's wrong?' she said, taking my hand.

'Wrong!' I cried.

In two seconds and three sentences my pretty Virland girl was up to date on everything. She remained silent for a few seconds. Was her heart pounding as hard as mine? I don't know, but the hand holding mine wasn't trembling. We continued for a hundred yards without a word.

'Axel,' she said at last.

'Darling Gräuben!'

'It'll be a wonderful journey.'

I jumped a mile.

'Yes, Axel. A journey worthy of a scholar's nephew. A man should try to prove himself by some great adventure!'

'What, Gräuben, you're not attempting to stop me going on such an expedition?'

'No, dear Axel, and I would gladly go with you and your uncle, but a poor girl would only be in the way.'

'Are you telling the truth?'

'Yes.'

O women, girls, feminine hearts, impossible to understand! When you are not the shyest of creatures, you are the most foolhardy. Reason has no influence over you. What, this child was encouraging me to take part in such an expedition! She wouldn't have been afraid to do the journey herself! She *wanted* me to do it, although she loved me!

I was put out and, I admit, a little ashamed.

'Gräuben,' I tried again. 'We'll see if you talk this way tomorrow.'

'Tomorrow, dear Axel, I'll be the same as today.'

We continued on our way, holding hands but not saying anything. I was exhausted by the day's events.

'After all,' I thought, 'the calends of July are still ages off, and before then any number of things can occur to cure my uncle of his craze for underground travel.'

Night had already fallen when we got home to Königstrasse. I expected to find the house quiet, with my uncle in bed as usual and Martha giving the dining-room one last feather-dusting.

But I had forgotten about the professor's impatience. I found him shouting and rushing round in the middle of a troop of porters all unloading goods on the garden path, with the old servant at her wits' end.

'Come on Axel, don't hang around like a drip,' shouted my uncle from afar as soon as he saw me. 'Your trunk is not packed, my papers are not in order, I have lost the key for the travelling-bag, and my gaiters have not yet arrived.'

I was overwhelmed, I couldn't find my voice. All my lips managed to produce was:

'So we're leaving?'

'Yes, my poor boy. You should be moving instead of just standing there.'

'Really leaving?' I repeated faintly.

'Day after tomorrow, crack of dawn.'

I couldn't bear to hear any more, and ran up to my little room.

There could no longer be any doubt. All afternoon my uncle had been buying the articles and utensils needed for his journey. The path was blocked with rope-ladders, knotted cords, torches, water-bottles, iron crampons, pickaxes, ice-picks, alpenstocks—the total needing at least ten men to carry it.

I spent an awful night. In the morning I was called early. I decided not to open the door. But how could I resist a gentle voice saying:

'Dear Axel.'

I came out. I thought that my dishevelled appearance, my pale face, my eyes reddened by the lack of sleep, would affect Gräuben and make her change her mind.

'So, darling Axel, I see you're in better form, and have calmed down during the night.'

'Calmed down!'

I rushed to the mirror. To my surprise I looked less bad than I'd thought. It was unbelievable.

'Axel,' said Gräuben. 'I've had a long talk with my guardian. He is a staunch scholar, a man of great courage, and you should always remember that you have his blood in your veins. He told me of his aims, his hopes: why he wants to achieve his goal, and how he's planning to go about it. He will get there, I'm sure. Dear Axel, it's such a fine thing to devote oneself to science! How famous Herr Lidenbrock will become, and his companion too. When you come back, Axel, you will be a man, his equal, free to speak, free to act, free at last to . . .'

The girl, turning red, could not finish. Her words gave me new energy. But I still couldn't believe that we were about to leave. I dragged Gräuben into the professor's study.

'So, Uncle,' I said. 'Are you really determined to go?'

'What, aren't you convinced?'

'Of course I am,' I said to pacify him. 'But I'm just wondering what all the hurry is.'

'*Time* is the hurry! Time fleeing with a speed nothing can alter!'

'But it is only 26 May, and the end of June is . . .'

'So you think, ignoramus, that it is as easy as that to get to Iceland? If you had not left me like a madman, I would have taken you with me to the branch-office of Liffender

& Co. of Copenhagen. There you would have seen that there is only one service from Copenhagen to Reykjavik, on the 22nd of each month.'

'Well then?'

'Well then, if we waited until 22 June, we would arrive too late to see the shadow of Scartaris playing along the crater of Snæfells! We have to get to Copenhagen as quickly as possible and try to find some means of transport there. Go and pack your trunk.'

There was nothing more I could say. I went back up to my room. Gräuben came with me. She immediately took charge, carefully packing into a small suitcase the things needed for my journey. She was no more excited than if it had been a day-trip to Lübeck or Heligoland. Her little hands went back and forth unhurriedly. She talked calmly, she gave me the most sensible reasons for doing our expedition. She beguiled me and I felt very angry at her. At times I felt like getting carried away, but she took no notice and continued her calm and methodical work.

Finally the last strap round the case had been tightened. I went downstairs again.

Throughout the day, more and more suppliers of scientific instruments, firearms, and electrical apparatus arrived. Martha was completely out of her depth.

'Is Sir mad?' she cried.

I nodded.

'And he's taking you with him?'

Affirmative.

'Where?'

I pointed to the centre of the Earth.

'Down to the cellar?'

'No, further!'

Evening came. I was no longer aware of the passing of time.

'See you tomorrow then,' said my uncle. 'Departure: six sharp.'

At ten o'clock I fell on my bed a lifeless mass.

During the night, terror took hold of me again.

I spent it dreaming of chasms. I was the creature of

delirium. I felt myself seized by the vigorous hand of the professor, dragged along, engulfed, bogged down. I was falling to the bottom of unfathomable pits with the increasing speed of bodies abandoned in space. My life was just one endless fall.

I woke at five, broken with fatigue and fear. I went down to the dining-room. My uncle was at table. He was wolfing down food. I looked at him with horror. But Gräuben was there, so I didn't say anything. But I couldn't eat.

At half past five, wheels were heard rumbling in the street. A large carriage arrived to take us to Altona station. It was soon piled up with my uncle's packages.

'But where's your trunk?'

'Everything's ready,' I replied, my knees weakening.

'Hurry up and bring it down or we'll miss the train.'

Fighting against destiny seemed impossible for the moment. Going up to my room I let my case slide downstairs, rushing headlong down after it.

Meanwhile my uncle was solemnly putting the reins of the house in Gräuben's hands. My pretty Virland girl was as calm as usual. She kissed her guardian, but she could not hold back a tear when she grazed my cheek with her sweet lips.

'Gräuben,' I said.

'Go, dear Axel, go. You are leaving a fiancée but you will come back to a wife.'

I held Gräuben briefly in my arms, then got into the carriage. She and Martha waved us a last goodbye from the front door. Then the two horses, urged on by the whistling of the driver, galloped off towards Altona.

8

IN less than 20 minutes, we had crossed the border into Holstein Province. Altona, really a suburb of Hamburg, is the terminus of the line from Kiel, along which we were due to travel to the coast of the Bælts.

At half past six the carriage pulled up in front of the station. My uncle's numerous packages and bulky cases were unloaded, carried in, weighed, labelled, and loaded into the luggage van. At seven o'clock we were sitting opposite each other in our compartment. The steam-whistle blew and the locomotive moved off. We had left.

Was I resigned to my fate? No, not yet. But the fresh morning air and the view constantly changing with the motion of the train soon took my mind off its main worry.

The professor's thoughts were obviously flying ahead of the train, moving too slowly for his impatience. We were alone in the carriage, but did not speak. My uncle checked his pockets and travelling-bag with the most painstaking care. I could see that not one of the items needed for carrying out his projects was missing.

Amongst them was a carefully folded sheet of headed notepaper from the Danish Consulate, signed by Mr Christiensen, Consul-General in Hamburg and a friend of the professor's. It was intended to afford us every facility in Copenhagen with a view to being granted recommendations for the Governor-General of Iceland.

I also glimpsed the famous document, carefully hidden away in the most secret compartment of my uncle's wallet. Still cursing it from the bottom of my heart, I began to examine the countryside. It was an endless succession of plains, lacking in interest: monotonous and silty, but relatively fertile and highly suitable for laying down a railway, given its potential for those straight lines so popular with the rail companies.

But the tedium did not have time to annoy me for, only three hours after leaving, the train stopped at Kiel, a stone's throw from the sea.

Since our luggage was registered for Copenhagen, we needed do nothing about it. Nevertheless the professor watched with an anxious expression as it was loaded on to the steamship. Then it disappeared into the bottom of a hold.

In his hurry, my uncle had very carefully calculated the connections between the train and the steamer. As a result we had nearly a whole day to kill, for the *Ellenora* was not due to leave until after nightfall. Hence a fever lasting nine hours, during which the cantankerous traveller rained curses on the shipping and railway companies and the governments which allowed such abuses to happen. I was forced to back him up while he berated the captain of the *Ellenora* on this very subject. He wanted to make him stoke the boilers without wasting a moment. The captain advised him to go for a walk.

In Kiel, as elsewhere, a day has to pass, eventually. By dint of walking along the luxuriant banks of the bay leading to the town, by trampling through the bushy woods which make the town look like a nest amidst a network of branches, by admiring the bungalows each with its own little cold-bath-house, and by rushing and cursing, we somehow managed to reach ten in the evening.

The whorls of smoke from the *Ellenora* rose into the sky; the deck trembled with the shivers issuing from the boiler; we had already embarked, the proud occupants of two superimposed berths in the only passenger cabin on board.

At quarter past ten the moorings were cast off, and the steamer moved rapidly over the dark waters of the Store Bælt.

It was a black night; there came a fine breeze and a strong sea; a few lights from shore perforated the darkness. Later, a flashing lighthouse shone briefly over the waves from some mysterious point—and that is all I can remember of our first crossing.

At 7 a.m. we disembarked at Korsør, a little town on the west coast of Zealand. There we quickly climbed into another train, which carried us over a countryside just as flat as the Holstein one.

It still took three more hours to reach the capital of Denmark. My uncle hadn't shut his eyes all night. In his impatience, I think he was even pushing the carriage along with his feet.

Finally he caught sight of an arm of the sea.

'The Sound!' he shouted.

On our left was a vast construction like a hospital.

'A lunatic asylum,' said one of our travelling companions.

Well, I thought, there's one establishment where we ought to end our days! And however big it is, that hospital would still be too small for all the professor's folly!

At 10 a.m., we finally alighted in Copenhagen. The luggage was loaded on to a cab and driven with us to the Phoenix Hotel in Bredgade, taking half an hour, for the station is out of town. Then, after a quick wash, my uncle dragged me out of my room. The hotel porter spoke German and English; but the professor, playing the polyglot, questioned him in good Danish and it was in good Danish that we were told where the Museum of Northern Antiquities was.

This curious establishment contained stacks of marvels allowing one to reconstitute the country's history, with its old stone weapons, its goblets, and its jewels. Professor Thomson, the director, was a scholar, and a friend of the Consul in Hamburg.

My uncle had a warm letter of recommendation to give him. Normally one scholar does not receive another very well at all. But here things were different. Professor Thomson, a man who liked to help, gave Professor Lidenbrock and even his nephew a kind welcome. To say that our secret was kept from the excellent director goes without saying. We wished simply to visit Iceland as disinterested amateurs.

Professor Thomson put himself entirely at our disposal, and together we combed the quays looking for a ship about to sail.

I had hoped that no means of transport would be available; but this was not to be. A little Danish schooner, the *Valkyrie*,* was due to sail for Reykjavik on 2 June. The captain, a Mr Bjarne, was on board. His future passenger, overjoyed, shook his hand hard enough to break it. This simple man was surprised by such a grip. He found it quite normal to go to Iceland—that was his job. But my uncle found it sublime. The worthy captain took advantage of his enthusiasm to make us pay double for the voyage. But we weren't bothered by such trifles.

'Be on board by 7 a.m. on Tuesday,' said Mr Bjarne, thrusting a wad of dollars into his pocket.

We thanked Mr Thomson for all his help and returned to the Phoenix Hotel.

'Everything's going well, very well indeed!' my uncle kept saying. 'What a stroke of luck to have found that vessel ready to leave! Now let's have breakfast and then we can visit the town.'

We headed for Kongens Nytorv, an irregularly-shaped square with a plinth containing two innocent cannon which have taken aim but in fact frighten nobody. Just beside it, at No. 5, there was a restaurant run by a French chef called Vincent. We ate our fill there for the modest price of four marks each.[1]

Then I took a childish pleasure in exploring the town, with my uncle allowing himself to be dragged along. In any case he saw nothing: not the insignificant Royal Palace, nor the pretty seventeenth-century bridge across the canal in front of the museum, nor the huge memorial to Thorvaldsen,* covered in hideous murals and with the works of this sculptor inside, nor the candy-box Rosenborg castle, nor the admirable Renaissance building of the Stock Exchange, nor the church spire made of the intertwined tails of four bronze dragons—nor even the great windmills on the ramparts, whose immense wings swelled up like a ship's sails in a strong sea-wind.

What delightful walks we could have gone on, my lovely Virland girl and I, around the port where the double-deckers and frigates slept peacefully under their red roofs, along the lush shores of the strait, through the bushy shade concealing the fortress, whose cannon push their black mouths through the branches of the elders and the willows . . .

But unfortunately my poor Gräuben was far away. Did I have any hope of ever seeing her again?

---

[1] About 2 francs 75 centimes (Author's note).

And yet, if my uncle noticed nothing of these enchanted sites, he was bowled over when he saw a certain church spire on the Island of Amager, in the southeastern* part of Copenhagen.

I was instructed to head in that direction. We climbed on to a small steam-powered boat serving the canals and soon it pulled in at the quay known as the 'Dockyard'.

Having made our way through narrow streets where convicts dressed in grey-and-yellow striped trousers were working under stick-wielding warders, we arrived at the Vor Frelsers Kirke. The church itself was not special in any way. But its high tower had caught the professor's eye: starting from the platform, an outside staircase worked its way round the spire, and its spirals were in the open air.

'Up we go,' said my uncle.

'But what if we get giddy?'

'All the more reason: we have to get used to it.'

'But . . .'

'Come on, I tell you, we're wasting time.'

There was no choice but to obey. A caretaker who lived on the other side of the street gave us the key, and our ascent began.

My uncle went first, treading firmly. I followed with great trepidation, as my head turned deplorably easily. I had neither the eagle's sense of balance nor its steady nerves.

As long as we were imprisoned in the staircase inside the tower everything went well. But after 150 spiral steps the air suddenly hit me in the face: we had arrived on the platform. This was where the open-air staircase began, protected by a thin rail, with the steps getting ever narrower, apparently climbing up to infinity.

'I can't!'

'You are not a coward, are you? Start climbing!' replied the pitiless professor.

The only option was to follow, hanging firmly on. The open air made my head turn. I could feel the tower swaying in the gusts of wind. My legs began to give way. Soon

I was climbing on my knees, then on my stomach. I closed my eyes, feeling space-sickness.

At last, with my uncle pulling me up by the collar, I arrived near the ball.

'Look,' he said, 'and look properly. You need to take lessons in precipices!'

I opened my eyes. Through the smoky mist I caught sight of houses without any depth, as if crushed by a great fall. Above my head passed dishevelled clouds which by some optical illusion seemed to have become stationary while the tower, the ball, and myself were being carried away at an incredible speed. In the distance, the green countryside stretched out on one side, while on the other the sea sparkled under a sheaf of rays of sunlight. The Sound unwound to the Point of Elsinore, speckled with a few white sails exactly like seagulls' wings, and in the mist to the east rolled the coast of Sweden, only slightly smudged. This huge expanse swirled every time I looked at it.

Nevertheless I had to get up, stand straight up, and look. My first lesson in dizziness lasted an hour. When at last I was allowed down and could set foot again on the firm paving of the streets, I was aching all over.

'We'll do the same tomorrow,' announced my professor.

In fact I practised this dizzy-making exercise each day for five days. Whether I liked it or not, I made noticeable progress in the art of 'contemplation from high places'.

9

THE time came when we were due to leave. The day before, the obliging Mr Thomson had brought the warmest letters of recommendation for Count Trampe, the Governor of Iceland, Mr Pictursson, the Bishop's Coadjutor, and Mr Finsen, the Mayor of Reykjavik. In return my uncle granted him his heartiest handshake.

At 6 a.m. on the 2nd our precious luggage was already stowed on board the *Valkyrie*. The captain led us down to cabins that were rather narrow and situated under a sort of deck-house.

'Is the wind with us?' enquired my uncle.

'Perfectly,' replied Captain Bjarne. 'From the southeast. We can leave the Sound with the wind on the quarter and all sails set.'

A few moments later, the schooner, with lower foresail, brigantine, topsail, and mizen topgallant sail unfurled, cast off and sailed full speed into the strait. An hour later the capital of Denmark sank below the distant waves as the *Valkyrie* cut past the coast of Elsinore. In the state of nerves I was in, I half-expected to see Hamlet's shadow stalking along the legendary terrace.*

'Sublime dreamer,' I said. 'You'd probably have given us your blessing! You might even have wanted to come with us to the centre of the globe to seek a solution to your eternal doubt!'

But nothing appeared on the aged ramparts. In any case, the castle is much younger than the heroic prince of Denmark. It serves now as a luxurious lodge for the watchman of this strait of the Sound, through which 15,000 ships of all nations pass each year.

Kronoberg Castle soon disappeared into the mist, as did Helsingborg Tower on the Swedish coast. The schooner leaned over slightly in the breeze from the Kattegat.

The *Valkyrie* was a fine sailing ship, but with sails you never know exactly what to expect. She was transporting coal, household utensils, pottery, woollen clothing, and a cargo of wheat to Reykjavik. Five crew members, all Danish, were enough to man her.

'How long will the voyage take?' asked my uncle.

'About ten days, if we don't have too many nor'westers windward of the Faroes.'

'But you don't normally encounter significant delays?'

'No, Professor Lidenbrock. Don't worry, we'll get there.'

Towards evening the schooner rounded Cape Skagen, the northernmost point of Denmark, then during the night crossed the Skagerrak, cut across the tip of Norway to windward of Cape Lindesnes and ventured into the North Sea.

Two days later, we sighted the coast of Scotland in the region of Peterhead, and the *Valkyrie* headed towards the Faroe Islands, passing between the Orkneys and the Shetlands.

Soon our schooner was lashed by the waves of the Atlantic; she had to tack against the north wind, and reached the Faroes only with some difficulty. On the 8th, the captain caught sight of Mykiness, the westernmost of the Faroes,* and from that moment on headed straight for Portland Cape, on the southern coast of Iceland.

The crossing did not involve any special incident. I resisted sea-sickness quite well; whereas my uncle, to his great annoyance and even greater shame, was ill all the time.

As a result, he was unable to raise the subject of Snæfells with Captain Bjarne, or the availability of means of communication and transport. He had to put off these questions until he arrived, and spent all his time lying in the cabin, whose walls creaked whenever the ship rolled. It must be admitted that he had partly deserved his fate.

On the 11th, we sighted Portland Cape. The weather, clear at this point, allowed us to see Mýrdals-jökull standing up behind the cape, which consists of a large steep-sided hill solitarily washed up on the beach.

The *Valkyrie* kept a reasonable distance from the coast, working its way round towards the west while encircled by numerous schools of whales and sharks. Soon there appeared a huge outcrop with daylight showing through a hole where the foaming sea furiously surged. The West-mann Islands looked as if they had emerged directly from the ocean, like rocks planted in the liquid plains. From this point on the schooner kept well out so as to leave a wide berth while rounding Cape Reykjanes, which forms the westernmost corner of Iceland.

The sea was very rough, stopping my uncle from coming on deck to admire the shattered coasts lashed by the southwesterly wind.

Forty-eight hours later, after leaving behind a storm which had forced the schooner to run with all sails furled, we sighted to the east the beacon of Point Skagen,* whose dangerous rocks extend a long way out under the waves. An Icelandic pilot came on board, and three hours later the *Valkyrie* dropped anchor in Faxa Bay, beside Reykjavik itself.

The professor finally came out of his cabin, a little pale, a little shaky, but still enthusiastic and with a gleam of satisfaction in his eye.

The population of the town, enthralled by the arrival of a ship in which each expected something, congregated on the quayside.

My uncle was in a hurry to flee his floating prison-cum-hospital. But before leaving the deck of the schooner, he dragged me for'ard; there, near the northern part of the bay, stood a high mountain with two points on top, a double cone covered with perpetual snows.

'Snæfells,' he roared. 'Snæfells!'

He made a sign indicating total secrecy, and then climbed down into the waiting boat. Soon we were standing on the soil of Iceland itself.

The first man to appear had a pleasant countenance and a general's uniform. He was in fact a mere civilian, the Governor of the island, Baron Trampe himself. The professor realized who he was dealing with. He presented the Governor with the letters from Copenhagen and launched into a short conversation in Danish, which I took no part in at all, for a very good reason. But the result of this first interview was that Baron Trampe put himself entirely at Professor Lidenbrock's disposal.

My uncle also received a warm welcome from the Mayor, Mr Finsen, whose uniform was no less military than the Governor's, but whose temperament and function were just as peaceful.

As for the Coadjutor, Mr Pictursson, he was at present carrying out an episcopal visit to the Northern Diocese, so we had to postpone being introduced to him. But a charming citizen, whose help became extremely precious, was Mr Fridriksson, who taught science at Reykjavik School. This humble scholar spoke only Icelandic and Latin: he came and offered his services in the language of Horace, and I felt that we were bound to understand each other. He was in fact the only person I could converse with during my entire stay in Iceland.

Of the three rooms making up his household, this excellent man put two at our disposal, and soon we were ensconsed there together with our luggage, whose quantity slightly surprised the inhabitants of Reykjavik.

'Well, Axel,' said my uncle, 'things are working out. We are over the worst.'

'What do you mean, the worst?'

'I mean it's downhill all the way!'

'In that sense, you're right; but having gone down, won't we eventually have to come back up?'

'Oh, that will present no problem! Look, there is no time to be lost. I am going to visit the library. It might contain some manuscript of Saknussemm's, and if so I would very much like to have a look at it.'

'Well then, during that time I'll visit the town. Aren't you going to have a look at it yourself?'

'To tell the truth, I am not very much drawn by all that. What is interesting in this country of Iceland is below ground, not above.'

I went out, and walked around at random.

To get lost in the two streets of Reykjavik would have been difficult. I did not therefore have to ask my way, which can cause certain problems in sign language.

The town stretches out over rather low and marshy ground between two hills. A huge lava bed protects it on one side as it descends in gentle stages towards the sea. On the other stretches the vast Faxa Bay, encircled to the north by the huge glacier of Snæfells, and where the *Valkyrie* lay at anchor, alone for the moment. Normally, the British and French fish-patrols remain at anchor further out; but at this period they were working on the eastern coastline of the island.

The longer of Reykjavik's streets runs parallel to the

shore. This is where the shopkeepers and traders work, in log cabins of horizontal red beams. The shorter street, lying more to the west, heads towards a little lake, passing between the houses of the Bishop and other notables not in trade.

I had soon finished my tour of these bleak, depressing avenues. From time to time I caught sight of a scrap of faded lawn, like an old woollen carpet threadbare through use, or else some semblance of an orchard. Its rare produce—cabbages and lettuces—would not have seemed out of place on a table in Lilliput. A few sickly wallflowers endeavoured to look as though taking the sun.

Not far from the middle of the residential street, I found the public cemetery, enclosed by an earthen wall and with plenty of room left inside. Then, only a few yards away, the Governor's house, a farmhouse in comparison with Hamburg Town Hall, but a palace beside the huts of the Icelandic population.

Between the little lake and the town lay the church, in the Protestant style, built out of scorched rocks generously provided by the volcanoes themselves. During the strong westerly winds, the red tiles of its roof clearly had the habit of flying into the air, to the considerable danger of the congregation.*

On a nearby hillock, I discovered the National School where, as our host later told me, Hebrew, English, French, and Danish were taught, four languages of which, to my shame, I knew not a single word. I would have been the last amongst the forty pupils at this tiny school, and unworthy to sleep with them in those two-compartment cabinets where more sensitive souls might easily have suffocated on the very first night.

In three hours, I had visited not only the town but even its surroundings. Their appearance was especially dismal. No trees, no vegetation to speak of. Everywhere the bare bones of the volcanic rocks. The Icelandic habitations are made of earth and peat, and their walls slope inwards. They look like roofs placed on the ground—except that the roofs themselves constitute relatively fertile fields.

Thanks to the heat from the houses, grass grows here in abundance. It is carefully cut at haymaking time, for otherwise the animals from the houses would come and gently graze on these lush cottages.

During my excursion, I encountered few locals. When I got back to the street containing the shops, I found most of the population busy drying, salting, and loading cod, the main export. The men seemed robust but heavy, like blond Germans with pensive eyes. They must feel slightly outcast from humanity: exiles on this frozen land, whom nature should really have made Eskimos when she condemned people to live on the Arctic Circle. I tried in vain to surprise a smile on their faces; they sometimes laughed in a sort of involuntary contraction of the muscles, but never actually smiled.

Their clothing consisted of a coarse jumper of the black wool known in Scandinavian countries as *vadmel*,* a hat with a very broad rim, a pair of trousers with red piping, and a piece of folded leather in the way of shoes.

The women wore sad, resigned faces, of a fairly pleasant type but rather expressionless, and were dressed in a bodice and skirt of dark *vadmel*. Unmarried girls wore a small brown knitted bonnet on their hair, which was plaited into garlands; married women, a coloured kerchief on their heads, with a crest of white linen on top.

After a good walk I returned to Mr Fridriksson's house: my uncle was already there, together with his host.

10

DINNER was ready; it was devoured with great gusto by Professor Lidenbrock, whose stomach had become a deep chasm during the forced abstinence on board. The meal, more Danish than Icelandic, involved nothing remarkable in itself; but our host, more Icelandic than Danish, reminded me of the heroes of Classical hospitality. It was clear that we were more part of his household than the man himself.

Conversation used the native tongue, interspersed for my sake with German by my uncle and Latin by Mr Fridriksson. It concerned scientific subjects, as is appropriate for scholars; but Professor Lidenbrock maintained a very strict reserve, and at each sentence his eyes told me to keep a total silence about our future plans.

First Mr Fridriksson questioned my uncle about the results of his research in the library.

'Your library! It consists of lonely books on almost deserted shelves.'

'What! We have 8,000 volumes, many of which are valuable and rare, including works in old Scandinavian, plus all the new books that Copenhagen sends each year.'

'Where do you keep those 8,000 volumes! For my part . . .'

'Professor Lidenbrock, they're all over the country. We enjoy studying in our frozen old land. Every farmer, every fisherman knows how to read, and does read. We believe that books, instead of mouldering behind bars, far from interested examination, are meant to be worn out by readers' eyes. So these books are passed from person to person, looked at, read and re-read; and often they do not come back to the shelves for a year or two.'

'In the meantime,' replied my uncle with some annoyance, 'poor foreigners . . .'

'It cannot be helped. Foreigners have their own libraries at home and, above all, our farm-labourers need to educate themselves. As I mentioned, the love of study is in the Icelandic blood. Thus in 1816, we founded a Literary Society which is still thriving; foreign scholars are honoured to become members; it publishes books for the enlightenment of our fellow citizens, and it performs a real service for the country. If you wished to be one of its corresponding members, Professor Lidenbrock, we would be delighted.'

My uncle, who already belonged to a hundred or so scientific societies, accepted with good grace, which greatly pleased Mr Fridriksson.

'Now,' said he, 'please indicate the books you hoped to

find in our library, and I can perhaps provide some information on them.'

I looked at my uncle. He could not decide whether or not to reply. This matter concerned his projects directly. However, after thinking for a while, he decided to speak.

'Mr Fridriksson, I wish to know whether you have, amongst the oldest works, those of a certain Arne Saknussemm?'

'Arne Saknussemm! You are referring to that scholar of the sixteenth century, who was a great naturalist, a great alchemist, and a great traveller?'

'Precisely.'

'One of the stars of Icelandic literature and science?'

'As you so well put it.'

'One of the most illustrious of men?'

'Most certainly.'

'And whose courage was as great as his genius?'

'I see you know him perfectly.'

My uncle was in ecstasy to hear his hero spoken of in this way. He was devouring Mr Fridriksson with his eyes.

'Well?' he asked. 'What about his works?'

'H'm . . . his works, we do not have.'

'What, even in Iceland?'

'They do not exist, in Iceland or anywhere else.'

'And why ever not?'

'Because Arne Saknussemm was persecuted for heresy, and his works were burned in Copenhagen in 1573 by the hand of the executioner.'

'Good! Splendid!' shouted my uncle, greatly shocking the science teacher.

'Eh?'

'Yes, everything is explained, everything fits together, all is clear, and now I understand why Saknussemm, having been put on the Index and forced to hide the discoveries of his genius, had to conceal the secret in an incomprehensible word-puzzle . . .'

'What secret?' enquired Mr Fridriksson keenly.

'A secret that . . . by means of which . . .' spluttered my uncle.

'Do you by any chance have some special document?'

'No . . . I was making a pure supposition.'

'Fine,' replied Mr Fridriksson, who had observed my uncle's confusion and was kind enough not to insist. 'I hope', he added, 'that you will not leave our island without delving into its mineral riches?'

'Certainly, but perhaps I arrive a little late in the day; have any scholars been through here already?'

'Yes, Professor Lidenbrock; the work of Olafsen and Povelsen, carried out by order of the King, Troil's studies, Gaimard and Robert's scientific mission on board the French corvette *La Recherche*,[1] and recently the observations of scholars on board the frigate the *Reine Hortense*,* have all contributed very considerably to our knowledge of Iceland. But believe me, there are still things to be done.'

'Do you really think so?' said my uncle a shade naively, trying to make his eyes shine less.

'Yes. How many mountains, glaciers, volcanoes there are to be studied, still hardly explored! Look, without going any further, consider that mountain on the horizon. It is called Snæfells.'

'Is it indeed? "Snæfells."'

'Yes, a most unusual volcano, whose crater is rarely visited.'

'Extinct?'

'Oh yes. Extinct for the last 500 years.'

'Well!' replied my uncle, frantically crossing and uncrossing his legs so as not to jump into the air. 'I feel like beginning my geological studies with this Snyfil . . . Feless . . . what did you call it?'

'Snæfells,' repeated the excellent Mr Fridriksson.

This part of the conversation took place in Latin. I had followed everything, hardly able to keep a straight face when I had seen my uncle trying to keep his satisfaction

---

[1] *La Recherche* was sent by Admiral Duperré in 1835 to find the traces of a lost expedition, that of M. de Blosseville and *La Lilloise*, of which no trace has ever been found.

in, flowing as it was from every pore. He had been trying to put on an innocent air which made him look like a grimacing old devil.

'Yes,' he said, 'your words have made up my mind! We will try and climb this Snæfells, perhaps even study its crater!'

'I very much regret that my duties do not allow me to leave Reykjavik; I would have willingly accompanied you with pleasure and profit.'

'No, no!' quickly replied my uncle. 'We wish to disturb nobody, Mr Fridriksson. I thank you with all my heart. To have a scholar like you with us would have been very useful, but your professional duties . . .'

I like to think that our host, in the innocence of his Icelandic soul, did not suspect my uncle's blatant tricks.

'It seems a very good idea, Professor Lidenbrock, to begin with this volcano. You will make many interesting observations there. But tell me, how are you planning to reach the Snæfells peninsula?'

'By sea, crossing the bay. It is the quickest route.'

'No doubt; but it cannot be taken.'

'Why not?'

'Because we do not have a single small boat in Reykjavik.'

'My God!'

'You will have to go by land, following the coast. It will take longer, but be more interesting.'

'Good. I will see to obtaining a guide.'

'As a matter of fact I have one to offer you.'

'Who is reliable and intelligent?'

'Yes, he lives on the peninsula. He is an eider hunter, highly skilled, and whom you will be pleased with. He speaks perfect Danish.'

'And when can I see him?'

'Tomorrow if you wish.'

'Why not today?'

'Because he will only be here tomorrow.'

'Tomorrow then,' with a sigh.

This decisive conversation finished a few moments later

with warm thanks from the German scholar to his Icelandic counterpart. During the dinner, my uncle had gathered some vital information, including the story of Saknussemm, the reason for his mysterious document, the fact that his host would not be accompanying him on the expedition, and the news that a guide would be at his orders the very next day.

11

IN the evening, I went for a brief walk along the sea-front of Reykjavik, came back early, and then retired to my bed of rough planks, where I slept the sleep of the just.

On waking up, I heard my uncle talking volubly in the next room. I quickly got up and joined him.

He was speaking Danish with a tall man, robustly built. This great strapping figure was clearly of unusual strength. His eyes, in a head of very considerable size and a certain *naïveté*, appeared intelligent to me. They were of a dreamy blue colour. Long hair, which would have passed for red even in Britain, fell on athletic shoulders. This native was supple in his movements, but moved his arms little, like a man who didn't know the language of gestures or didn't bother to use it. Everything about him revealed a perfectly calm nature, not lazy, but composed. You felt that he didn't require anything from anyone, that he worked as it suited him, that his philosophy of life couldn't be astonished or disturbed by anything in this world.

I was able to detect the nuances of the Icelander's character by the way he listened to the passionate flow of words addressed to him. He remained with his arms crossed, not moving despite my uncle's repeated gesticulations; to say no, his head turned from left to right, to say yes, downwards; but so little that his long hair hardly moved. He was not so much economical with his movements as tight-fisted.

Certainly, looking at this man, I would never have

guessed that he was a hunter. He wouldn't frighten the game, for sure, but how could he possibly get near it?

Everything became clear when Mr Fridriksson reminded me that this calm person was only a hunter of eider, a bird whose plumage constitutes the main resource of the island. Called eiderdown, you do not need to move a great deal to collect it.

During the first days of summer, the female eider, a kind of prettified duck, goes and builds her nest amongst the rocks of the fjords[1] which fringe the coast. The nest built, she carpets it with fine feathers that she tears out of her stomach. Straightaway the hunter, or rather merchant, arrives, takes the nest, and the female starts her work again. This continues as long as she has any down left. When she is completely bare, it is the male's turn to contribute his. But as the hard, rough feathers of the male have no commercial value, the hunter does not bother to steal his future brood's bed. So the nest is completed; the female lays her eggs; the babies hatch; and, the following year, the hunting of the eiderdown starts again.

However, since the eider does not choose steep rocks to build her nest on, but easy, horizontal ones sloping down into the sea, the Icelandic hunter can practise his profession without too much commotion. He is a farmer who doesn't have to sow his seed or cut his harvest, but merely gather it in.

This serious, phlegmatic, silent type was called Hans Bjelke; and he came with Mr Fridriksson's recommendations. He was our future guide—whose manner contrasted singularly with my uncle's.

Nevertheless they got on well from the start. Neither of them discussed prices; the one ready to accept whatever was offered, the other to pay whatever was asked. Never was a deal easier to reach.

According to their agreement, Hans undertook to guide us to the village of Stapi, on the southern coast of the Snæfells peninsula and at the very foot of the volcano.

---

[1] The name given to the long narrow inlets in Scandinavian countries.

The distance by land was about 22 miles, or two days' journey according to my uncle's reckoning.

But when he learned that these were Danish miles, of 24,000 feet apiece, he had to readjust his calculations, and plan on seven or eight days' travel, given the poor quality of the tracks.

Four horses were to be put at our disposal, two for riding and two for luggage. Hans would travel on foot, which he was used to. He knew this part of the coast like the back of his hand, and promised to take us by the shortest route.

His contract with my uncle did not expire when we arrived at Stapi. He remained in his service for the total time necessary for his scientific excursions, at the price of three rix-dollars per week.[1] It was expressly agreed that this sum would be paid to the guide each Saturday evening, failing which his contract would be null and void.

It was decided to leave on 16 June. My uncle wanted to give the hunter an advance on the agreement, but was rebuffed with a single word.

'Efter.'*

'After,' said the professor for my edification.

Once the agreement had been reached, the hunter promptly left.

'He's perfect,' exclaimed my uncle. 'But he can hardly realize the brilliant part he is going to play.'

'So he's coming with us . . .'

'. . . to the centre of the Earth.'

There were still forty-eight hours left, but to my great regret, I had to use them for the preparations. All our intelligence was employed organizing the things in the most useful way, the instruments here, the firearms there, the tools in this package, the food in that. Four groups in all.

The instruments included:

1. A centigrade thermometer made by Eigel, graduated to 150°, which didn't seem quite right to me. Too

[1] 16 francs 98 centimes.

much if the temperature went up as far as that, since we would be cooked. But not enough to measure the temperature of hot springs or other molten substances.

2. A manometer operated by compressed air, designed to show pressures greater than that at sea-level. An ordinary barometer would not have been sufficient, given that the atmospheric pressure was due to increase proportionally with our descent underground.

3. A chronometer by Boissonas Junior of Geneva, perfectly set to the Hamburg meridian.

4. Two compasses to measure positive and negative inclination.

5. A night-glass.

6. Two Ruhmkorff* lamps which used an electric current to give a highly portable source of light, reliable and not too bulky.[1]

The arms consisted of two rifles from Purdley More & Co. and two Colt revolvers. Why take them? I didn't imagine we were going to encounter all that many savages or wild beasts. But my uncle seemed very attached to his arsenal and his instruments, and especially to a considerable quantity of guncotton, which is unaffected by damp and whose explosive power is far greater than that of ordinary powder.

[1] The Ruhmkorff apparatus consists of a Bunsen battery, activated by means of potassium dichromate, which is odourless; an induction coil transmits the electricity produced by the battery to a lantern of a particular nature. In this lantern there is a glass coil under vacuum, in which there remains only a residue of CO_2 and nitrogen. When the apparatus is in operation, this gas becomes luminous, producing a continuous white light. The battery and coil are placed in a leather bag that the traveller wears over one shoulder. The lantern, placed outside, provides more than sufficient light in total darkness. It allows one to venture without fear of explosion amongst the most inflammable gases, and does not go out even when immersed in the deepest rivers. M. Ruhmkorff is a learned and skilful physicist. His great discovery is that of the induction coil, which allows high-tension electricity to be produced. He has just obtained, in 1864, the prize of 50,000 francs that France awards every five years for the most ingenious application of electricity.

The tools were two ice-picks, two pickaxes, one ladder made of silk, three alpenstocks, one axe, one hammer, a dozen iron wedges and pitons, and several long knotted ropes. This could not help making a large packet, for the ladder alone was 300 feet in length.

Finally there were the provisions. The parcel was not a big one, but was reassuring, for I knew that it contained six months' supply of dried meat and biscuits. Gin was the only liquid, with water totally absent: we had flasks, and my uncle counted on springs to fill them. The objections I raised as to their quality, temperature, and even existence were ignored.

To complete the list of our travel items, I will mention a portable medical kit containing blunt-bladed scissors, splints for fractures, a strip of holland material, bandages and compresses, sticking plaster, a basin for blood-letting—terrifying objects in themselves; but in addition a whole series of bottles containing dextrin, surgical spirit, liquid acetate of lead, ether, vinegar, and ammonia, all drugs of a frightening nature; and finally the materials necessary for the Ruhmkorff lamps.

My uncle was careful not to forget a supply of tobacco, powder for hunting, and tinder, nor a leather belt he wore round his waist and which contained an adequate supply of money in gold, silver, and paper form. Six stout pairs of shoes, waterproofed by means of a coating of tar and gutta-percha, fell into the category of 'miscellaneous items'.

'With such clothing, shoes, and equipment, there is no reason we shouldn't go far,' declared my uncle.

The 14th was entirely taken up with organizing the various items. In the evening we dined at Baron Trampe's, in the company of the Mayor of Reykjavik and Dr Hyaltalin, the most distinguished physician in the country. Mr Fridriksson was not amongst the guests; I learned later that the Governor and he were in disagreement on an administrative matter and did not speak to each other. As a result I didn't have the opportunity of understanding a single word of what was said during this semi-official dinner. I noticed only that my uncle spoke all the time.

The following day, our preparations were finished. Our host delighted the professor by presenting him with a chart of Iceland which was incomparably better than Handerson's: it was the map drawn up by Mr Olaf Nikolas Olsen, on a scale of 1:480,000, published by the Icelandic Literary Society and based on Mr Scheel Frisac's geodesic work and Mr Bjorn Gumlavgson's topographical survey. It constituted a precious document for a mineralogist.

The last evening was spent in close conversation with Mr Fridriksson, for whom I felt the warmest sympathy; after the talk came a rather agitated sleep, for me at least.

At five o'clock, I was woken up by four horses whinnying and prancing directly below my window. I dressed quickly and went outside. Hans was finishing loading the luggage, almost without moving a finger. He worked, however, with an unusual degree of skill. My uncle was producing more heat than light and the guide seemed to be taking very little notice of his recommendations.

Everything was ready by six. Mr Fridriksson shook our hands. With a great deal of warmth and in Icelandic, my uncle thanked him for his kind hospitality. As for myself, I strung together a cordial farewell in my best Latin. Then we climbed into the saddles, and Mr Fridriksson accompanied his final goodbye to me with that line from Virgil that seemed ready-made for us, uncertain travellers on the road:

Et quacumque viam dederit fortuna sequamur.[*]

12

WE had left in overcast but settled weather. No exhausting heat to fear, no disastrous rain. Weather for tourists.

The joy of riding through an unknown land made me easy to please at the beginning of our venture. I was caught up in the happiness of those who go on journeys, a feeling of hope mixed with a sense of freedom. I began to feel involved in the trip.

'In any case, what do I risk? Travelling through a fascinating country, going up a remarkable mountain, at worst climbing down an extinct crater! It's clear that that's all Saknussemm ever did. As for the existence of a tunnel leading straight to the centre of the globe: pure fantasy, totally impossible! So let's get whatever good we can out of this expedition, and not quibble too much about the rest.'

By the time my thoughts had got this far, we had left Reykjavik.

Hans walked in front, at a quick but regular and unchanging pace. The two horses followed with our luggage, without his having to lead them. My uncle and I came last, trying not to make too much of a sight of ourselves on our small but hardy mounts.

Iceland is one of the biggest islands in Europe. It covers 1,400 square 'miles',* but has only 60,000 inhabitants. Geographers have divided it into four parts, and it was the Region of the Southwest Quarter, 'Sudvestr Fjordùngr', that we had to cross, almost diagonally.

On leaving Reykjavik, Hans had immediately followed the sea-shore. We crossed thin pastures that made great efforts to be green: but yellow had more success. The rugged summits of the trachytic* hills faded away amongst the mists on the eastern horizon. From time to time, patches of snow, concentrating the diffuse light, shone on the slopes of distant mountains. A few peaks, standing up more firmly, pointed through the grey clouds, to reappear above the shifting mists like bare reefs in an open sky.

Often these chains of dry rocks pushed out towards the sea, eating into the pasture, but there was always room to get past. In any case our horses instinctively chose the best route without ever slowing their pace. My uncle did not even have the consolation of using his voice or whip to urge his mount forward: he had no excuse to be impatient. I couldn't help smiling when I saw him so big on his little horse for, with his long legs skimming the ground, he looked like a six-legged centaur.

'Nice animal, nice animal!' he kept saying. 'You will see, Axel, that a creature more intelligent than the Icelandic horse does not exist. Snow, storms, blocked paths, rocks, glaciers—nothing stops him. He is brave, he is cautious, he is reliable. Never a foot wrong, never a false reaction. Should a stream appear, a fjord to be crossed— and they *will* appear—you will see him throw himself unhesitatingly into the water like an amphibian and swim across to the other side. If we do not upset him, if we let him do as he wishes, we shall cover our 25 miles a day, the one carrying the other.'

'*We* will, I'm sure; but what about the guide?'

'Oh, I am not worried about him. That sort of person walks without noticing. Our guide moves so little that he cannot possibly get tired. In any case, I will give him my horse if need be. I would soon get cramps if I did not take some exercise. My arms feel all right, but one must not neglect one's legs.'

We meanwhile carried on at a considerable pace. The countryside was already virtually deserted. Here and there an isolated farm, a lonely *boer*[1] built of wood, earth, and blocks of lava, appeared like a beggar beside a rough track. These dilapidated huts seemed to be imploring the charity of passers-by, and one would almost have offered them alms. In this region, roads and even paths were completely lacking, and the vegetation, however slow-growing, soon hid the traces of the infrequent travellers.

And yet this part of the province, a stone's throw from the capital, was considered one of the inhabited and cultivated parts of Iceland. What were the areas like then that were more deserted than this desert? After half a mile we had still not seen a single farmer at the door of his cottage, nor a single wild shepherd grazing a flock less wild than himself; only some cows, plus a few sheep left to their own devices. What would the regions in turmoil

---

[1] The house of an Icelandic peasant-farmer.

be like, broken by the eruptions, born of volcanic explosions and underground upheavals?

We were due to make their acquaintance later; but when I consulted Olsen's map, I saw that we were avoiding them by following the winding edge of the shore. The main eruptive movements are in fact concentrated in the interior of the island. There, the horizontal strata of superimposed rocks called *trapps* in the Scandinavian languages, the trachytic strips, the eruptions of basalt, of tuff,* of all the volcanic aggregates, the streams of lava and of molten porphyry, have produced a country of supernatural horror. I hardly realized at this stage what a sight awaited us on the Snæfells peninsula, where the damage wrought by an impulsive Nature forms a fearsome chaos.

Two hours after leaving Reykjavik, we arrived at Gufunes 'aoalkirkja' ('main church' or 'settlement'). It contained nothing special. Just a handful of houses. Hardly enough for a hamlet in Germany.

Hans decided to stop there for half an hour; he shared our frugal breakfast, replied 'yes' or 'no' to my uncle's questions about the nature of the road, and when asked where he intended to spend the night:

'Garðar,' was all he would say.

I looked at the map to know what Garðar was. I found a small community of this name on the shore of the Hvalfjörd, four 'miles' away from Reykjavik. I showed it to my uncle.

'Only four miles!' he said. 'Four out of 22! This is just a pleasant stroll.'

He tried to say something to the guide, who did not reply but took up his position at the head of the horses and set off again.

Three hours later, still travelling over the faded grass of the pastures, we had to work our way around the Kollafjörd, as detouring round this estuary was easier and quicker than crossing it. Soon we had reached a 'pingstar' ('tiny administrative unit') called Ejulberg, whose tower would have struck twelve, if the Icelandic churches had been rich enough to possess a clock; but they closely resemble their parishioners, who have no watches, but manage quite well without.

The horses were watered there; and afterwards took us along a shore squeezed in between the sea and a chain of hills, then carried us without stopping to the 'aoalkirkja' of Brantär, and then a mile further to Saurböer* Annexia ('church annex'), situated on the southern shores of the Hvalfjörd.

It was now four o'clock, and we had covered four 'miles'.[1]

The fjord was at least half a 'mile' wide at this point; the waves crashed noisily on to the sharp rocks; this bay opened out between high rocky walls, a sort of vertical scarp 3,000 feet high, with remarkable brown strata separated by tuff beds of a reddish tinge. However intelligent our horses were, I was not looking forward to crossing a real sea-estuary on the back of a four-legged animal.

'If they really are smart,' I said, 'they won't try and cross. In any case, I'm planning to be smart for them.'

But my uncle didn't want to wait. He spurred his horse on towards the shore. His mount sniffed slightly at the swell lapping at the edge, and stopped. My uncle, who had his own instinct, urged it on all the more. Another refusal from the beast, who shook his head. Next, oaths and an application of the whip, but kicks from the creature, who began to unsaddle the rider. Finally the small horse, bending his knees, withdrew from the professor's legs and left him standing there on two sea-shore rocks, like the Colossus of Rhodes.

'Cursed animal!' shouted the rider, suddenly converted into a pedestrian, as humiliated as a cavalry officer turned infantryman.

'Färja,'* said the guide, touching him on the shoulder.

'What, a ferry?'

'Der,' replied Hans, pointing to a boat.

'Yes,' I called out, 'there's a ferry.'

'You should have said so earlier! Well, come on!'

[1] Twenty miles.

'Tidvatten.'

'What's he saying?'

'He's saying "tide",' translated my uncle from the Danish.

'We presumably have to wait for the tide?'

'Förbida?'

'Ja.'*

My uncle stamped his foot, while the horses headed for the ferry.

I perfectly understood the need to wait for a particular moment of the tide before starting to cross the fjord: the moment when the sea has reached its highest level and so is not moving. The ebb and flow are not felt then and the ferry is not in danger of being carried to the bottom of the bay or out to the open sea.

The right time only arrived at six o'clock. My uncle, myself, the guide, two ferrymen, and the four horses had got on to a sort of flatboat which looked rather fragile. Accustomed as I was to the steam-ferries on the Elbe, I found the boatmen's oars an unimpressive mechanical device. It took more than an hour to cross the fjord; but finally we arrived without incident.

Half an hour later, we had reached the 'aoalkirkja' of Garðar.

13

It should have been dark, but on the 65th parallel, I was not surprised by light during the night in the Arctic regions: in June and July in Iceland the sun never sets.

Nevertheless, the temperature had gone down. I was cold and above all hungry. Most welcome was the 'boer' which hospitably opened to receive us.

It was a peasant's house but worth a king's in terms of hospitality. When we arrived, the master came to shake our hands and, without further ado, indicated we should follow him into the house.

'Follow him', for it would have been impossible to go in at the same time. A long, narrow, dark passage led into this dwelling constructed of beams that had hardly been squared off. It gave access to each of the rooms: the kitchen, the weaving workshop, the 'badstofa' (family bedroom), and, the best of all, the visitors' bedroom. My uncle, whose height had not been remotely considered when the house was built, duly hit his head three or four times against the projections of the ceiling.

We were shown into our room, which was quite large and had an earthen floor and a window with panes made of rather opaque sheep membranes. The bed was dry straw heaped into two wooden frames painted red and ornamented with maxims in Icelandic. I was not expecting such comfort; but the house was pervaded with a strong smell of dried fish, marinated meat, and soured milk which rather upset my nose.

After setting down our travellers' saddlery, we heard our host's voice inviting us into the kitchen, the only room with a fire, even during the very coldest weather.

My uncle hastened to follow his hospitable suggestion. I followed suit.

The kitchen chimney was of the classical sort: just a stone as a hearth in the middle of the room, with a hole in the roof to let the smoke out. The kitchen also served as the dining-room.

When we came in, our host, as if seeing us for the first time, greeted us with the word 'sællvertu', which means 'be happy', and came and kissed us on the cheek.

His wife pronounced the same word in turn, accompanied by the same greeting; then the two of them, putting their right hands on their hearts, bowed deeply.

I hasten to add that the Icelandic woman was the mother of nineteen children, some small and some big and all chaotically teeming in the spirals of smoke filling the room from the hearth. At each moment I caught sight of another little blond head of some melancholy emerging from the cloud. It was exactly like a line of angels who had forgotten to wash their faces.

My uncle and I gave a very warm welcome to the brood; soon we had three or four of the urchins on our shoulders, the same number on our laps and the others between our knees. Those who could speak repeated 'sællvertu' in all imaginable pitches. Those who could not merely shouted louder.

The concert was interrupted by the meal being announced. At this moment the hunter came back, having seen to the horses' food, by thriftily letting them out on the countryside. The poor beasts had to be satisfied with chewing the rare mosses on the rocks and some seaweed without much sustenance: the following day they would be sure to come of their own accord to continue the work of the day before.

'Sællvertu,' said Hans.

Then, calmly, automatically, without one kiss being different from another, he greeted the host, the hostess, and their nineteen children.

Once the ceremony was finished, we moved to table, all twenty-four of us, and consequently some literally on top of the others. The luckiest ones had only two urchins on their knees.

However, silence fell across the whole community when the soup was served, and the natural Icelandic taciturnity, even amongst the youngsters, came back. Our host served us a lichen soup which was not unpleasant, then an enormous portion of dried fish swimming in some butter that had been soured for twenty years, and was consequently much to be preferred to fresh butter according to the gastronomic ideas of Iceland. With it was 'skyr', a sort of soured milk, served with biscuits and sweetened with the juice of juniper berries; and finally, as a drink, whey mixed with water, called 'blanda' in this country. If this remarkable food was good or not, I was unable to judge. I was hungry and, when the dessert came, swallowed every last mouthful of the thick buckwheat porridge.

After the meal was finished, the children disappeared; the adults grouped round the hearth which was burning with peat, heather, cowpats, and the bones from the dried fish. Then, after this 'taking of the heat', the various groups went to their respective rooms. The hostess, as was the custom, offered to take off our stockings and trousers; but, following our gracious declining of this offer, did not insist, and I was finally able to curl up in my straw bedding.

The following day, at five o'clock, we bade the Icelandic farmer farewell, although my uncle had great difficulty in making him accept sufficient payment; and finally Hans gave the signal for departure.

Less than a hundred yards from Garðar, the appearance of the landscape began to change: the ground became marshy and the going less easy. On the right, the chain of mountains extended indefinitely, in a huge system of natural fortifications, of which we were following the counterscarp; often there were streams, which had to be forded, and without getting the bags too wet.

The wasteland was getting more and more deserted. Sometimes, nevertheless, a human shadow in the distance seemed to be shunning contact. If the bends of the path unexpectedly brought us near one of these ghosts, I felt a sudden disgust at the sight of a swollen head with shiny skin devoid of hair and repulsive wounds showing through the rents in the miserable rags.

The unhappy creature did not come to tend his deformed hand; he ran away instead, but not before Hans had had time to greet him with the customary 'sællvertu'.

'Spetelsk,'* he said.

'A leper!'

This single word produced a frightful effect. The horrible affliction of leprosy is relatively common in Iceland; it is not contagious, but is hereditary: accordingly the wretched creatures are forbidden to marry.

These wraith-like figures were hardly calculated to add joy to the countryside, which was becoming deeply depressing, as the last patches of grass died under our feet. Not a single tree, if one excludes a few thickets of dwarf birches similar to brushwood. Not a single animal, except a few horses that their owner could not feed and which wandered over the sad plains. Sometimes a falcon glided amongst the grey clouds and fled in full flight towards some southern clime; I let myself become absorbed in the melancholy of this untamed nature, and my memories took me back to my native land.

Soon we had to cross several insignificant little fjords, and finally a real bay; the tide, steady at this time, allowed us to traverse without waiting and thus reach the hamlet of Alftanes, a 'mile' further on the other side.

In the evening, after fording across two rivers teeming with trout and pike, the Alfa and Heta,* we were obliged to spend the night in a tumbledown abandoned cottage, worthy of being haunted by all the goblins of Scandinavian mythology; the god of cold had clearly taken up residence there, and he was up to his tricks the whole night.

The following day presented no particular incident. Still the same marshy ground, the same uniform view, the same sad features. In the evening we had covered half the total distance, and slept in the 'Annexia' at Krösolbt.

On 19 June, a bed of lava extended beneath our feet for about a 'mile'; this shape of ground is called *hraun* locally; the lava, wrinkled on the surface, produced shapes like thick ropes, either simply stretched out or coiled up on themselves. A huge lava flow came down from the neighbouring mountains, volcanoes now extinct, but whose remnants testified to the violence of the past. A few wreaths of steam from hot springs still crept here and there.

We had little time to marvel at these phenomena; we had to push on. Soon the marshy ground came back under our horses' feet, criss-crossed by little lakes. We were now proceeding in a westerly direction; we had worked our way round the great Faxa Bay, and the two white peaks of Snæfells stood erect amongst the clouds less than five 'miles' away.

The horses were moving well; the problems of the terrain did not stop them. For my part I was beginning to feel very tired; my uncle remained as stiff and as upright as on the first day; I could not help admiring him as much as the hunter, who considered this expedition a simple stroll.

On Saturday, 20 June, at 6 p.m., we got to Büdir, a village on the sea-coast, and the guide asked for his agreed pay. My uncle settled the sum. It was Hans's own family—his uncles and first cousins—who offered their hospitality. We were kindly welcomed, and without wishing to abuse the generosity of these good people, I would have been very glad to recover from the fatigues of the journey in their house. But my uncle, who had nothing to recover from, didn't see it that way; and the following day we had to straddle our good old mounts once more.

The ground was affected by being near the mountain, with granite roots emerging from the earth like those of an old oak. We were working our way round the huge base of the volcano. The professor couldn't take his eyes off it; he waved his arms, he seemed to be sending challenges at it, as if saying: 'That's the giant I am going to slay!' Finally, after four hours' ride, the horses stopped of their own accord at the front door of the Stapi parsonage.

14

STAPI is a settlement of about thirty shacks, built on the lava itself and under the rays of the sun reflected from the volcano. It lies at the end of a little fjord which forms part of a basalt wall of a most curious appearance.

It needs no repeating that basalt is a dark brown rock of igneous origin. It takes on regular forms which produce surprising patterns. Nature proceeds geometrically here, working in the human fashion, as if she had used a set-square, a pair of compasses and a plumb-line. If in every other case her art consists of great heaps strewn in disorder, barely-formed cones, imperfect pyramids, strange collections of lines—here, wanting to provide an example of regularity, and working before the architects of the first ages, she has constructed a severe order which has never been surpassed, even by the marvels of Babylon or the wonders that were Greece.

I had of course heard of the Giants' Causeway in Ireland and Fingal's Cave on one of the Hebrides, but I had never actually seen the display of a basalt construction.

Here, at Stapi, I was able to appreciate the full beauty of the phenomenon.

The walls of the fjord, like the whole coast of the peninsula, were made up of a series of vertical columns, thirty feet high. These straight shafts of perfect proportions supported an archivolt, made of horizontal columns whose overhang produced a half-vault over the sea. At intervals under this natural impluvium, one's eye detected arched openings of a superb design, through which the waves from the open sea rushed and foamed. A few basalt sections, torn off by the ocean's furies, were stretched out on the ground like the remains of a Classical temple, ruins eternally young, over which the centuries would pass without leaving any mark.

This was the last overnight stop of our overland journey. Hans had brought us here with intelligence, and I drew some reassurance from the thought that he was to accompany us further.

When we arrived at the door of the Rector's house, a simple low-built croft that was no finer and no more comfortable than its neighbours, I found a man shoeing a horse, hammer in hand and dressed in a leather apron.

'Sællvertu,' the hunter said.

'God dag,' replied the shoeing-smith in perfect Danish.

'Kyrkoherde,' said Hans, turning to my uncle.

'The Rector! It seems, Axel, that this good man is the Rector.'

In the meantime the guide had been explaining the situation to the 'Kyrkoherde': interrupting his work, this man shouted out in a way presumably designed for horses and horse dealers, and immediately a big, ugly woman came out of the croft. If she was not six foot tall, the difference wasn't worth mentioning.

I was afraid that she might offer the travellers an Icelandic kiss; but this didn't happen and nor did she demonstrate very good grace in showing us into her house.

The guest-room seemed to me the worst in the vicarage, narrow, dirty, and foul-smelling. But we had no choice. The Rector apparently didn't practise the traditional hospitality. Far from it. Before the day was out, I could see that we were dealing with a blacksmith, a fisherman, a hunter, a carpenter, and not at all with a minister of the Lord. We were in mid-week, it has to be admitted. Perhaps he made up for it on Sundays.

I do not wish to criticize these poor priests who are, after all, perfectly wretched: they get a ludicrous income from the Danish Government and receive a quarter of a tithe from their parish, which does not even add up to 60 marks at present-day values.[1] Hence the need to work for a living. But by fishing, hunting, and shoeing horses, one ends up adopting the manners, tone, and habits of hunters, fishermen, and other slightly rustic people. That same evening I noticed that amongst our host's virtues, sobriety did not figure.

My uncle quickly understood what sort of man he was dealing with: instead of a fine, worthy scholar, he found a heavy, rude countryman. He accordingly resolved to initiate his great expedition as soon as possible and to leave this inhospitable rectory. Ignoring his tiredness, he decided we would spend a few days in the mountains.

Preparations for leaving were accordingly made the day after arriving at Stapi. Hans hired the services of three Icelanders to replace the horses carrying the luggage; once we got to the bottom of the crater, these locals would have to turn back, leaving us on our own. That point was made clear.

At this juncture, my uncle had to tell the hunter of his intention to continue his exploration of the volcano to its furthermost limits.

Hans merely inclined his head. Whether he went there

---

[1] Hamburg unit, worth about 90 francs.

or somewhere else, whether he plunged into the innards of his island or travelled over its surface, made no difference to him. I myself had rather forgotten about the future, distracted until this point by the events of the journey—but now felt my feelings taking hold of me more than ever. What could I do? If I had wanted to try and stand up to Professor Lidenbrock, it ought to have been in Hamburg and not at the foot of Snæfells.

One idea above all others worried me tremendously, a terrifying idea that would unsettle nerves stronger than mine.

'So,' I said to myself, 'we're going to go up Snæfells. Fine. We're going to have a look at its crater. Good. Others have done it and lived to tell the tale. But that is not all. If a path appears going down into the bowels of the Earth, if that wretched Saknussemm told the truth, we're going to get lost in the underground galleries of the volcano. But there's nothing to say that Snæfells really is extinct! What proves that an eruption is not in preparation? Because the monster has been asleep since 1229,* does it necessarily follow that it won't wake up again? And if it does wake up, what will happen to us?'

It was certainly worth thinking about; which I was doing most seriously. I couldn't sleep without dreaming of eruptions. And playing the part of scoria seemed to me rather a difficult one.

In the end I couldn't stand it any more. I decided to put the case to my uncle as skilfully as possible, presenting it as a hypothesis which couldn't possibly be put into practice.

I went and found him. I shared my fears with him, and then retreated so that he could explode unhindered.

'I've been thinking about it,' was his only reply.

What did these words mean? Was he going to listen to the voice of reason? Was he thinking of giving up his projects? It seemed much too good to be true.

After a few moments of silence, during which I did not dare to question him, he continued:

'I had thought of it. Since we arrived in Stapi, I have

anxiously considered the critical question you have just put to me, for we must not be hasty.'

'No, we mustn't,' I said emphatically.

'Although Snæfells has been silent for 600 years, it might speak again. But eruptions are always preceded by perfectly well-known phenomena. I have therefore questioned the local inhabitants, I have surveyed the ground, and I can assure you, Axel, that there will not be an eruption.'

I stood flabbergasted at this statement, and was not able to reply.

'Do you not believe me?' said my uncle. 'Well then: follow me.'

I obeyed without thinking. Leaving the Rectory, the professor took a direct route which led through a gap in the basalt rock-face, heading inland. Soon we were out in the open country, if that term can be used for a huge waste-ground of discarded volcanic material. The country appeared flattened under a hail of huge rocks, of trapp, basalt, granite, and all the pyroxenic rocks.*

Here and there I could see exhalations rising in the air: these white mists, called 'reykir' in Icelandic, came from hot springs, and their intensity showed the volcanic activity of the ground. This seemed to me to justify my fears. So I fell off my stool when my uncle said:

'Do you see all that steam, Axel? Well, it proves that we have nothing to fear from the fury of the volcano!'

'I don't believe it!'

'Listen carefully. When an eruption is on the way, the steam increases considerably; but then disappears completely when the phenomenon is actually happening, for the expanding gas no longer has the required pressure, and heads for the craters instead of escaping through the cracks of the globe. If therefore this steam stays in its normal state, if its force does not increase, if you add to such an observation that the wind and the rain are not replaced by a heavy, calm atmosphere, you can safely say that there will not be an immediate eruption.'

'But . . .'

'Enough. When science has spoken, one can only remain silent thereafter!'

I returned to the parsonage a little hangdog. My uncle had defeated me by means of scientific arguments. I had one remaining hope, however: that once we had got to the bottom of the crater, it would be impossible, for lack of gallery, to go any deeper, in spite of all the Saknussemms in the world.

I spent the night in the clutches of a nightmare; I was in the middle of a volcano in the depths of the Earth, I felt as if I was being thrown into interplanetary space in the form of eruptive rock.

The following day, 23 June, Hans was waiting for us with his companions, who were loaded down with food, tools, and instruments. Two of the iron-tipped sticks, two rifles, and two cartridge-belts were set aside for my uncle and myself. Hans, a man of foresight, had added to our bags a full goatskin water-bottle which, together with our flasks, meant we had water for a week.

It was 9 a.m. The Rector and his huge bad-tempered wife were waiting in front of the door. They presumably wished to give us the last farewell that a host addresses to the traveller. But this farewell took the unexpected form of a formidable bill, which charged even for the air of the pastoral house, far from fresh air I may say. The worthy couple held us to ransom like a Swiss innkeeper and put a high price on their overrated hospitality.

My uncle paid without quibbling. A man who was leaving for the centre of the Earth sniffed at a few rix-dollars.

The matter being settled, Hans gave the signal for departure, and a few moments later we had left Stapi.

15

SNÆFELLS is 5,000 feet high. Its double cone marks the end of a trachytic strip which branches off the main relief system of the island. From our point of departure we couldn't see its two peaks in profile against the greyish background of the sky. I could only see an enormous snowy cap lowered on the giant's forehead.

We were walking in single file, following the hunter; he was climbing up narrow paths where two men couldn't have proceeded abreast. All conversation therefore became more or less impossible.

Beyond the basalt wall of Stapi fjord we encountered first a peaty soil, fibrous and herbaceous, the remains of the age-old vegetation of the marshes on the peninsula; these quantities of fuel which have never been put to use would be sufficient to heat the whole population of Iceland for a century. The huge peat-bog, to judge from the bottom of the ravines in it, was often 70 feet thick and consisted of successive layers of charred refuse, separated by thin sheets of pumiceous tuff.

As a nephew of Professor Lidenbrock's, and despite my worries, I examined with interest the mineralogical curiosities displayed in this vast natural history collection. At the same time my mind ran through the whole geological history of Iceland.

This extraordinary island clearly emerged from the watery depths at a relatively recent period. It is perhaps still rising imperceptibly. If indeed so, its origin can only be attributed to the work of underground fires. Accordingly, in such a case, Sir Humphry Davy's theory, Saknussemm's document, my uncle's claims, all went up in smoke. This hypothesis led me to examine the nature of the ground closely, and I was soon able to observe the successive phenomena governing its formation.

Iceland, which has no sedimentary terrain at all, is

composed uniquely of volcanic tuff, that is of an agglomeration of stones and rocks of a porous texture. Before the volcanoes appeared, it consisted of a trappean massif, slowly lifted above the waves by the pressure of the forces in the centre. The central fires had not yet burst out.

But later a wide slit cut its way diagonally from the southwest to the northeast of the island, and the whole trachytic magma gradually poured out. At that time the phenomenon happened without violence, for the exit was very large, and the molten matter, thrown up by the vitals of the globe, spread quietly out in vast sheets or mammary bulges. The feldspars, syenites, and porphyries appeared during this period.

But thanks to this effusion, the thickness of the island increased considerably, and consequently its resistance. One can imagine what quantities of gas under pressure were built up in its breast when there was no longer any way out after the cooling of the trachytic crust. There came therefore a moment when the mechanical force of these gases was such as to lift up the heavy crust and to create high chimneys. Hence this volcano's raising of the outermost crust, and then the sudden piercing of a crater at the top of the volcano.

After the eruptive phenomena came the volcanic ones. Through the openings recently made escaped, first the basaltic dejecta, of which the plain we were crossing at that moment offered the most splendid specimens. We were walking over these heavy, dark-grey rocks that the cooling down had moulded into prisms with hexagonal bases. In the distance could be seen a large number of flattened cones, each of which was formerly a fire-breathing mouth.

Then, when the basaltic eruption was exhausted, the volcano, which drew its strength from that of the extinct craters, gave passage to the lavas and to those tuffs made up of cinders and scoria whose long spread-out rivulets I could see on its shoulders like an opulent head of hair.

Such were the successive phenomena that had constructed Iceland. All of them came from the effect of the internal fires, and to suppose that the interior did not remain in a permanent state of white-hot flux was pure madness. It was madness, especially, to claim to be able to reach the centre of the globe!

So I was reassuring myself about the result of our undertaking as we moved in to attack Snæfells.

The route was becoming more and more difficult; the ground was climbing; the loose rocks were easily moved and it needed the most careful concentration to avoid dangerous falls.

Hans carried calmly on, as if moving over unbroken ground. Sometimes he passed behind huge boulders and we lost sight of him for a moment—but then a piercing whistle would spring from his lips to tell us which way to go. Often he would stop, pick up loose pieces of rock and arrange them into beacons in a recognizable fashion, so as to mark the way back. An admirable precaution in itself, but one that would be made useless by future events.

Three hours' tiring march had only brought us as far as the base of the mountain. At this point Hans called a halt, and we all shared a quick lunch. My uncle took double mouthfuls to save time. But since this halt was also a rest period, he was forced to wait until the guide was completely ready: he gave the signal for departure an hour later. The three Icelanders, as taciturn as their hunter companion, didn't say a single word and ate soberly.

We now began to move up the slopes of Snæfells. By an optical illusion common with mountains, its snow-covered summit seemed to me very close; and yet, how many long hours it took to reach it! Above all, what fatigue! The stones, not held together by earth or grass, rolled away from under our feet and disappeared towards the plain with the speed of an avalanche.

At certain places, the sides of the mountain made an angle of at least 36° with the horizon. It was impossible to climb them, and we had to work our way round these steep rock-strewn slopes with considerable difficulty. In such cases we helped each other by means of the sticks.

I have to say that my uncle kept as close to me as possible. He never lost sight of me and on quite a few occasions his arm provided solid support. He himself undoubtedly had an intrinsic sense of balance for he never hesitated. The Icelanders climbed with the sure-footedness of highlanders, despite their heavy loads.

To judge from the height of the peak of Snæfells, I assumed it was impossible for us to reach it from this side, unless the angle of the slope decreased. Fortunately, after an hour of tiring efforts and considerable feats, a sort of staircase suddenly appeared in the middle of a vast carpet of snow built up on top of the volcano, and this helped our climb. It was formed by one of those rivers of stones (called *stinâ* in Iceland) thrown out by the eruptions. If this river hadn't been stopped dead by the form of the mountain's flanks, it would have thrown itself into the sea, and thus formed new islands.

As it was, it helped a great deal. The steepness of the slope increased, but the stone steps meant that it could be climbed without problem. So quick was our progress that, remaining behind for a moment while my companions carried on up, I saw that they were already reduced to microscopic size by the distance.

By seven in the evening we had climbed the 2,000 steps of the staircase. We stood at the top of a big swelling of the mountain, a sort of base on which rested the cone forming the crater.

The sea stretched out at a depth of 3,200 feet. We were above the line of the perpetual snows, at a relatively low level in Iceland because of the constant humidity of the climate. It was bitterly cold. The wind blew hard. I felt utterly exhausted. The professor saw clearly that my legs were refusing to carry me and decided to stop, despite his impatience. He therefore made a sign to the hunter, who shook his head saying:

'Ofvanför.'

'Apparently we need to go higher.'

He asked Hans the reason for his reply.

'Mistour.'

'Ya, mistour,' repeated one of the Icelanders in a frightened tone.

'What does the word mean?' I asked anxiously.

'Look there,' replied my uncle.

I turned to look at the plain. An immense column of ground-up pumice-stone, sand, and dust was climbing, swirling like a waterspout. The wind was driving it against the flank of Snæfells, which we were now clinging on to. This opaque curtain, spread out in front of the sun, threw a large shadow over the whole mountain. If the waterspout leaned over, it would inevitably embrace us in its swirls. Such a phenomenon, called 'mistour' in Icelandic, is quite common when the wind blows in from the glaciers.

'Hastigt, hastigt,'* shouted the guide.

Without knowing Danish, I understood that we had to follow Hans as quickly as possible. He began to work his way round the cone of the crater, at an angle for easier going. Soon the waterspout crashed down on the mountain, which quivered at the shock; the stones caught up in the eddies rained down as if in an eruption. Fortunately we were on the other side and sheltered from all danger. If it hadn't been for the guide's precaution, our torn bodies would have been pulverized and dropped far away like the product of some unknown meteor.

However, Hans didn't consider it prudent to spend the night on the side of the cone. We continued our zigzagging ascent. The 1,500 feet still to be covered took nearly five hours, for the detours, diagonal paths, and retreats measured at least 8 miles. I couldn't go on: I was overcome by cold and hunger. The air was slightly rarefied and insufficient to fill my lungs.

Finally, at eleven at night, very much in darkness, we reached the summit of Snæfells. Before going to shelter inside the crater, I caught sight of the midnight sun at the lowest point in its life's course, sending its pale rays over the island asleep at my feet.

16

DINNER was quickly swallowed and the mini-expedition settled down as well as it could. The ground was very hard, the shelter fragile, the situation very uncomfortable at 5,000 feet above sea-level. But my sleep was especially calm that night, one of the best I'd spent for a long time. I didn't even dream.

In the morning we woke up half-frozen by a glacial temperature but in the rays of a fine sun. I got up from my granite bed to go and enjoy the magnificent spectacle laid out before my eyes.

I was standing on the southern summit of Snæfells' twin peaks. The panorama extended over most of the island. As at all great heights, the perspective lifted up the shores while the central parts seemed to have sunk. You would have thought that one of Helbesmer's relief-maps was spread beneath my feet. I saw deep valleys criss-crossing in every direction, chasms opening up like wells, lakes turned into ponds, rivers become brooks. On my right were endless glaciers and repeated peaks, some of them plumed with light smoke. The undulations of these infinite mountains, whose layers of snow made them appear foaming, reminded me of the surface of a rough sea. If I turned towards the west, the ocean spread out its magnificent expanse like a continuation of the white horses of the summits. I could hardly see where the land stopped and the swell began.

I plunged into that high-blown ecstasy produced by lofty peaks, without feeling dizzy this time, as I was finally getting used to these sublime contemplations. My dazzled eyes bathed in the clear irradiation of the sun's rays. I forgot who I was, where I was, and lived the life of elves and sylphs, the imaginary inhabitants of Scandinavian mythology. I was intoxicated by the voluptuous pleasure of the heights, oblivious of the depths my fate was shortly going to plunge me into. But I was brought back to reality by the arrival of the professor and Hans, who joined me at the sharp summit.

Turning to the west my uncle pointed to a slight mist, a haze, a hint of land above the line of the waves.

'Greenland.'

'Greenland?'

'Yes, we're less than 90 miles away,* and during the thaws the polar bears come as far as Iceland, carried down from the north on ice-floes. But that is of little importance. We are at the summit of Snæfells, with its twin peaks, one to the north and the other to the south. Hans will tell us what the Icelanders call the one bearing us at this instant.'

The hunter duly replied to his question:

'Scartaris.'

My uncle looked at me in triumph.

'To the crater!'

The crater of Snæfells formed an inverted cone whose mouth was probably slightly more than a mile across. It seemed to me to be about 2,000 feet deep. One should imagine the state of such a receptacle when it was filling up with thunder and flames. The bottom of the funnel was only about 500 feet in circumference, so its relatively gentle slopes allowed one to reach the lower part with ease. I couldn't help comparing this crater to an enormous widened-out blunderbuss; and the comparison terrified me.

'To climb down into a blunderbuss,' I thought, 'when it may be loaded and could go off at the least shock, you've got to be crazy.'

But there was no going back. With an indifferent expression, Hans took the lead. I followed him without a word.

In order to make the going easier, Hans described greatly lengthened ellipses on the inside of the cone. We had to pass amongst stones from eruptions, some of which, when loosened from their crevices, would rebound and rush down to the bottom of the chasm. Their fall produced waves of strange-sounding echoes.

Parts of the cone were covered with internal glaciers. Hans moved forward here with tremendous caution, prodding the ground with his iron-tipped stick, looking for crevasses. At some of the difficult parts, we had to tie ourselves together with a long rope, so that if by chance one of us happened to slip, he would be held up by his companions. This solidarity constituted a useful precaution, but did not remove all danger.

Despite the difficulties of climbing down slopes unknown to the guide, we covered the distance without incident, except for the fall of a packet of rope which slipped from the hands of one of the Icelanders, and took the shortest route towards the bottom of the chasm.

We arrived at midday. I looked up and saw the high mouth of the cone framing part of the sky: an almost perfect circle, but with a dramatically reduced circumference. Only at one point did the peak of Scartaris stand out and plunge into the huge space.

At the bottom of the crater opened three vents through which, at the time when Snæfells used to erupt, the central fire forced its lava and its steam. Each of these chimneys was about 100 feet across. There they were, wide open, beneath our feet. I didn't dare look down into them. As for Professor Lidenbrock, he had quickly examined their shape and size. He was breathing heavily, running from one to the other, waving his arms and shouting unintelligible words. Hans and his companions sat on hummocks of lava and watched: they clearly took him for a madman.

Suddenly my uncle cried out. At first I thought he had lost his footing and fallen into one of the three holes. But then I saw him, standing arms outstretched and legs apart in front of a granite boulder placed at the centre of the crater, like an enormous pedestal designed for a statue of Pluto.* He stood like a man dumbstruck, but it soon turned instead into an insane happiness.

'Axel, Axel! Come here, down here!'

I ran down. Hans and the Icelanders stayed exactly where they were.

'Look!' said the professor.

Dumbstruck like him, but markedly less happy, I read on the western side of the boulder, in runic characters gnawed by time, the thousand-times-accursed name:

ᚴᛐᚾᛐ   ᛋᛁᛏᛚᚴᛋᛋᛐᚴ

'Arne Saknussemm!' shouted my uncle. 'Can you have any doubt now?'

I didn't reply, but came back to my lava seat in a state of total confusion. I was crushed by the evidence.

How long I spent sunk in my thoughts I don't know. All I'm certain of is that when I looked up again I found my uncle and Hans alone at the bottom of the crater. The Icelanders had been dismissed, and were now climbing down the outer slopes of Snæfells on their way back to Stapi.

Hans was quietly sleeping at the foot of a rock, in a lava channel where he had improvised a bed. My uncle was walking up and down the floor of the crater, like some wild animal in a trap dug by a hunter. I had neither the strength nor the desire to get up, and, imitating the guide, slipped into a harrowing doze, thinking I could hear noises or feel shivers in the sides of the mountain.

That was how our first night at the bottom of the crater was spent.

The following day, a grey sky, cloudy and heavy, lowered over the summit of the cone. I noticed this less from the darkness of the chasm than from the anger that took hold of my uncle.

I understood why, and a last feeling of hope came back to me. The reason was as follows:

Of the three routes open under our feet, only one had been followed by Saknussemm. According to the Icelandic scholar, it was to be identified by the particularity described in the cryptogram, namely that the shadow of Scartaris came and played along its edge during the last few days of the month of June.

This sharp peak could thus be considered the style of a

huge sundial, whose silhouette on a given day marked the way to the centre of our globe.

If by chance the sun was not there, no shadow. Consequently no sign. It was 25 June. Should the sky stay overcast for six more days, the observation would have to be put off to another year.

I will not attempt to describe Professor Lidenbrock's impotent rage. The day passed without a shadow coming down to the bottom of the crater. Hans didn't move from where he was, although he must have wondered what we were waiting for—if he wondered anything! My uncle didn't address a single word to me. His eyes, invariably turned to the sky, blended into the grey and misty background.

On the 26th, still nothing. Rain mixed with snow fell during the day. Hans built a hut with pieces of lava. I took some pleasure from watching the thousands of improvised cascades running down the sides of the cone, with each stone adding to the deafening murmur.

My uncle could no longer hold himself back. The most patient man could legitimately be irritated, for this really was sinking while coming into harbour.

But Heaven constantly mixes great joys with great sorrows, and it was preparing a satisfaction for Professor Lidenbrock equal to his terrible disappointments.

The sky was still covered the following day. But on Sunday, 28 June, the third last day of the month, the change of moon coincided with a change in the weather. The sun poured its abundant rays down into the crater. Each hummock, each rock, each boulder, each bump, had its share of the luminous flow and instantly cast its shadow on the ground. That of Scartaris, especially, stood out like a sharp stone and began to turn imperceptibly with the radiant orb.

My uncle turned with it.

At the middle of the day, when it was shortest, it came and gently kissed the edge of the middle chimney.

'It is there! There it is!' shouted the professor. 'To the centre of the globe!' he added in Danish.

I looked at Hans.

'Forüt!'* he said calmly.

'Forward!' replied my uncle.

It was thirteen minutes past one.

17

THE real journey began. Until now things had been more tiring than difficult; but henceforth problems were literally going to spring forth under our feet.

I had still not looked down at the fathomless pit into which I was going to engulf myself. The moment had arrived. I could still either take part in the venture or else refuse to try it. But I felt ashamed to turn back in the hunter's presence. Hans accepted the adventure so calmly, with such indifference, such unconcern at all danger, that I blushed at the idea of being less brave than him. On my own, I would have launched into a whole series of important arguments, but since the guide was there I remained silent. My memory flew back towards my pretty Virland girl, and I approached the middle chimney.

As mentioned already, it was 100 feet across, or about 300 feet right round. I leant over an overhanging rock, and looked. My hair stood on end. An impression of void took hold of my being. I felt the centre of gravity moving through me and dizziness going to my head like a heady brew. Nothing more intoxicating than this attraction of the abyss. I was going to fall. A hand held me back. Hans's. Decidedly, I hadn't had enough 'lessons in chasms' at the Frelsers Kirke in Copenhagen.

But however little I'd dared look down into the well, I had realized what shape it was. Its walls, almost perpendicular, had many projections which were certainly going to make them easier to climb down. But, if there was an adequate staircase, there was no banister. A rope attached at the mouth would have provided sufficient support, but how to untie it when we got to the end?

My uncle employed a very simple method to get round this difficulty. He unrolled a rope as thick as a thumb and 400 feet long. First he dropped half of it down, then wound it round a block of lava which projected out, and finally threw the other half into the chimney. Each of us could then climb down while holding the two halves of the rope together, which couldn't slip. Two hundred feet further down, nothing would be easier than bringing it down by letting one end go and pulling on the other. We would then be able to repeat this exercise *ad infinitum*.

'Now,' said my uncle, 'having finished these preparations, let's think about the luggage. It will be split into three, and each of us will strap one package to his back— I refer only to the fragile objects.'

The bold professor clearly didn't include us in the last category.

'Hans will carry the tools and a third of the food; you, Axel, another third of the food and the firearms; I will take the rest of it and the delicate instruments.'

'But what about the clothing and this great pile of ropes and ladders, who will take charge of them?'

'There is no need.'

'Why?'

'You will see.'

My uncle liked to employ strong-arm methods, and without hesitating. On his command, Hans tied the non-fragile objects into a single packet, which was roped solidly together, and then quite simply dropped down into the abyss.

I heard the lowing sound produced by the movements of layers of air. My uncle, leaning over the gulf, watched the descent of our luggage with a satisfied air, and stood up again only after losing sight of it.

'Right. We are next.'

I ask any man of good faith if it was possible to listen to such words without getting cold shivers.

The professor attached the package of instruments to his back; Hans took the implements, myself the firearms. The descent began in the following order: Hans, my uncle, myself. It proceeded in a deep silence, broken only by rock debris falling into the abyss.

I allowed myself to flow, so to speak, with one hand desperately holding on to the double rope, and the other using my alpenstock to slow me down. A single idea obsessed me: I was afraid of losing all means of support. This rope seemed to me very fragile for bearing the weight of three people. I used it as little as possible, performing miracles of balance on the lava projections that my foot tried to hold on to like a hand.

When one of these precarious steps happened to dislodge under Hans's feet, he would say in his calm voice:

'Gif akt!'

'Careful!' repeated my uncle.

After half an hour we had reached the top of a boulder solidly attached to the wall of the chimney.

Hans pulled one of the ends of the rope, and the other rose in the air. Having gone round the rock at the top, it fell back, dragging down pieces of rock and lava, a sort of rain or rather hail, full of danger.

Leaning over our narrow platform, I noticed that the bottom of the hole could still not be seen.

The rope manœuvre began again, and half an hour later we had got 200 feet deeper.

I don't know if the most fanatical geologist would have tried to study the nature of the rocks surrounding him during such a descent. As for me, I hardly thought about them: I was not really bothered whether they were Pliocene, Miocene, Eocene, Cretaceous, Jurassic, Triassic, Permian, Carboniferous, Devonian, Silurian, or Primitive. But the professor undoubtedly made observations or else took notes, for during one of our halts he said:

'The further I go, the more confident I become. The arrangement of these volcanic rocks absolutely confirms Davy's theory. We are in the middle of Primordial ground, the ground where the chemical reaction of the metals burning on contact with the air and water occurred. I absolutely refuse to accept the theory of a heat in the centre. In any case we will see for ourselves.'

Still the same conclusion. It goes without saying that I didn't bother to discuss it. My silence was taken for agreement, and the descent began again.

After three hours, I had still not caught a glimpse of the bottom of the chimney. When I looked up I could see the mouth, which was getting quite a lot smaller. Because of the small angle between the walls, they looked as though they were coming together. It was slowly getting darker and darker.

We were still going down. It seemed to me that the rocks disturbed from the walls were swallowed up with a duller reverberation and that they ought to be reaching the bottom of the abyss more quickly.

As I had carefully noted the operations of the rope, I was able to calculate the precise depth and time elapsed.

We'd used the rope fourteen times, taking half an hour each time. So we'd spent seven hours, plus fourteen rest periods of fifteen minutes, or three-and-a-half hours. Ten-and-a-half in total. Since we had left at one, it had to be about eleven now.

As for the depth reached, the fourteen operations of the rope gave 2,800 feet.

At that moment Hans's voice was heard:

'Halt!'

I stopped dead at the moment my feet were about to collide with my uncle's head.

'We are there,' he said.

'Where?' I asked, slipping down beside him.

'At the bottom of the perpendicular chimney.'

'And there's no way out?'

'Yes, I can just see a sort of corridor at an angle towards the right. We will have a look at it tomorrow. Let's eat, and then we can sleep.'

It was still not completely dark. We opened the food bag, ate, and lay down, each doing his best to make a bed out of the stone and lava debris.

Lying on my back, I opened my eyes and caught sight of a brilliant object at the other end of the 3,000-foot-long tube, converted into a gigantic telescope.

It was a star, but not twinkling at all. According to my calculations it was Beta of the Little Bear.

Then I fell into a deep sleep.

18

AT eight in the morning, a ray of daylight came and woke us up. The thousand facets of the lava on the walls picked it up on the way down and scattered it everywhere like a rain of sparks.

These gleams were enough for us to be able to distinguish the surrounding objects.

'Well, Axel, what do you say?' shouted my uncle, rubbing his hands together. 'Have you ever spent a more peaceful night in our house on Königstrasse? No noise of cartwheels, no cries from the market, no yelling boatmen!'

'It is admittedly very calm at the bottom of this well, but such quiet has itself rather a frightening effect.'

'Come now. If you are frightened already, what will you be like later? We have not gone a single inch into the bowels of the earth!'

'What do you mean?'

'I mean that we have only reached ground-level on the island! This long vertical tube leading down from the crater of Snæfells stops at approximately sea-level.'

'Are you certain?'

'Absolutely. Have a look at the barometer.'

The mercury, after rising in the instrument as we descended, had indeed stopped at 30 inches.

'You see. The pressure is still only 1 atmosphere, and I am looking forward for the manometer to replace the barometer.'

The barometer was indeed going to become useless when the weight of the air was greater than its pressure as calculated at sea-level.

'But shouldn't we be afraid that the ever-increasing pressure will become highly uncomfortable?'

'No, we will descend slowly, and our lungs will get

used to breathing a denser atmosphere. Aeronauts eventually lack air when they climb up into the highest layers but we ourselves may perhaps have too much. But I prefer that. Let's not waste a moment. Where is the parcel that came down the inside of the mountain before us?'

I remembered then that we had looked for it the evening before but not found it. My uncle questioned Hans who looked carefully with his hunter's eyes, then replied:

'Der huppe!'

'Up there.'

It was indeed hanging from a projecting rock a hundred feet above our heads. The agile Icelander immediately climbed up like a cat and, a few moments later, the package had caught up with us.

'Now,' said my uncle, 'let's have breakfast—but a breakfast like people who perhaps have a long journey ahead of them.'

The dried meat and biscuit were washed down with a few mouthfuls of water mixed with gin.

Once we had finished, my uncle pulled from his pocket a notebook designed for observations. He examined each of the various instruments in turn and wrote down the date:

*Monday, 1 July**

Chronometer: 8.17 a.m.
Barometer: 29$\frac{7}{12}$"
Thermometer: 6° C
Direction: ESE

The last observation referred to the dark corridor, as indicated by the compass.

'Now, Axel,' cried the professor enthusiastically, 'we are going to penetrate the globe's bowels proper. This is the precise moment when our journey begins.'

Saying that, with one hand he took the Ruhmkorff lamp, which was hanging round his neck. With the other he applied the electric current to the filament of the lamp, and a brightish light chased the darkness from the tunnel. Hans carried the second lamp, which was also switched on. This ingenious application of electricity allowed us to go for a long time in artificial daylight, even through the most inflammable of gases.

'Off we go!' said my uncle.

Each of us picked up his bundle. Hans took charge of pushing the packet of ropes and clothing in front of him, and with me in third position we entered the gallery.

Just as I plunged into the black passage, I raised my head and looked through the long tube at the sky of Iceland, 'that I would never see again'.

During its last eruption in 1229, the lava had forced its way through the tunnel. It had carpeted the inside with a thick, shiny coating: the electric light was now reflected in it, becoming a hundred times brighter.

The only difficulty consisted of not sliding down the slope too quickly, for it was at an angle of about 45°. Fortunately, worn-away parts and blisters acted as steps, and all we had to do was let our packages slide, held back by a long rope.

But what acted as steps under our feet became stalactites on certain walls. The lava, porous in places, was covered with little round bulbs; crystals of opaque quartz, decorated with clear drops of glass, hung from the vaulted ceiling like chandeliers, and seemed to light up as we passed. It was as if the spirits of the underground were lighting up their palace to welcome their guests from the Earth.

'It's magnificent!' I shouted in spite of myself. 'What a sight, Uncle! Look at the colours in the lava which go from reddish-brown to bright yellow absolutely continuously. And these crystals that look like luminous globes!'

'You're getting there, Axel! So you admire all that, my boy? You will see lots more, I hope. Come on, off we go!'

He should have said 'off we slide', for we were able to simply let ourselves go on these inclined slopes, without taxing ourselves. It was Virgil's *facilis descensus Averni*.* The compass, which I often consulted, showed the direction as southeast with an unflinching precision. The lava flow deviated to neither side. It had the inflexibility of the straight line.

Meanwhile it wasn't getting any appreciably warmer. This confirmed Davy's theories, and several times I looked at the thermometer with surprise. Two hours after we had left, it still only indicated 10°, in other words an increase of 4°. That made me think that our journey was more horizontal than vertical. As for knowing the exact depth reached, nothing was easier. The professor measured the precise vertical and horizontal angles of our route—but kept the results to himself.

At about eight in the evening, he gave the signal to stop. Hans immediately sat down. The lamps were hung from convenient pieces of lava. We were in a sort of cavern where there was no lack of air. On the contrary: we felt a wind blowing. What was causing it? What movement in the atmosphere did it come from? I wasn't really interested in answering the question at that moment. Hunger and tiredness made me unable to think. A descent of seven hours without stopping produces a great depletion of energy. I was exhausted, and had been very glad to hear the word 'Halt'. Hans spread out a few things to eat on a block of lava and each of us dined hungrily. One thing worried me, though: half our supply of water had been used up. My uncle planned to replenish it at underwater springs, but there hadn't been a single one so far. I couldn't help mentioning it to him.

'Are you surprised by the absence of streams?'

'Yes, and even worried. We have water left for only five days.'

'Don't worry, Axel, my reply is that we *will* find water, and more than we want.'

'When?'

'When we have left the lava envelope. How do you think that springs can get through these walls?'

'But the lava-flow may continue to a great depth. And we don't seem to have gone very far yet in the vertical direction.'

'What makes you say that?'

'Because if we had gone a long way into the interior of the earth's crust, the heat would be greater than it is.'

'According to your system. What does the thermometer say?'

'Hardly 15°, which is only 9° more than when we left.'

'And your conclusion?'

'I conclude as follows. From the most precise observations, we know that the temperature increases by one degree for every 100 feet you go into the interior of the globe. But local conditions can sometimes alter that figure. Thus in Yakutsk in Siberia, it has been observed that the increase is one degree for every 36 feet. The difference clearly depends on the conductivity of the rock. One can also add that in the neighbourhood of an extinct volcano, through the gneiss, the increase is only one degree for every 125 feet. Let us therefore take this last hypothesis, which is the most favourable, and let us calculate.'

'Calculate on, my boy.'

'It's child's play,' I said, jotting the figures down in my notebook. 'Nine times 125 feet gives 1,125 feet deep.'

'So it does.'

'Well?'

'Well, according to my observations, we are now 10,000 feet below sea-level.'

'Are we really?'

'Yes—or else figures are no longer figures!'

The professor's calculations were correct. We had gone 6,000 feet further than the greatest depths achieved by man, such as the mines of Kitzbühel in the Tyrol or those of Wuttemberg in Bohemia.*

The temperature, which should have been 81° at this spot, was barely 15°. It made you think.

19

A T 6 a.m. the following day, Tuesday, 30 June, the journey began again.

We were still following the lava gallery, truly a natural ramp, as gentle as those inclined planes that still replace staircases in old houses. This continued until 12.17, the precise moment when we caught up with Hans, who had just stopped.

'Ah,' exclaimed my uncle, 'we have reached the end of the chimney.'

I looked around. We were in the middle of an inter-section, with two paths heading forward, both of them dark and narrow. Which one were we to take? We had a problem.

But my uncle didn't want to be appearing to hesitate before either me or the guide: he pointed to the eastern tunnel, and soon all three of us had plunged into it.

In any case, any deliberation about the choice of path could have gone on indefinitely, for no sign could possibly determine the choice of one or the other—we had to trust entirely to chance.

The slope of the new gallery was very gentle, and the cross-section varied a great deal. Sometimes a succession of arches unfolded in front of us like the aisles of a Gothic cathedral.* The artists of the Middle Ages could easily have studied here all the forms of religious architecture generated by the ogive. A mile further on, we had to bow our heads under low semicircular arches in the Roman style, with thick pillars, forming part of the rock itself, bending under the spring of the vaults. At certain places, these forms gave way to low substructures that looked like beavers' work, and we crawled and slid through narrow intestines.

The heat stayed at a tolerable level. I couldn't help thinking about its intensity when the lavas vomited by Snæfells rushed through this path, today so peaceful. I imagined the rivers of fire producing breakers at the bends in the tunnel and the build-up of superheated steam in this enclosed space!

'Provided', I thought, 'that the old volcano doesn't decide to give in again to a senile fantasy!'

I didn't mention these ideas at all to Uncle Lidenbrock: he wouldn't have understood. His sole thought was to go forward. He walked, he slid, he even tumbled down, with a degree of conviction that after all it was better to admire.

At 6 p.m., after a relatively easy march, we had covered five miles in a southerly direction, but scarcely a quarter of a mile in depth.

My uncle gave the signal to stop. We ate without talking very much, and then went to sleep without thinking very much.

Our arrangements for the night were very simple: travelling-rugs in which we rolled ourselves up were our sole bedding. We had no fear of cold, nor of surprise visits. Those travellers who penetrate to the middle of the deserts of Africa or the heart of the forests of the New World are forced to watch over each other during the hours of sleep. But here, absolute solitude and complete safety. Savages or wild beasts: none of these harmful races were to be feared.

In the morning we woke fresh and revitalized. We started off again. We were following a lava route like the day before. Impossible to recognize what sort of terrains we were passing through. Instead of going down into the bowels of the globe, the tunnel was becoming more and more horizontal. I even thought it was heading back up towards the surface of the Earth. At about 10 a.m., the tendency became so clear and consequently so tiring, that I had to slow down our progress.

'Well, Axel?' the professor said impatiently.

'Well, I'm totally exhausted.'

'What, after three hours of strolling along such an easy route!'

'Easy, perhaps, but most certainly tiring.'

'But all we have to do is descend!'

'Climb, with respect!'

'Climb?' said my uncle, raising his shoulders.

'Definitely. For the last half-hour, the gradient's been different, and were we to follow it to the end, we'd certainly get back to the soil of Iceland.'

The professor shook his head like someone who is unwilling to be convinced. I tried to pursue the conversation. He didn't reply, but just gave the signal for departure. I saw clearly that his silence was nothing but concentrated ill humour.

All the same I valiantly picked up my burden and hurried after Hans, who was following my uncle. I didn't want to be left behind for I was tremendously worried about losing sight of my companions. I trembled at the thought of getting lost in the depths of the labyrinth.

In any case, if the ascending route was becoming more difficult, I consoled myself by thinking that it was bringing me closer to the surface of the Earth. It was a hope. Every step confirmed it, and I rejoiced at the idea of seeing my little Gräuben again.

At midday the walls of the tunnel changed appearance. I noticed this from the dimming of the electric light reflected from them. The covering of lava was replaced by bare rock. The massif was made up of layers at an angle, often in fact completely perpendicular. We were in the middle of the Transition Era, in full Silurian Period.[1]

'It's obvious,' I said to myself. 'During the Second Era of the Earth, the sediment from the water formed these schists, these limestones, these sandstones! We're turning our backs on the granite massif. We're like people from Hamburg who take the Hanover road to go to Lübeck.'

I should have kept my remarks to myself. But my temperament as a geologist overcame my caution, and Uncle Lidenbrock overheard my exclamations.

'What is the matter then?'

'Look!' I replied, showing him the successive varieties

[1] So called because the rocks of this period are very common in the parts of Britain formerly inhabited by the Celtic tribe, the Silures.

of sandstones and limestones and the first signs of the shale terrains.

'Well?'

'Here we are at the period when the first plants and animals appeared!'

'Do you really think so?'

'But look, examine, observe!'

I made the professor shine his lamp on each of the walls of the tunnel. I expected some exclamation from him. But he didn't say a word—merely continued on his way.

Had he understood me or not? Didn't he want to admit, because of his self-regard as an uncle and a scientist, that he had made a mistake in choosing the eastern tunnel; or did he want to explore the passage to the end? It was clear in any case that we had left behind the route taken by the lava, and that this path couldn't lead to the source of Snæfells's heat.

However, I wondered whether I wasn't placing too much importance on the change in the terrain. Was I not deluding myself? Were we really crossing the layers of rock superimposed on the granite foundation?

If I'm right, I thought, I'll surely find traces of primitive plants, and it will be self-evident to anyone. Let's look.

I hadn't gone a hundred yards further before incontrovertible proof appeared in front of my eyes. It was to be expected, for during the Silurian Period there were more than 1,500 species of vegetables and animals in the seas. My feet, used to the hard ground of the lava, were suddenly treading on a dust composed of fragments of plants and shells. On the walls could be clearly seen the outlines of seaweeds and club-mosses.* Professor Lidenbrock could no longer entertain any doubt—but he closed his eyes, I imagine, and continued on his way at a steady pace.

This was obstinacy taken beyond all limits. I couldn't stand it any more. I picked up a perfectly preserved shell, one that had belonged to an animal more or less like the present-day woodlouse. Then I caught up with my uncle and said to him:

'See!'

'Well,' he replied calmly, 'it is the shell of a crustacean of the extinct order of trilobites. Nothing else.'

'But do you not conclude from that . . . ?'

'What you conclude yourself? Yes. Fine. We have left the granite stratum behind, together with the route followed by the lava. It is possible that I made a mistake; but I will only be certain of my error when I have reached the end of the gallery.'

'You're right to follow such a course of action, Uncle, and I would support it, if we weren't in greater and greater danger.'

'What danger?'

'The shortage of water.'

'Well, we will ration it, Axel.'

20

RATIONING was indeed essential. We didn't have enough water left for more than three days, as I found out that evening at dinner-time. Nor could we have much hope of coming across an open spring in the ground of the Transition Era—a dismal perspective.

The whole of the following day, the tunnel lined up its endless arches in front of us. We walked almost without a word. Hans's silence was catching.

The route was not climbing, at least not noticeably. Sometimes it even seemed to be going down. But such a tendency, in any case very slight, can't have reassured the professor, for the nature of the strata didn't change, and the signs of the Transition Era became more and more obvious.

The electric lamp produced a wonderful sparkling on the schists, the limestone, and the old red sandstone of the walls. You might have thought you were in a trench excavation in Devon, the county which gave its name to this sort of terrain. Magnificent marble specimens covered the walls, some an agate grey with white veins standing out in various places, others crimson or yellow with red spots. Further on were samples of griotte marble in dark colours, but with limestone providing bright highlights.

Most of the marble displayed the outlines of primitive animals. Since the day before, creation had made clear signs of progress. Instead of rudimentary trilobites, I spotted evidence of a more perfect order: amongst others, Ganoid fish and those saurians where the palaeontologist's eye has discerned the first reptile forms. The Devonian seas were inhabited by a large number of animals of this latter species, and deposited thousands and thousands of them on to the newly formed rocks.

It became plain that we were moving back up the scale of animal life, of which man forms the peak. But Professor Lidenbrock didn't seem to be paying attention to this.

He was hoping for one of two things: either that a vertical shaft would somehow open up beneath his feet and thus allow him to descend again; or that he would be blocked by some obstacle. But evening came without either hope being fulfilled.

On the Friday, after a night when I began to be tortured by thirst, our little team plunged again into the tunnel's meanders.

After ten hours' march, I noticed that the reflection of our lamps on the surfaces was decreasing to a remarkable degree. The marble, the schist, the limestone, and the sandstone on the walls were giving way to a dark covering not giving off any light. At a moment when the tunnel was especially narrow, I leaned on the left-hand wall.

When I withdrew my hand, it was black all over. I looked closer. We were in the middle of a coal-deposit.

'A coal-mine!' I exclaimed.

'A mine without miners.'

'Who knows?'

'*I* know,' replied the professor firmly. 'And I am certain that this tunnel cutting through the coal seams was not made by human hands. But I do not really care whether it is nature's work or not. The time for dinner has arrived. Let us therefore dine.'

Hans prepared some food. I hardly ate anything, but drank the few drops of water that made up my ration. The guide's half-full flask was all that remained for three men.

After the meal, my two companions stretched out on their blankets and found a remedy to their tiredness in sleep. I myself couldn't doze off, and merely counted the hours till morning.

On Saturday we left at six. Twenty minutes later, we arrived at a huge excavation. I realized then that human hands could not have hollowed out this coal-pit, for in that case the arches would necessarily have been underpinned. Here they literally held up only by some miracle of equilibrium.

This cavernous space was 100 feet wide by 150 feet high. The earth had been violently pushed aside by some underground upheaval. The solid ground, subjected to some huge force, had split wide open, leaving this spacious void, never before penetrated by the inhabitants of the Earth.

On these dark walls was written the whole history of the coal period, and a geologist could easily read its successive stages. The beds of coal were separated by strata of sandstone or compacted clay, as if crushed under the uppermost layers.

During this age of the world which preceded the Secondary Era, the Earth became covered in immense vegetation due to the tropical heat combined with a permanent humidity. An atmosphere of steam enveloped all parts of the globe, shielding it from the sun's rays.

Hence the conclusion that the high temperatures could not have come from that new source of heat. Perhaps the sun was not ready to play its brilliant role. But in any case 'climates' did not yet exist, and a torrid heat spread across the entire surface of the globe, the same at the poles as at the equator. Where did it come from? The centre of the globe.

Despite Professor Lidenbrock's theories, a violent fire smouldered in the bowels of the spheroid. Its effects were felt even in the outermost layers of the Earth's crust. The plants, shielded from the life-giving radiation of the sun, did not produce flowers or scent, but their roots drew vigorous life from the burning soils of the first days.

There were few trees, only herbaceous plants, huge grassy areas, ferns, club-mosses, and *Sigillarias* and Asterophyllites,* rare families whose species were then numbered in thousands.

It was this exuberant vegetation which produced the coal. The Earth's crust, still elastic, followed the movements of the liquid mass it encased. Hence a large amount of cracking and subsiding. The plants, dragged under water, gradually built up considerable piles of matter.

Next came the action of nature's chemistry: on the bottom of the seas, the vegetable masses became peat. Then, thanks to the effect of the gases, and in the heat from the fermentation, they underwent a complete mineralization.

In this way were formed the huge layers of coal. These, however, will be used up by over-consumption in less than three centuries, if the industrialized nations are not careful.

These ideas passed through my mind while I looked at the coal riches accumulated in this section of the Earth's mass. Such riches will probably never be opened up. The exploitation of these far-away mines would require too much effort. What would be the point in any case, when coal is spread over the Earth's surface, so to speak, in a large number of countries? So these untouched strata I saw will probably remain exactly the same when the Earth's last hour sounds.

We carried on walking meanwhile, and I was the only one of the three companions to forget how long the route was, deeply engrossed as I was in my geological considerations. The temperature remained virtually the same as during our passage through the lavas and the schists. On the other hand, my nose was distressed by a very pronounced smell of hydrocarbon. I immediately realized that in this tunnel there was a significant amount of the dangerous gas which miners call fire-damp, and whose explosions have so often caused such terrible disasters.*

Fortunately, our lighting came from the ingenious Ruhmkorff lamps. If, by misfortune, we had carelessly explored this tunnel holding torches, an awful explosion would have terminated the journey by destroying those carrying it out.

Our excursion through the coal lasted until evening. My uncle could hardly control the impatience that the horizontality of the route was generating in him. The darkness, impenetrable at more than twenty yards, prevented any estimation of how far the tunnel ran. I was beginning to believe that it must be endless, when suddenly and without warning, at 6 p.m., a wall appeared right in front of us. There was no way through, to the left or to the right, above or below. We had reached the end of a cul-de-sac.

'Well so much the better!' bellowed my uncle. 'At least I know what I'm up against. We are not on Saknussemm's route, and our only choice is to turn round and go back. Let's rest for a night, and within three days we will be back at the point where the two tunnels fork.'

'Yes, if we are strong enough.'

'And why should we not be?'

'Because tomorrow there will be no water left at all!'

'And no courage left either?' asked the professor, looking at me sternly.

I did not dare reply.

21

THE following day, we left very early. Speed was of the essence. We were five days' march from the parting of the ways.

I will not dwell on our suffering during the return. My uncle bore it with the anger of a man who knows that he is less strong; Hans with the resignation of his peaceful nature; myself, I must admit, with complaints and despair, for I was unable to just grin and bear it.

As I foresaw, the water ran out completely at the end of our first day's march. Our supplies of liquid were limited to gin, but this diabolical spirit burned your throat, and I couldn't even bear to look at it. I found the heat stifling. Tiredness prevented me from moving. More than once, I almost fell down in a faint. On such occasions a halt was called, and my uncle or the Icelander comforted me as best they could. But I could see that the professor was already reacting with difficulty against the extreme fatigue and the torment produced by the lack of water.

Finally on Tuesday, 7 July, dragging ourselves along on our hands and knees, half-dead, we reached the point where the two tunnels split. I lay there a lifeless mass, stretched out on the lava floor. It was ten in the morning.

Hans and my uncle, leaning back on the walls, tried to nibble a few crumbs of biscuit. Long groans escaped from my swollen lips. I fell into a deep faint.

After a time, my uncle drew near and lifted me up in his arms.

'Poor child,' he murmured in tones of real pity.

I was touched by these words, not being used to such tenderness from the tough professor. I seized hold of his trembling hands in mine. He allowed me to do this, while looking at me. His eyes were damp.

I then saw him take the flask hanging at his side. To my amazement, he put it to my lips:

'Drink.'

Had I heard properly? Had my uncle gone mad? I looked at him with a wild expression. I couldn't take in what he said.

'Drink,' he repeated.

And tilting the flask, he emptied it between my lips.

Oh infinite ecstasy! A mouthful of water came and wetted my fiery lips and tongue, only one, but it was enough to bring back the life that was tiptoeing away from me.

I thanked my uncle by putting my hands together.

'Yes, one mouthful of water. The last, do you hear? The very last! I carefully kept it at the bottom of my flask. Twenty times, a hundred times, I had to resist a terrible wish to drink it. But no, Axel, I was keeping it for you.'

'Uncle!' I whispered as large tears formed in my eyes.

'Yes, poor child, I knew that when you arrived at this junction, you would drop down half-dead, and I kept my last drops of water to bring you back to life.'

'Thank you, thank you!'

However little my thirst was quenched, I had nevertheless got back some strength. The muscles in my throat, contracted until this point, now relaxed, and the burning in my lips diminished. I could speak again:

'Look, we now have only one course of action: since we have no water, we must retrace our path.'

While I spoke, my uncle avoided looking at me. He hung his head, and his eyes avoided mine.

'We have to turn round, and follow the path back to Snæfells. May God give us the strength to climb back up to the peak of the crater!'

'Go back!' said my uncle, as if replying to himself rather than to me.

'Yes, go back, without wasting a moment.'

There came a long silence.

'So as a consequence, Axel,' said the professor in a strange tone, 'those few drops of water have not given you back your courage and energy?'

'Courage!'

'I see you are as overcome as before, giving voice to words of despair!'

What sort of man was I dealing with, and what plans was his fearless spirit still hatching?

'What, you don't want to . . . ?'

'. . . give up the expedition, at a moment when all the signs show it can succeed? Never!'

'So we must prepare to die?'

'No, Axel, no! Go if you want. I do not wish your death! Hans will go with you. Leave me alone!'

'On your own?'

'Leave me, I tell you! I began this journey: I will carry it out to the bitter end, or else not come back at all. Off you go, Axel. Go!'

My uncle spoke very agitatedly. His voice, tender for a moment, had now become hard and threatening. He was struggling with a sombre energy against the impossible! I did not want to abandon him at the bottom of this chasm; but, from another point of view, the instinct of self-preservation urged me to flee.

The guide followed this scene with his usual indifference. Yet he understood what was happening between his two companions. Our gestures were enough to show the different ways that each of us wanted to drag the other. But Hans did not appear to be especially interested in this question where his life was at stake: he seemed ready to leave if the signal was given, ready to remain at the least wish of his master.

What I would have given at that moment to be able to speak to him! My words, my complaints, my tone would have won his cold nature over. These dangers that the guide did not seem to suspect—I would have made him understand them in the most literal way. The two of us together might perhaps have convinced the stubborn professor. If need be, we could have forced him to return to the heights of Snæfells!

I went over to Hans. I put my hand on his. He did not move. I pointed to the route up to the crater. He still remained motionless. My gasping face showed all my suffering. The Icelander gently shook his head, and, calmly indicating my uncle:

'Master,' he said in Icelandic.

'No, you fool! He's not the master of your life! We must flee, we must drag him with us! Do you hear, do you understand?'

I seized Hans by the arm, trying to make him get up. I was wrestling with him. My uncle intervened.

'Calm yourself, Axel. You will not get anything out of this impassive servant. So hear what I have to offer.'

I crossed my arms, looking squarely at my uncle.

'Only the lack of water puts an obstacle to the achievement of my aims. In that eastern tunnel, made of lavas, schists, and coals, we did not find a single liquid molecule. We may possibly be more fortunate in the western tunnel.'

I shook my head with a look of utter disbelief.

'Hear me out,' continued the professor in a louder voice. 'While you were lying there without moving, I went to reconnoitre the shape of the tunnel. It forces its way directly into the bowels of the Earth and will lead us, in a few hours, to the granite rock-formations. There we should meet abundant springs. The nature of the rock implies this, and intuition and logic combine to support my conviction. Now here is what I have to offer you. When Columbus asked his crews for three more days to reach the new lands, his crews, ill and terror-stricken, nevertheless granted his request, and he discovered a new world. Myself, the Columbus of these underground regions, I am asking for only one more day. If at the end of that time I have not encountered the water we need, I swear to you that we will return to the surface of the Earth.'

In spite of my irritation, I was touched by these words and by the way my uncle had to force himself to speak in such a way.

'All right!' I cried. 'Let it be as you wish, and may God reward your superhuman energy. You have only a few hours left in which to tempt fate. Let us go!'

22

WE set off again, this time down the other tunnel. Hans led the way as usual. We hadn't gone further than 100 yards, when the professor, shining his lamp along the walls, bellowed:

'These are Primitive terrains! We're on the right route, come on, come on!'

When the Earth slowly cooled during the first days of

the world, the decrease in volume produced disruptions, breakages, shrinkages, and cracks in the crust. Our present corridor was a fissure of this sort, through which the eruption of the liquid granite had formerly poured out. Its thousand paths formed an impossible maze through the primeval ground.

As we went further down, the succession of strata making up the Primitive terrain appeared more and more clearly. Geological science considers the Primitive terrain as the base of the mineral crust, and has analysed it into three different strata: schists, gneisses, and mica schists resting on that immovable rock called granite.

Never had mineralogists been in such perfect circumstances for studying nature *in situ*. The drill, a brutal and unintelligent machine, could not bring its internal texture back to the surface of the globe—but we were going to examine it with our eyes, touch it with our hands.

Through the layer of schists, coloured in wonderful green shades, there meandered metallic seams of copper and manganese, with traces of platinum and gold. I dreamed when I saw these riches hidden away in the bowels of the Earth, which human greed would never enjoy! These treasures were so deeply buried by the upheavals of the first days, that neither pick nor drill will ever be able to tear them from their tomb.

After the schists came the gneisses, with a stratiform structure, remarkable for their regularity and their parallel *folia*;* then the mica schists laid out in huge laminae, standing out because of the scintillations in the white mica.

The light from the lamps, reflected by the tiny facets of the mass of rock, shone its fiery flashes at all angles, and I imagined I was travelling through a hollowed-out diamond with the rays disintegrating into a thousand dazzling lights.

At about six, this festival of light reduced noticeably and then almost stopped. The rock-faces took on a crystallized tint, but of a dark shade. The mica mixed more intimately with feldspar and quartz, to form that most rock-like of all rocks, the stone that is the hardest of them all, the one that holds up the four layers of the globe's terrains without being crushed. We were walled up in a huge granite prison.

It was eight in the evening. There was still no water. I was in terrible pain. My uncle walked ahead. He wouldn't stop. He kept turning his head in order to detect murmurs from any spring. But none came!

Meanwhile my legs refused to carry me any further. I resisted the agony so that my uncle would not have to call a halt. It would have been a blow of despair for him, as the day was coming to an end, the last one he had.

Finally my strength left me. I uttered a cry and fell down.

'Help! I'm dying!'

My uncle came back. He examined me, crossing his arms. Then the leaden words came from his lips:

'It is finished!'

A terrifying gesture of anger struck my eyes one last time, and I closed them.

When I opened my eyes again, I saw my two companions motionless, rolled up in their blankets. Were they asleep? For my part, I could not find a moment's repose. My distress was too great, and above all the thought that my sufferings were not going to find any relief. My uncle's last words rang out in my ears: 'It is finished!'—since in such a weak state, we couldn't even think about reaching the surface of the Earth again.

There were more than four miles of Earth's crust! This mass seemed to be leaning with all its weight on my shoulders. I felt crushed, and I wore myself out with violent struggles to turn over on my granite bed.

A few hours went by. A deep silence hung around us, the silence of the grave. Nothing reached us through these walls each of which was at least five miles thick.

Nevertheless, in the middle of my lethargy, I thought I heard a noise. It was dark in the tunnel. I looked more carefully and thought I could see the Icelander slipping away with the lamp in his hand.

Why was he going? Was Hans leaving us to our fate? My uncle was asleep. I tried to cry out. My voice could not find a way through my dried-up lips. It was now very dark, and the last sounds had just died away.

'Hans is leaving us!' I cried. 'Hans, Hans!'

These words, I shouted them inside myself. They went no further. But after the first moment of terror, I felt ashamed of my suspicion of a man whose conduct had been beyond reproach until now. His departure could not be running away. Instead of going up the tunnel, he was heading down. Evil intentions would have taken him towards the top, not the bottom. This argument calmed me down a little, and I came back to another order of ideas. Only a serious reason could have torn Hans, that peaceful man, from his rest. Was he in search of something? Had he heard some murmur during the silent night, one which had not reached me?

23

FOR an hour, my delirious brain ran through all the conceivable reasons that could have made the calm hunter act in this way. The most absurd ideas intersected in my head. I thought I was about to go mad!

But finally the sound of feet could be heard in the depths of the chasm. Hans was coming back up. An indefinite light began to slide along the rock-face, then flowed through the mouth of the corridor. Hans reappeared.

He went up to my uncle, put a hand on his shoulder and gently woke him up. My uncle sat up.

'What is it?'

'Vatten,' replied the hunter.

It must be the case that, under the inspiration of extreme suffering, everyone becomes multilingual. I did not know a single word of Danish, and yet I instinctively understood our guide's utterance.

'Water, water!' I shouted, clapping my hands and gesticulating like a lunatic.

'Water!' repeated my uncle. 'Hvar?'

'Nedat,' replied Hans.

Where? Below! I could understand everything. I had seized hold of the hunter's hands, and was holding them tight, while he looked calmly at me.

The preparations for departure didn't take long, and soon we were moving down a corridor whose slope was one in three.

An hour later, we had covered about a mile-and-a-quarter and gone down about 2,000 feet.

At that moment, I distinctly heard an unusual sound running along the side-walls of the granite rock-face, a sort of muffled rumbling like distant thunder. During the next half-hour of walking, not meeting the promised spring, I felt anxiety taking hold of me again; but then my uncle told me where the noise was coming from.

'Hans was not wrong. What you hear is the roaring of fast-flowing water.'

'A stream?'

'There can be no doubt about it. An underground river is flowing around us!'

We walked faster, overstimulated by hope. I forgot about my tiredness. The sound of babbling water was already refreshing me. It was increasing noticeably. The water, having for a long time remained over our heads, was now running behind the left-hand rock-face—roaring and splashing. I frequently touched the rock with my hand, hoping to find traces of condensation or water oozing through. But in vain.

Another half-hour went by. Another mile-and-a-quarter was covered.

It became clear at this point that, while he had been away, the hunter hadn't been able to continue his search any further. Guided by an instinct peculiar to mountain men, to water-diviners, he had 'felt' the presence of a stream through the rock, but had certainly not seen the precious liquid: and he had not drunk any.

Soon it became obvious that, if we continued walking, we would be moving away from the current, whose murmuring was now tending to diminish.

We turned back. Hans stopped at the precise point where the stream seemed to be the closest.

I sat near the rock-wall, while the waters ran with great violence only two feet away from me. But a granite wall stood between us.

Without thinking, without wondering whether some way didn't exist of getting to this water, I gave in to an immediate feeling of despair.

Hans looked at me, and I thought I could see a smile playing on his lips.

He rose and picked up the lamp. I followed. He went up to the rock-face. I watched him. He put his ear to the dry stone, and slowly moved it around, listening with great concentration. I understood that he was looking for the precise point where the noise from the stream was loudest. He located this spot in the left-hand wall, three feet above the ground.

I was highly excited. I didn't dare guess what the hunter planned to do. But I had to understand, and applaud, and embrace him passionately, when I saw him lift up the pickaxe to attack the very rock.

'Saved!' I cried out.

'Yes,' repeated my uncle in a frenzy. 'Hans is right. Oh the excellent hunter! We would never have thought of that!'

I cannot disagree. Such a solution, however simple, would not have entered our minds. Nothing could be more dangerous than striking a blow with a pick into the structure of the globe. What if a landslide happened and crushed us to death? What if the water, bursting through the rock, drowned us? These fears were far from imaginary; but at such a moment the danger of landslide or flood couldn't stop us. Our thirst was so strong that to quench it we would have dug into the ocean bed itself.

Hans set to work, a task which neither my uncle nor I

could have completed. Our hands would have been so impatient that the rock would have flown into pieces under our hurried blows. The guide, in contrast, was calm and moderate, slowly chipping away at the rock with a long series of little blows, creating an opening six inches wide. I heard the noise of the stream increase, and I could already feel the life-giving water spurting on my lips.

Soon the pick had gone two feet into the granite wall. The work had lasted over an hour. I was writhing with impatience. My uncle wanted to bring in the big guns. I had difficulty holding him back, and he was already seizing his pickaxe, when suddenly a whistling noise was heard. A jet of water shot out of the rock and hit the opposite face.

Hans, almost knocked down by the blow, could not hold back a cry of pain. I understood why when I thrust my hand into the liquid jet, and in turn uttered a wild exclamation. The spring was boiling.

'Water at 100°!' I shouted.

'It will soon cool down,' replied my uncle.

The corridor filled with steam, while a brook formed, and headed off into the underground meanders. Soon we were drinking our first mouthfuls.

Oh, what ecstasy! What indescribable gratification! What was this water? Where did it come from? I didn't care. It was water and, although still hot, gave back to our hearts the life that was escaping from them. I drank without stopping, without even tasting.

It was only after a minute of delight that I shouted:

'But it's full of iron!'

'Excellent for the stomach,' replied my uncle, 'and full of minerals! Our journey is as good as a trip to Spa or Tœplitz!'*

'Oh, how satisfying it is!'

'I am not surprised, water from five miles below ground. It tastes of ink, which is not unpleasant. A vital commodity Hans has given us! I propose therefore to call this brook after the person who was our salvation.'

'Agreed!'

The name 'Hans-Bach'* was decided on the spot.

Hans did not become any the prouder because of this. Having drunk in moderation, he sat back in a corner with his usual calm.

'Now,' I said, 'we mustn't let the water be lost.'

'Why bother? I do not imagine this source will ever dry up.'

'It makes no difference. Let's fill the water-bottle and flasks, and then try to block up the hole.'

My advice was followed. Using granite chips and coarse cloth, Hans tried to block the gash made in the wall. It was not easy. Our hands got scalded to no avail; there was too much pressure, and our attempts produced no result.

'It's obvious,' I said, 'that the water-bearing beds are at too great a height, to judge from the strength of the jet.'

'There can be no doubt about it. If this water column is 32,000 feet high, it will be at a pressure of 1,000 atmospheres. But I have an idea.'

'What is it?'

'Why are we trying so hard to block the hole?'

'But, because . . .'

I would have been hard put to find a reason.

'When our flasks are empty, would we be certain to be able to fill them again?'

'Clearly not.'

'Well then, we will let the water flow. It will work its way down naturally, and guide those who drink from it on the way!'

'Good idea! With this stream as companion, there is no reason for our projects not to succeed.'

'You are getting there, my boy,' said the professor, laughing.

'I'm doing better than that, I'm there already.'

'Not so quick! Let's begin by taking a few hours' rest.'

I had in truth forgotten that it was night-time. The chronometer soon confirmed the fact. Shortly afterwards, each of us, having eaten and drunk his fill, fell into a deep sleep.

24

THE following day, we had already forgotten about our difficulties. I was amazed at first not to feel thirsty, and wondered why. The stream flowing and gurgling at my feet gave me the answer.

We ate and drank from the excellent ferrous water. I felt like a new man, determined to go a long way. Why should a man as convinced as my uncle not succeed, with a hard-working guide like Hans and a committed nephew like myself? These were the wonderful ideas which slid into my brain. Had someone suggested going back up to the top of Snæfells, I would have indignantly refused.

But fortunately the only item on the agenda was descending.

'Let's go!' I shouted, waking with my enthusiastic cries the old echoes of the globe.

We started off again at 8 a.m. on the Thursday. The granite corridor, twisting and turning in sinuous paths, produced unexpected corners, taking on the complexity of a maze; but, overall, its general direction was still towards the southeast. My uncle continually consulted his compass with the greatest care, so as to be able to note the ground covered.

The gallery proceeded almost horizontally, with a gradient of at the very most 1 in 35. The stream followed unhurriedly at our feet, murmuring. I compared it to some familiar spirit guiding us down into the Earth, and I caressed the warm water-nymph whose song accompanied our steps. When I was in a good mood, my mind often took a mythological turn.

As for my uncle, he was cursing the horizontality of the route, as 'the man of the perpendiculars'.* His route was being indefinitely extended, and instead of 'sliding down the Earth's radius', as he put it, he was almost going off at a tangent. But we had no choice, and as long as we were getting nearer the centre, no matter how slowly, there was no reason to complain.

In any case from time to time the slopes got steeper: the water-nymph would start tumbling down and moaning, and we would go down deeper with her.

In sum, during that and the following day, we covered a great deal of ground horizontally, but relatively little vertically.

On Friday evening, 10 July, according to our estimates we were about 70 miles southeast of Reykjavik and at a depth of just over six miles.

Under our feet at this point opened a rather frightening shaft. My uncle couldn't resist clapping his hands when he calculated the steepness of the slope.

'It will take us a very long way,' he exclaimed, 'and easily, for the projections of the rock form a veritable staircase.'

The ropes were placed in position by Hans in such a way as to prevent all accidents. The descent began. I do not dare call it a perilous descent because I was already familiar with this sort of operation.

The shaft was a narrow slit cut into the mass of the rock, of the sort called 'faults'. It had clearly been pro-duced during the contraction of the Earth's very structure, at the period when it was cooling down. If it had formerly served as a way through for the eruptive matters vomited by Snæfells, I couldn't explain to myself how it was that these materials had left no trace. We were going down a sort of spiral staircase that you'd have said was made by human hands.

Every quarter of an hour we were forced to stop and take a rest to allow our knees to recover. We invariably sat down on some projection with our legs dangling over it; we ate while chatting; and we drank at the brook.

It goes without saying that the Hans-Bach had become a waterfall in this fault and had lost much of its volume, but it was still more than sufficient to quench our thirst. In any case, when the slope became less steep, it would soon have to adopt its more peaceful course again. At this point it reminded me of my worthy uncle, with his fits of impatience and anger, whilst, when following the gentler slopes, it was like the Icelandic hunter's calm.

On 11 and 12 July we worked our way round the spirals of the fault, penetrating five miles further into the Earth's crust, which made nearly 12 miles below sea-level. But on the 13th, at about midday, the fault took on a much gentler slope, about 45°, heading towards the southeast.

The path became quite easy then, and very boring. It would have been hard for it to have been anything else. There was no way that the journey could be varied by charges in the countryside.

Finally, on Wednesday the 15th we were 17 miles below ground and about 120 miles from Snæfells. Although we were a little tired, our health was still in a reassuring state and the portable medical kit had not yet been used.

Every hour my uncle noted the measurements of the compass, the chronometer, the manometer, and the thermometer: the same notes that he published later in his scientific account of the journey. In this way he could easily deduce what our position was. When he told me that we'd done this horizontal distance of 120 miles, I couldn't hold back an exclamation.

'What's the matter?' he asked.

'Nothing. I was just thinking.'

'Thinking what, my boy?'

'That if our calculations are correct, we are no longer under Iceland.'

'Do you believe so?'

'It is easy to check.'

I used my compasses to measure on the map.

'I was right,' I said. 'We have gone right past Portland Cape and these 120 miles towards the southeast mean that we are now on the open sea.'

'*Under* the open sea,' said my uncle, rubbing his hands.

'So,' I exclaimed, 'the ocean stretches above our heads!'

'Well, Axel, perfectly normal. At Newcastle, are there

not coal-mines which extend a great distance under the waves?'

The professor might find the situation perfectly normal, but the thought of walking under the great weight of the waters wouldn't stop worrying me. And yet, whether the plains and mountains of Iceland were suspended over our heads or the waves of the Atlantic, made very little difference in the end, provided that the granite structure remained solid. In any case, I quickly got used to the idea, for the corridor—which was sometimes straight, sometimes winding, as capricious in its slopes as in its detours, but running regularly towards the southeast and working its way constantly down—was quickly leading us to great depths.

Four days later, on the evening of Saturday, 18 July, we arrived at a sort of grotto, of considerable size. My uncle gave Hans his three weekly rix-dollars; and it was decided that the following day would be a day of rest.

25

ACCORDINGLY I woke up on the Sunday morning without the normal worry about leaving immediately and, although we were amongst the deepest chasms, this was all the same very pleasant. In any case we had got used to our troglodytes' existence. I hardly thought about the sun, the stars, the moon, the trees, the houses, the towns—all the unnecessary aspects of earthly life which terrestrial beings consider a necessity. Since we were fossils, we didn't care a fig about such useless marvels.

The grotto formed a huge hall. Over its granite floor gently flowed the faithful stream. At such a distance from its source, its water was only the same temperature as the air, and we could drink it without difficulty.

After breakfast the professor wanted to spend a few hours putting his daily notes into order.

'First of all,' he said, 'I am going to make a few calculations in order to find out exactly what our position is.

When we get back, I want to be able to draw a map of our journey: a sort of vertical section of the globe giving the profile of the expedition.'

'That'll be fascinating, Uncle, but will your observations be sufficiently precise?'

'Yes, I have carefully noted down the angles and the gradients. I am sure I have not made any mistakes. Let us first see where we are: take the compass and note the direction it indicates.'

I considered the instrument and after a careful examination replied 'east-a-quarter-southeast'.*

'Good,' said the professor, noting down the observation and making a few quick calculations. 'I conclude that we have covered 210 miles from the point where we started.'

'So we're travelling underneath the Atlantic?'

'Correct.'

'And at this moment a storm is perhaps raging up there, with ships being shaken about above our heads by waves and hurricanes?'

'It is possible.'

'And the whales are coming to knock their tails on the roof of our prison?'

'Don't worry, Axel, they will not do it any harm. But let's get back to our calculations. We are 210 miles from the base of Snæfells in a southeasterly direction, and, according to my previous notes, I estimate the depth reached to be 40 miles.'

'Forty miles?' I shouted.

'In all probability.'

'But that's the furthest limit that science has ascribed to the thickness of the Earth's crust!'

'I will not contradict you.'

'And here, according to the law of increasing temperature, there should be a temperature of over 1,500°?'

'"Should be", my boy.'

'And all this granite couldn't remain in a solid state and would be completely melted?'

'You can see that this is not the case and that as usual the facts are able to contradict the theories.'

'I am forced to agree, but it still astonishes me.'

'What temperature does the thermometer indicate?'

'27.6°.'

'The scientists are only out, therefore, by 1,474.4°.* So the proportional increase in the temperature is an error. So Sir Humphry Davy was right. So I was not wrong to listen to him. What have you to say to that?'

'Nothing.'

In fact, I would have had quite a few things to say. I didn't accept Davy's theories at all: I still believed in the heat in the centre, although I could not feel any of its effects. To tell the truth, I preferred to think that this vent was the chimney of an extinct volcano: one that the lava had covered over with a coating that was refractory and did not allow the temperature to spread through its walls.

But without stopping to seek new arguments, I merely accepted the situation as it was.

'Uncle,' I tried again, 'I believe that all your calculations are accurate, but allow me to draw a logical conclusion from them.'

'Go on, my boy, feel free.'

'At the point where we are now, on the same latitude as Iceland, the radius of the Earth is about 3,935 miles, isn't it?'

'Three thousand nine hundred and thirty-six.'

'Let's say 4,000 as a round figure. Out of a journey of 4,000 miles we've done 40?'*

'As you say.'

'And this has been achieved at the expense of 210 miles in a diagonal direction?'

'Perfectly.'

'In about twenty days?'

'In twenty days.'

'Now, 40 miles is a hundredth of the radius of the Earth. If we continue in this way we will therefore take 2,000 days, or nearly five-and-a-half years to get down.'

The professor did not reply.

'And that's not counting the fact that, if the vertical journey of 40 miles has been at the expense of a horizontal one of 210, that will make 20,000 miles towards the southeast, and we will have come out through a point on the circumference long before we reach the centre.'

'The devil take your calculations!' cried my uncle with an angry gesture. 'The devil take your hypotheses. What do they rest on? Who can tell you that this corridor does not go straight to our goal? In any case, I have a precedent on my side. What I am doing here, someone else has already done, and where he succeeded I will also succeed.'

'I hope so. But finally, I have the right . . .'

'You have the right to keep quiet, Axel, when you attempt to reason in that way.'

I could see clearly that the terrible professor was threatening to reappear under the skin of the uncle, and so I considered myself duly warned.

'Now,' he said, 'consult the manometer: what does it indicate?'

'A considerable pressure.'

'Good. You can see that by going down gradually, by slowly getting used to the density of the atmosphere, we have not had any problems at all.'

'None at all, apart from a few earaches.'

'That's nothing, and you can get rid of the pain by putting the external air in rapid communication with the air contained in your lungs.'

'Fine,' I replied, having decided not to upset my uncle any more. 'There is even a real pleasure in being plunged into this denser atmosphere. Have you noticed how intensely the sound is propagated?'

'Indeed; a deaf man would end up hearing perfectly.'

'But this density will undoubtedly increase?'

'Yes, following a law which has not been completely determined. It is true that the force of gravity will decrease in proportion to our descent. You know that it is at the surface itself of the Earth that its action is most strongly felt, and that objects no longer have any weight at the centre of the globe.'

'I know, but tell me, will this air not finish up having the density of water?'

'Probably, under a pressure of 710 atmospheres.'

'And further down?'

'Further down this density will increase still further.'

'How will we carry on then?'

'Well, we will just have to put stones in our pockets.'

'Indeed my uncle, you have a reply for everything.'

I didn't dare venture any further into the area of hypotheses, for I would again have come up against some impossibility that would have made the professor hopping mad.

It was clear, however, that the air, under a pressure which could reach thousands of atmospheres, would end up solidifying, and then, even supposing that our bodies could have resisted this, we would have to stop, in spite of all the reasoning in the world.

But I did not communicate this argument; my uncle would have counter-attacked again with his perpetual Saknussemm, a precedent without value, for, even accepting the journey of the learned Icelander as true, there was a very simple thing that could be replied.

In the sixteenth century, neither the barometer nor the manometer had been invented; so how did Saknussemm know when he had reached the centre of the globe?

But I kept this objection to myself and waited to see what the future would bring.

The rest of the day was spent calculating and chatting. I was always in agreement with Professor Lidenbrock; and I envied the perfect indifference of Hans who, without seeking causes and effects to such an extent, carried blindly on wherever fate took him.

26

It must be admitted that things had gone well until now and it would have been ungracious of me to complain. But if the average difficulty didn't increase, we couldn't avoid reaching our goal. And what glory then! I had reached the point where I reasoned in the same way as

Lidenbrock. Quite seriously. Was this due to the strange environment in which I was living? Perhaps.

For a few days, steeper gradients, some of them even of an alarming perpendicularity, brought us deeper into the internal rock massif. On some days we gained between four and five miles towards the centre. Perilous descents, during which Hans's skill and marvellous sang-froid were very useful to us. The impassive Icelander gave of himself with an incomprehensible straightforwardness and, thanks to him, we survived more than one tricky situation which we wouldn't have got out of on our own.

What was surprising was that his silence increased every day. I believe that we were even catching it. External objects have a real effect on the brain. The person who shuts himself up between four walls finishes up losing the ability to associate ideas and words. How many people in prison cells have become idiots, if not madmen, through lack of use of their faculties of thought?

For the two weeks that followed our last conversation, nothing worth reporting happened. I can only find in my memory a single event of an extreme seriousness—but with reason. It would be difficult for me to forget the smallest detail of it.

On 7 August our successive descents had brought us to a depth of 70 miles, in other words above our heads lay 70 miles of rocks, of ocean, of continents, and of towns. We must have been about 500 miles from Iceland.

That day the tunnel was following a relatively gentle slope.

I was walking ahead. My uncle carried one of the Ruhmkorff lamps and myself the other one. I was examining the granite strata.

Suddenly, turning round, I noticed that I was alone.

'So,' I thought, 'I've walked too quickly: or else Hans and my uncle have stopped on the way. It's best to join up with them again. Fortunately, the path does not climb very much.'

I went back the way I had just come. I walked for a quarter of an hour. I looked. Nobody. I called out. No reply. My voice was lost in the middle of the cavernous echoes that it suddenly awakened.

I began to feel worried. A shiver ran through my whole body.

'Let's be calm,' I said out loud. 'I'm certain to be able to find my companions again. There's only a single path. Now I was ahead—let's go back.'

I went up for half an hour. I listened out to see if some call was not addressed to me. In such a dense atmosphere it might reach me from a long way away. An extra-ordinary silence reigned in the immense tunnel.

I stopped. I couldn't believe my isolation. I wanted to think I was just astray, not lost. When you've strayed from your path, you can find yourself again.

'Let's see,' I repeated. 'Since there's only one route, since they're following it, I must meet up with them again. All I have to do is go further up. Unless, not having seen me, forgetting that I was ahead of them, they didn't think they had to come back. Well, even in that case, I'll find them again if I hurry. It's obvious.'

I repeated these last words like a man who is not convinced. What is more, to put together such simple ideas and form them into reasoning, I had to employ a great deal of time.

A doubt then took hold of me. Was I really ahead? Certainly Hans had been following me, and he was in front of my uncle. He'd even stopped for a few seconds to adjust the bags on his shoulder. The detail came back to me. It was at that very moment that I must have con-tinued on my way.

'In any case,' I thought, 'I have a sure means of not getting lost: a thread to guide me through this labyrinth, one which can never break: my faithful stream. All I have to do is go back up its course and I will automatically find my companions' traces again.'

This reasoning brought me back to life: I resolved to start off again without losing a second.

How I blessed, then, the foresight of my uncle when he prevented the hunter from blocking up the cut made in the granite wall. In this way the health-giving source, having quenched our thirst *en route*, was going to guide me through the meanders of the Earth's crust.

Before starting back up, I thought a wash would do me good.

I bent over to wet my forehead in the water of the Hans-Bach.

My stupefaction can be imagined.

Under my feet was dry and uneven granite. The stream was no longer flowing at my feet!

27

I CANNOT depict my despair. No word in any human language would be adequate to describe my feelings. I was buried alive with the prospect of dying in agonies of hunger and thirst.

Without thinking I moved my burning hands over the ground. How dried up this rock seemed to me!

But how could I have left the stream's course?—for it just wasn't there. I understood then the reason for the strange silence when I had listened the last time to see if some call from my companions might not reach my ear. At the point when I had first started off on the wrong route, I hadn't noticed at all that the stream wasn't there. Clearly, at that moment, a forking in the gallery must have appeared in front of me, whilst the Hans-Bach, obeying the whims of another slope, had gone off with my companions towards unknown depths.

How could I get back? There were no tracks at all. My feet left no imprint on the granite. I cudgelled my brain, looking for a solution to this insoluble problem. My position could be summed up in a single word: lost!

Yes, lost at a depth which seemed immeasurable to me: those 70 miles of Earth's crust weighed down on my shoulders with a terrible weight. I felt I was being flattened.

I tried to take my mind back to things on Earth. I could

hardly do so. Hamburg, the house in Königstrasse, my poor Gräuben, this whole world under which I was lost, went quickly through my terrified brain. I relived the incidents of the journey in a brilliant hallucination, the events of the crossing, Iceland, Mr Fridriksson, Snæfells. I said to myself that if, in the present situation, I still kept the shadow of a hope, it would be a sign of madness;* that it was better to give in to despair.

For, what human power could bring me back up to the surface of the globe or break up the enormous vaults which buttressed each other over my head? Who could put me on the route back and thus help me rejoin my companions?

'Oh, my uncle,' I shouted, in a tone of despair.

It was the only word of reproach that came from my mouth, for I understood that the unfortunate man must himself be suffering while looking for me.

When I saw myself beyond all human help, unable to try and do anything to save myself, I thought of the help of Heaven. Memories of my childhood, of my mother whom I had known only at the time of kisses, came back into my mind. I resorted to prayer, however little right I had to be heard by a God whom I was addressing so late; and I implored him with fervour.

This return to Providence made me a little calmer and I was able to concentrate all the forces of my mind on the situation.

I had three days' food left, and my flask was full. However, I could not remain alone any longer. But should I go up or down?

Go up, clearly, up all the way.

I would have to reach the point where I'd left the stream, the fateful dividing of the ways. There, once I had the stream beside my feet, I would still be able to get back up to the summit of Snæfells.

Why hadn't I thought of this sooner? There was clearly a chance of being saved. The first priority was to find the course of the Hans-Bach again.

I got up and, leaning on my iron-tipped stick, went

back up the tunnel. The slope was quite steep. I walked with hope and without hindrance, like a man who has no choice of path to follow.

For half an hour no obstacle stopped me. I tried to recognize my route from the form of the tunnel, from the shape of some of the rocks, from the patterns some of the crevices made. But no particular indication struck my mind and soon I had to admit that this gallery could not lead me back to the fork. It was a cul-de-sac. I collided with an impenetrable wall and fell against it.

With what horror, with what despair I was seized then, I would not be able to say. I lay there overwhelmed. My last hope had just broken against this granite wall.

Lost in the labyrinth, whose multiple meanderings criss-crossed in all directions, I could no longer try an imposs-ible flight. I had to die from the most terrifying of deaths and—strangely enough—it came into my mind that if one day my fossilized body was found again, encountering it 70 miles into the bowels of the Earth would raise serious scientific questions.

I wanted to speak out loud, but only rough sounds came out through my dried-up lips. I lay there panting very heavily.

In the midst of that anguish, a new terror came and took hold of my mind. My lamp had broken when it fell; and I had no means of repairing it. Its light was getting dimmer and was just about to give up.

I watched the luminous current as it diminished in the filament of the apparatus. A procession of moving shadows flickered past on the darkened walls. I no longer dared blink or move my eyes, afraid to lose the least molecule of this fleeing light. At each moment it seemed to me that it was going to vanish and that blackness would take hold of me.

Finally, a last gleam trembled in the lamp. I followed it, I breathed it in with my eyes, I concentrated the whole power of my vision on it, as if on the last sensation of light that it would ever be able to see—and then was plunged into the depths of an immense darkness.

What a terrible shout came from me. On Earth, in the middle of the darkest nights, light never entirely gives up its rights. It is diffuse, it is subtle, but however little remains, the retina ends up receiving it. Here: nothing. Absolute darkness made me a blind man in the full sense of the word.

I lost my head. I raised my arms in front of me, trying to feel my way in the most painful fashion. I started fleeing, rushing at random through this inextricable labyrinth, going down all the time, running through the Earth's crust like an inhabitant of the underground faults, calling, shouting, screaming, soon bruised on the rock projections, falling and getting up covered with blood, trying to drink the blood flooding over my face, but constantly waiting for some wall of rock to come and offer an obstacle for my head to break on.

Where did this mad running take me? I shall never know. After several hours, undoubtedly at the end of my strength, I fell like an inert mass along the wall and lost all awareness of existence.

28

WHEN I came back to life, my face was wet with tears. How long this state of unconsciousness had lasted, I cannot say. I no longer had any way of keeping track of time. Never had there been loneliness like mine, never such complete abandon.

After my fall, I had lost a great deal of blood. I could feel myself covered in it. Oh, how I regretted not being dead and that 'it all still had to be done'. I no longer wanted to think. I pushed every idea out of my head and, overcome by pain, rolled over towards the opposite wall.

Already I could feel unconsciousness taking hold of me again, and with it the supreme annihilation—when a loud noise struck my ear. It was like long rolling thunder; and I listened as the soundwaves slowly disappeared into the far depths of the gulf.

Where was this noise coming from? Undoubtedly from some phenomenon happening in the heart of the Earth's mass. The explosion of gas or the collapse of some major buttress of the globe.

I listened again. I wanted to find out whether this noise would occur again. A quarter of an hour went by. Silence reigned in the tunnel. I couldn't even hear the sound of my own heart beating any more.

Suddenly my ear, by chance applied to the wall, seemed to detect words: vague, imperceptible, distant. I shuddered. 'It's a hallucination,' I thought.

But no—by concentrating harder on listening, I distinctly heard voices murmuring. I was too weak to understand what was being said. Someone was speaking though. I was quite certain of that.

For a moment I was terrified that it might be my own words coming back to me through an echo. Perhaps I had been crying out without knowing. I tightly closed my mouth, and once more placed my ear on the granite wall.

Yes, it's voices for sure! Definitely voices!

By moving only a few feet along the side of the tunnel, I could hear distinctly. I managed to make out strange, uncertain, incomprehensible words. They reached my ear as if spoken in a low voice—murmured, as it were. The word *förlorad* was repeated several times in a sorrowful tone.

What could it mean, and who was speaking? It had to be my uncle or Hans! But if I could hear them, they might easily be able to hear me.

'Help!' I cried with all my strength. 'Help!'

I then listened, I laid watch in the darkness for a reply, a cry, a sigh. But nothing could be heard. A few minutes passed. A whole flood of ideas burgeoned in my mind. I feared that my weakened voice might not reach my companions.

'It must be them,' I repeated. 'What other men can be buried 75 miles underground?'

I began to listen again. By moving my ear along the side-wall, I found the mathematical point where the voices appeared to attain their maximum intensity. The word *förlorad* again reached my ear; then that rolling of thunder which had dragged me from my torpor.

'No, no. These voices are not reaching my ears through the solid rock. The walls are solid granite, and wouldn't allow the most fearful explosion to pass through. The sound must be coming along the gallery itself. There must be some peculiar acoustic effect here.'

Again I listened; and this time—yes, this time—I heard my name distinctly projected through space.

It was my uncle who was speaking. He was conversing with the guide, and *förlorad* was a Danish word.

Then everything became clear. To make myself heard, I too had to speak along the side of the gallery, which would carry the sound of my voice just as wires carry electricity.

But there was no time to lose. If my companions were only to move a few feet away from where they stood, the acoustic effect would be destroyed. So I again moved towards the wall, and said as distinctly as I could:

'Uncle Lidenbrock!'

I then waited for a reply with the greatest possible anxiety. Sound does not travel very quickly. Besides, the density of the layers of air did not add to its speed; only to the volume. Several seconds, several ages, elapsed, and finally these words reached my ears:

'Axel, Axel! Is it you?'

. . . .

'Yes, yes!'

. . . .

'Where are you, my boy?'

. . . .

'Lost, in the most complete darkness!'

. . . .

'And your lamp?'

. . . .

'Out.'

. . . .

'And the stream?'

. . . .

'Lost!'

. . . .

'Axel, my poor Axel, courage.'

. . . .

'Please wait a moment, Uncle. I'm exhausted. I no longer have the strength to reply. But carry on speaking to me!'

. . . .

'Courage,' said my uncle. 'Do not speak, but listen to me. We have been searching for you both upwards and downwards in the tunnel. But with no success at all. I shed many tears for you, my child. Finally, we assumed that you were still following the Hans-Bach down, and descended again, firing our guns. Now, if our voices are in contact, this is only an acoustic effect: our hands cannot touch. But do not despair, Axel. It is already something to be able to hear each other.'

While he was speaking I was thinking. A hope, still faint, was coming back to me. Before anything else, there was one thing I had to know. I therefore put my mouth close to the wall, and said: 'Uncle?'

. . . .

'My boy,' came back after a while.

. . . .

'We must first of all find out how far we are apart.'

. . . .

'It is not difficult.'

. . . .

'Do you have your chronometer to hand?'

. . . .

'Yes.'

. . . .

'Well, have it ready. Pronounce my name, noting exactly the second at which you speak. I will repeat it as soon as it gets to me—and you will then note down the exact moment when my reply reaches you.'

. . . .

'Very good; and half the time between my call and your answer will be the time my voice takes to reach you.'

. . . .

'Exactly, Uncle.'

'Ready?'

'Yes.'

'Well, stand by, I am about to pronounce your name.'

I applied my ear to the gallery, and as soon as the word 'Axel' reached me, I repeated the word, then waited.

. . . .

'Forty seconds,' said my uncle. 'Forty seconds between the two words. Sound therefore takes twenty seconds to arrive. Now, at 1,020 feet per second, that makes 20,400 feet: almost four miles.'

. . . .

'Almost four miles . . .'

. . . .

'Which can be covered, Axel!'

. . . .

'But do we know whether to go up or down?'

. . . .

'Down, and I will tell you why. We have reached a vast open space, where a large number of galleries culminate. The one you followed must necessarily take you to this point, for it appears that all these fissures, these fractures of the globe, radiate out from the vast cavern we are in. Get up, then, and continue walking. If necessary drag yourself along—slide on the steep slopes, and you will find our open arms at the end of your journey. Off you go like a good fellow, go!'

These words brought me back to life.

'Farewell, Uncle, I am starting off. As soon as I leave here, our voices will not be able to communicate. Farewell then!'

. . . .

'Goodbye, Axel! See you soon!'

. . . .

These were the last words I heard.

This surprising conversation, transmitted through the vast mass of the Earth, exchanged over almost four miles, ended with these words of hope. I offered thanks to God, for he had led me through the dark vastnesses to perhaps the only point where my friends' voices could reach me.

This astounding acoustic effect can easily be explained by simple natural laws; it arose from the peculiar shape of the gallery and the conductibility of the rock. There are many instances of this propagation of sounds, not perceptible in intermediate positions. I remembered that the phenomenon can be observed in various places, including the Whispering Gallery at St Paul's in London, and especially the curious caverns in Sicily, those stone quarries near Syracuse, of which the most remarkable is known as the Ear of Dionysus.

These memories came into my mind, and I realized that since my uncle's voice reached my ears, no obstacle could exist between us. By following the path of the sound, logically I had to be able to reach him too, provided my strength did not fail me.

I accordingly got up. I dragged myself along more than I walked. The slope was very steep; but I allowed myself to slide down.

Soon the speed of the descent began to increase alarmingly; and threatened to become a real fall. I no longer had the strength to stop myself.

Suddenly the ground disappeared from under my feet. I felt myself rolling and hitting the projections of a vertical gallery, a veritable well. My head bounded against a sharp rock, and I lost consciousness.

29

WHEN I came to, I found myself in semi-darkness, lying on thick covers. My uncle was watching—his eyes fixed intently on my face, looking for any sign of life. At my first sigh he took hold of my hand. When he saw my eyes were open, he uttered a cry of joy:

'He's alive, he's alive!'

'Yes,' I said in a weak voice.

'My dear boy,' said my uncle, clasping me to his breast, 'you are saved!'

I was deeply touched by the tone in which these words were uttered, and even more by the devotion that accompanied them. But such trials were necessary to produce a display of emotion like this in the professor.

At that moment Hans joined us. He saw my hand in my uncle's, and I venture to say that his eyes showed a lively satisfaction.

'God dag,' he said.

'Good day, Hans, good day,' I murmured. 'And now, Uncle, tell me where we are.'

'Tomorrow, Axel, tomorrow. You're still too weak today. I've bandaged your head with compresses which mustn't be disturbed. Sleep, my boy, sleep, and tomorrow I will tell you everything.'

'At least', I cried, 'tell me what time it is, what day it is?'

'Eleven o'clock at night, Sunday, 9 August, and I forbid you to ask any more questions until the tenth of this month.'

I was, if the truth be told, very weak indeed, and my eyes soon closed of their own accord. I did need a good night's rest, and dozed off with the thought that my isolation had lasted two long days.

When I woke up the next morning I looked around. My berth, composed of all our travelling rugs, was in a charming grotto, adorned with magnificent stalagmites, and with a floor covered in soft sand. There reigned a semi-darkness. No torch, no lamp was lighted, and yet a certain inexplicable light entered from the outside through a narrow opening in the grotto. I also heard a vague and indefinite murmur, like the moaning of waves breaking upon a strand, and occasionally the whistling of the wind.

I began to wonder if I had woken up properly, if I wasn't still dreaming, if my brain, cracked by my fall, was not registering purely imaginary noises. However, neither my eyes nor my ears could be mistaken to that extent.

'It's a ray of daylight,' I thought, 'coming through that crack in the rocks. That really is the murmur of waves! And that is the whistle of the wind! Am I imagining things, or have we returned to the surface of the Earth? Has my uncle given up his expedition, then, or has it come to a satisfactory conclusion?'

I was puzzling over these insoluble questions, when the professor came in.

'Good day, Axel,' he cried happily. 'I'm willing to bet you are quite well.'

'I am indeed,' I replied, sitting up in bed.

'I thought as much, for you slept calmly. Hans and I have each taken turns to watch over you, and we have seen you recovering by leaps and bounds.'

'I really feel much better now; to prove it, I'll do justice to the breakfast you're going to put in front of me!'

'You shall eat, my boy! The fever has left you. Hans has been rubbing your wounds with some sort of ointment known only to Icelanders, and they have closed up marvellously. He's a grand chap, is our hunter.'

While speaking, my uncle prepared a few items of food, which I devoured, despite his advice. While I was eating I overwhelmed him with questions, to which he did not hesitate to respond.

I then learned that my providential fall had brought me to the end of an almost perpendicular shaft. As I had come down in the middle of a torrent of stones, the smallest of which would have been enough to crush me, it followed that a section of the rock-face must have slid down with me. This terrifying vehicle had carried me straight into my uncle's arms, where I had fallen, unconscious and covered in blood.

'It is truly incredible that you weren't killed a thousand times over. But, good God, let's stay together from now on, otherwise we would be in danger of never seeing each other again.'

Stay together from now on! The journey wasn't over, then? My eyes widened, which immediately prompted the question:

'What is the matter, Axel?'

'I want to ask you a question. You say that I'm safe and sound?'

'Undoubtedly.'

'I have all my limbs intact?'

'Certainly.'

'And my head?'

'Your head, apart from one or two bruises, is exactly where it ought to be—on your shoulders.'

'Well, I think my mind must have gone.'

'Gone?'

'Yes. We haven't returned to the surface of the Earth, have we?'

'Most certainly not!'

'Then I must be mad, for I can see the light of day, I can hear the wind blowing and the breaking of the sea.'

'Oh! Is that all?'

'Will you please explain?'

'I will not explain anything, for it is inexplicable. But you shall see, and you will realize that geological science has not yet said its last word.'

'Let's go out then,' I cried, suddenly getting up.

'No, Axel, no! The open air might be bad for you.'

'Open air?'

'Yes, the wind is rather strong. I don't want you to put yourself in danger like that.'

'But I tell you I feel wonderful.'

'Patience, my boy. A relapse would put us in an awkward position. We have no time to lose, as the crossing could take a long time.'

'Crossing?'

'Yes. Have another rest today, and tomorrow we shall sail.'

'Sail?'

The word shocked me.

Sail! Did we have a river, a lake, or a sea at our disposal? Was there a ship anchored at some interior port?

My curiosity was aroused to fever-pitch. My uncle tried in vain to restrain me. When he realized that my impatience would do me more harm than the fulfilment of my longings, he gave in.

I dressed quickly. As an excessive precaution, I wrapped myself in one of the covers and went out of the grotto.

30

AT first I saw nothing. My eyes, no longer used to the light, snapped shut. When I was able to open them again, I stood still, far more stupefied than delighted.

'The sea!' I cried.

'Yes. The Lidenbrock Sea, and I like to believe that no other navigator will contest the honour of having discovered it and the right to name it with his own name.'

A vast expanse of water, the beginning of a lake or ocean, stretched away out of view. The shoreline, greatly indented, offered the lapping water a fine golden sand, dotted with those small shells that housed the first beings in creation. The waves broke over it with that sonorous murmur peculiar to vast enclosed spaces. A light foam was swept off by the breath of a moderate wind, and some of the spray was blowing into my face. On this gently sloping shore, about 200 yards from the edge of the waves, expired the last spurs of large cliffs that soared, widening, to an immeasurable height. Some of them, piercing the shoreline with their sharp edges, formed capes and promontories worn away by the teeth of the surf. Further on, the eye was drawn by their shapes clearly outlined against the hazy distant horizon.

It was a real ocean, with the capricious contours of the coastlines of the surface. It was empty, though, and looked horribly wild.

If I was able to look so far across this sea, it was because of a special light which revealed the smallest details. It was not the light of day with its dazzling beams and splendid halo of rays, nor the pale indistinct illumination of the night star, which is only a reflection without heat. No, the luminous power of this light, its flickering diffusion, its clear dry whiteness, the lowness of its temperature, its brilliance, superior indeed to the moon's, all pointed to an electrical origin. It was like an aurora borealis, a continuous cosmic phenomenon, filling this cavern big enough to hold an ocean.

The vault suspended above my head, the sky as it were, seemed to be made of vast clouds, mobile and changeable water-vapours which, due to condensation, surely burst into torrential rain on certain days. I would have thought that under such extreme atmospheric pressure, evaporation could not take place; yet by some physical law which was beyond me, there were great clouds filling the air. But at this moment 'it was a fine day'. The electric layers produced an astonishing play of light amongst the high clouds. Clear shadows stood out on their lower curves and often, between two separate strata, a ray of remarkable intensity slipped through to us. And yet it was not the sun, for its light gave no heat. The effect was sad, sovereignly melancholy. Instead of a firmament bright with stars, I felt the granite vault above these clouds weighing down on me: this space, immense as it was, would not have sufficed for the orbit of even the humblest satellite.

I remembered then that theory of a British captain's which compared the Earth to a vast hollow sphere, inside which the air was kept luminous by reason of the great pressure, while two heavenly bodies, Pluto and Proserpina,* traced their mysterious orbits. Had he perhaps been telling the truth?

In reality we were imprisoned in a vast excavation. It was impossible to say how wide it stretched, since the shore broadened until it was out of sight, nor how long, for the eye was soon restricted by a slightly uncertain horizon. Its height must have been several miles at the very least. It was impossible to make out where the vault rested on its granite buttresses, as there was so much cloud floating in the atmosphere, which had to be over two miles up, a height greater than on Earth. This was due no doubt to the considerable density of the air.

The word 'cavern' is clearly insufficient for my attempt to convey this immense place. The words which make up human language are inadequate for those who venture into the depths of the Earth.

I could not think what geological event might explain the existence of such a hollow. Could the cooling down of the globe have produced it? I was acquainted, through the tales of travellers, with several famous caverns, but none had such dimensions as this.

Although the grotto of Guachara, in Colombia, visited by the learned Humboldt, had not divulged the secret of its depth to him, although he explored it for 2,500 feet, its extent could not in all plausibility have been much more than that. The vast Mammoth Cave in Kentucky* was an example of gigantic proportions, since its ceiling rose 500 feet above an unfathomable lake, and travellers had explored more than 25 miles inside without ever reaching the end. But what were these holes compared to the one I was now admiring, with its sky of clouds, its electric illumination, and a vast ocean imprisoned in its breast? My imagination felt powerless before this immensity.

I reflected upon all these marvels in silence. Words to

describe my feelings failed me completely. I felt as if I was on some distant planet, observing Uranus or Neptune, phenomena which my 'Earthman' nature had no knowledge of. New words were needed for new sensations, and my imagination could not provide them. I looked, I thought, I admired, in a stupefaction mingled with a certain amount of fear.

The unexpectedness of this spectacle had restored the flush of health to my cheeks; I was in the process of treating myself by means of astonishment, bringing about my cure by means of this novel therapy; besides, the vigour of the very dense air was reviving me, by providing more oxygen for my lungs.

It will not be difficult to understand that after being confined in a narrow gallery for forty-seven days, it was infinite ecstasy to breathe in this breeze loaded with wet and salty emanations.

I could not possibly regret leaving my dark grotto. My uncle, already used to these marvels, was no longer astonished.

'Do you feel strong enough to go for a little walk?' he asked.

'Yes, certainly, nothing would give me greater pleasure.'

'Well then, take my arm, Axel, and we'll follow the meanders of the shoreline.'

I accepted eagerly, and we began to skirt this new ocean. On the left, precipitous rocks, humped one upon the other, formed a tremendous pile of a titanic appearance. Innumerable cascades wound down their sides, stretching away in limpid and echoing sheets of water. A few light vapours, springing from rock to rock, pointed to where hot springs lay; and streams flowed gently towards their shared lagoons, seeking the opportunity of the slopes to murmur more sweetly.

Amongst these streams I recognized our faithful travelling companion, the Hans-Bach, which came to melt peacefully into the sea as if it had never done anything else since the beginning of the world.

'We shall miss it in future,' I said with a sigh.

'Bah!' replied the professor. 'That or another one, what difference does it make?'

I found his reply a trifle ungrateful.

But at that moment my attention was distracted by an unexpected sight. Five hundred paces away, beyond a high promontory, appeared a tall, thick, dense forest. It consisted of trees of medium height, shaped like regular sunshades, with neat and geometric silhouettes; the air currents seemed to have no influence on their foliage, and in the midst of the breezes they stayed as still as a clump of petrified cedars.

I hurried forward. I could find no name for these singular varieties. Did they belong to the 200,000 known vegetable species, or would we have to give them a special place in the flora of water-based vegetation? No: when we arrived under their shade, my surprise turned to admiration.

I was in the presence of fruits of the Earth, but constructed on a gigantic scale. My uncle named them immediately:

'It is just a forest of mushrooms.'

He was right. It may be imagined how big these plants grew in their preferred hot, humid environment. I knew that the *Lycoperdon giganteum* reached, according to Bulliard,* eight or nine feet in circumference; but here we had white mushrooms 30 or 40 feet high, with caps of the same width. There were thousands of them. No light could pierce their dense cover, and complete darkness reigned beneath those domes, crowded together like the round roofs of an African city.

I still wanted to push further in. A mortal chill seeped down from these fleshy vaults. We wandered about for half an hour in these dank shadows, and it was with a real rush of well-being that I got back to the sea-shore.

But the vegetation of this subterranean land was not confined to mushrooms. Further on there arose in groups a great many other trees with faded leaves. They were easily recognizable; common shrubs of the Earth, of phenomenal size, Lycopodia a hundred feet high, giant

Sigillarias, tree-ferns as tall as pines from northern climes, Lepidodendrons with cylindrical forked stalks ending in long leaves bristling with coarse hairs like monstrous meaty plants.

'Astonishing, magnificent, splendid!' cried my uncle. 'Here we have the complete flora of the Secondary Period of the world, the Transition Era. Here we have those humble garden plants which became trees in the first centuries of the Earth. Look, Axel, and admire! No botanist has ever been invited to such a display!'

'Yes, Uncle. Providence seems to have wanted to preserve in this enormous hothouse all the antediluvian plants which have been reconstructed so successfully by the scholars.'

'You are right there, my boy, it is a hothouse; but you could add that it may be a menagerie too.'

'A menagerie?'

'Without a doubt. Look at this dust we are treading on, look at the bones scattered on the ground.'

'Bones? Why, yes, the bones of prehistoric animals!'

I swooped down on the age-old remains, made of some indestructible mineral substance.[1] I unhesitatingly put a name to these gigantic bones which resembled dried-up tree trunks.

'Here is the lower jaw-bone of a mastodon,' I said, 'here are the molars of a dinotherium; and here we have a thigh-bone which can only have belonged to the biggest of these animals, the megatherium. Yes, it really is a menagerie—these skeletons were definitely not carried here by some cataclysm. The animals they belonged to lived on the shores of this subterranean sea, in the shade of these arborescent plants. Look, I can see whole skeletons. And yet . . .'

'And yet?'

'I cannot understand how such quadrupeds came to be in this granite cavern.'

'Why not?'

---

[1] Calcium phosphate.

'Because animal life only existed on Earth at the Secondary Period, when the sedimentary soil was formed by the alluvial deposits, replacing the red-hot rocks of the Primitive Era.'

'Well, Axel, there's a very simple answer to your objection; namely that this soil *is* sedimentary.'

'What! So far below the surface of the Earth!'

'Without a doubt, and it can be explained geologically. At a certain period, the Earth consisted only of an elastic crust, subjected to alternate upward and downward movements, by virtue of the laws of gravity. These probably gave rise to landslides, and a section of the sedimentary terrains was carried down to the bottom of newly opened chasms.'

'That must be true. But if prehistoric animals lived in the subterranean regions, who is to say that one of those monsters is not still wandering around in one of these dark forests or behind these steep rocks?'

At the idea, I scanned the horizon with a certain dread; but no living creature appeared on the deserted shores.

I felt a little tired, and went and sat down right at the end of a promontory, at whose foot the waves were noisily breaking. From there I could see right round the bay, formed by an indentation in the coast. At the end there had formed a little harbour enclosed by pyramid-shaped rocks. A brig and two or three schooners might have anchored there with room to spare. I almost expected to see some ship coming out, all sails set, making for the open sea on the southerly breeze.

But this illusion soon faded. We really were the only living creatures in this subterranean world. At times, when the wind dropped, a silence deeper than the silence of the desert fell upon these arid rocks and weighed upon the surface of the ocean. I tried, then, to penetrate the distant mists, to tear apart the curtain which had fallen over the mysterious depths of the horizon. What questions rushed from my lips! Where did this sea end? Where did it begin? Would we ever be able to sight the shores on the other side?

My uncle, personally, had no doubts about the matter. I, for my part, both desired and feared it.

After an hour spent in contemplation of this marvellous sight, we set off once more along the path of the strand to return to the grotto, and it was in the grip of the strangest thoughts that I fell into a deep sleep.

31

I WOKE up the next day completely cured. I thought a bathe would do me a great deal of good, and so went and plunged for a few minutes in the waters of this Mediterranean Sea. Such a name, surely, suited the sea better than any other.

I returned and lunched with a healthy appetite. Hans knew perfectly how to cook our limited menu; and was equipped with fire and water, so could vary our usual fare a little. With the pudding he served us cups of coffee, and never had this delicious beverage tasted better.

'Now,' said my uncle, 'it's time for the tide, and we must not miss the opportunity to study this phenomenon.'

'What! A tide?'

'Of course.'

'Can the influence of the moon and the sun be felt down here then?'

'Why not? Are not all bodies subject to the force of gravity? This mass of water must therefore be subject to that universal law. So, despite the atmospheric pressure on the surface, you will see it rise like the Atlantic itself.'

During this time we were walking along the sand, and the waves were creeping slowly up the shore.

'Look, there's the tide beginning,' I cried.

'Yes, Axel, and judging from the tidemark of foam, you can see that the water rises about ten feet.'

'That's fantastic!'

'No, it's natural.'

'Say what you like, Uncle, this all seems extraordinary

to me, and I can hardly believe my eyes. Who would ever have thought that there could be a real ocean inside the Earth's crust, with its own ebb and flow, its own sea-breezes and storms!'

'And why not? Is there some physical reason to prevent it?'

'Not that I can see, if we abandoned the theory of the heat at the centre.'

'So up to this point Davy's theory appears to be confirmed?'

'It looks like it, and if that is the case there is nothing to oppose the existence of seas or lands inside the Earth.'

'No doubt, but uninhabited.'

'But why shouldn't these waters shelter a few fish of some unknown species?'

'Well at any rate we haven't found a single one so far.'

'We could rig up some lines and see if a hook has the same success here as in the sublunary oceans.'

'We'll try that, Axel, for we must unravel all the mysteries of these new territories.'

'But where are we, Uncle, for I haven't yet asked you that question, which the instruments must have answered for you?'

'Horizontally, 880 miles from Iceland.'

'As much as that?'

'I think I am right to the nearest mile.'

'And the compass is still pointing southeast?'

'Yes, with a deviation to the west of 19° 42', just like on the surface. As to its "dip" there is something very peculiar happening which I have been observing most carefully.'

'What's that?'

'The needle, instead of dipping towards the Pole as it does in the northern hemisphere, is pointing upwards instead.'

'That means that the point of magnetic attraction lies somewhere between the surface of the Earth and the place we have reached?'

'Exactly, and it is quite probable that if we reached the

polar regions, near the 70th parallel where Sir James Ross* discovered the magnetic pole, we would see the needle point stand straight up. Therefore this mysterious centre of attraction is not located at any great depth.'

'And that's something that science has never even suspected.'

'Science, my boy, is composed of errors, but errors that it is right to make, for they lead step by step to the truth.'

'How far down are we?'

'Eighty-seven miles.'

'So,' I said, examining the map, 'the Scottish Highlands are above us, and up there the snow-covered peaks of the Grampians are rising to prodigious heights.'

'Yes,' replied the professor with a laugh, 'it's a bit heavy to hold up, but the vault is solid; the Great Architect of the universe built it of good firm stuff, and man would never have been able to give it such a span! What are bridge arches and cathedral vaults next to this nave 40 miles in diameter, beneath which an ocean and its storms can behave as they wish?'

'Oh, I'm not afraid of the sky falling on my head. Now, Uncle, what are your plans? Don't you intend to go back to the surface of the Earth?'

'Go back! What an idea. On the contrary, my intention is to continue our journey, since everything has gone so well to date.'

'But I can't see how we are going to find our path underneath that liquid plain.'

'I have no intention of diving in head first. But if, properly speaking, oceans are nothing but lakes, since they are surrounded by land, then all the more reason for this inner sea to be surrounded by granite banks.'

'There's no doubt about that.'

'Well then! I'm sure to find other exits on the opposite shore.'*

'So how long would you guess this ocean to be?'

'Eighty or a hundred miles.'

'Ah,' I said, thinking to myself that this estimate could well be inaccurate.

'Consequently we have no time to lose, we will set sail tomorrow.'

I looked instinctively round for the ship which would carry us.

'So,' I said, 'we're going on board. Good! And which ship are we to travel on?'

'No ship, but a good solid raft.'

'A raft!' I cried. 'A raft is just as impossible to build as a ship, and I can't see . . .'

'You can't see, Axel, but if you were listening you'd be able to hear!'

'Hear?'

'Yes, hammer blows, which would tell you that Hans is already at work.'

'Building a raft?'

'Indeed.'

'What! Has he already been chopping down some trees?'

'The trees were already down. Come along, and you will see him at it.'

Quarter of an hour's walk later, I spotted Hans at work on the other side of the promontory which formed the small natural harbour. After a few more steps I was beside him. To my astonishment, a half-finished raft lay on the sand; it was made from timbers of a distinctive wood, and a great number of beams, knees, and frames were strewn over the ground.

'Uncle,' I cried, 'what wood is this?'

'Pine, fir, birch, all sorts of northern conifers, petrified by the sea water.'

'Is that possible?'

'It is what is called *surtarbrandur*, or fossilized wood.'

'In that case, like lignite, it must be as hard as stone, and unable to float.'

'Sometimes that is the case: some of these woods have become true anthracites; but others, such as these, have only just begun to be transformed into fossils. Watch this,' added my uncle, throwing one of the precious spars into the sea.

The piece of wood disappeared for a moment, then

bobbed up again to the surface of the water and floated up and down following its movements.

'Are you convinced?' said my uncle.

'Convinced that what I see is incredible!'

By the following evening, thanks to Hans's skill, the raft was finished; it was ten feet long by five feet wide; the beams of *surtarbrandur*, bound together with stout ropes, formed a solid surface. Once it had been launched, the improvised vessel floated serenely on the waters of the Lidenbrock Sea.

32

ON 13 August we woke up early. We were now going to inaugurate this new sort of transport, fast and not too tiring.

A mast, made of two pieces of wood fastened together, a yard made from another, and a sail borrowed from our blankets made up the rigging of our raft. There was no lack of rope, and the whole thing was solid.

At six o'clock the professor gave the signal to embark. Our provisions, luggage, instruments, and weapons, along with a good supply of fresh water collected among the rocks, were already on board.

Hans had fitted a rudder which allowed him to steer the floating construction. He took the helm. I unhitched the mooring line attaching us to shore. The sail was trimmed, and we set off at a rate of knots.

As we were leaving the little harbour, my uncle, who was very attached to his geographic nomenclature, wanted to give it a name and proposed mine, amongst others.

'Well, I have another to suggest.'

'And what's that?'

'Gräuben's. Port Gräuben will look very good on the map.'

'Port Gräuben it is.'

And that was how the memory of my dear Virland girl became linked to our adventurous expedition.

The wind was blowing from the northwest.* We ran before the wind at a good speed. The very dense atmospheric layers had great propulsive power and acted on the sail like a powerful fan.

After an hour, my uncle had been able to estimate our speed relatively precisely.

'If we continue to advance at the present rate,' he said, 'we will cover at least 75 miles each 24 hours, and it won't be too long before we reach the opposite shore.'

I did not reply, and made my way to the front of the raft. The northern coastline was already disappearing behind the horizon. The two limbs of the shore were spread wide apart, as if to assist our departure. An immense ocean stretched before my eyes. Massive clouds scooted along, casting their grey shadows on the surface; shadows which seemed to weigh down upon that dismal water. The silvery rays of electric light, reflected here and there by drops of spray, picked out glittering points in the vessel's wake. We were soon out of sight of land, without any point of reference, and had it not been for the frothy wake of the raft, I could have believed that we were totally motionless.

At about midday, immense patches of algae appeared, floating on the surface of the waves. I was aware of the extraordinarily prolific power of these plants, which creep along the bottom of the sea at a depth of more than 12,000 feet, reproduce under pressures of 400 atmospheres, and often form masses large enough to impede the progress of ships. But there can never, I believe, have existed algae as gigantic as those in the Lidenbrock Sea.

Our raft swept along beside pieces of seaweed some three to four thousand feet in length, immense snakes which stretched out far beyond our horizon; it gave me great amusement to gaze along their infinite ribbon-like lengths, thinking each moment that I had reached the end. Hour after hour passed. If my astonishment increased, my patience was well-nigh exhausted.

What natural force could have produced such plants? What must the Earth have looked like during the first centuries of its formation when, acted upon by heat and humidity, the vegetable kingdom was developing solitarily on its surface?

Night came; but as I had noticed the evening before, the luminosity of the atmosphere did not reduce at all. It was a consistent phenomenon whose permanence we could count on.

After supper, I stretched out at the foot of the mast, and soon, idly dreaming, fell asleep.

Hans, motionless at the tiller, let the raft run. As the wind was aft, he did not even have to steer it.

After leaving Port Gräuben, Professor Lidenbrock had given me the job of keeping the 'ship's log', with instructions to put down even the most trivial observations, to note interesting phenomena, the direction of the wind, our speed, the distance covered: in a word, every incident of our fantastic voyage.

I will confine myself, therefore, to reproducing here those daily notes, written as it were at the dictation of events, in order to give a more precise account of our crossing.

Friday, 14 August. Steady breeze from the NW. Raft progressing with extreme rapidity, going perfectly straight. Coast about 75 miles to leeward. Nothing on the horizon. The intensity of the light never varies. Weather fine; i.e. the clouds are very high, light, and fleecy, and surrounded by an atmosphere resembling molten silver. Thermometer: 32°C.

At midday Hans ties a hook to the end of a line. He baits it with a morsel of meat and casts it into the sea. He doesn't catch anything for two hours. Are there no fish in this sea? Yes, there is a tug on the line. Hans draws it in, and then pulls out a fish, which is wriggling furiously.

'A fish,' cries my uncle.

'A sturgeon!' I shout in turn, 'definitely a small sturgeon.'

The professor is examining the animal carefully, and he does not agree with me. This fish has a flattened, curving head, and the lower parts of its body are covered with bony plates; its mouth is wholly without teeth; quite well-developed pectoral fins are fitted to its tailless body. This animal certainly belongs to the order in which naturalists classify the sturgeon, but it differs from that fish in many fairly basic details.

My uncle is not mistaken, after all. Following a short examination he says:

'This fish belongs to a family which has been extinct for centuries, and of which only fossil traces remain, in the Devonian strata.'

'What! Have we really captured alive an authentic inhabitant of the Primitive seas?'

'We have,' said the professor, continuing his observation, 'and you may notice that these fossil fish are distinct from any existing species. To hold a living specimen of the order in one's hand is a great joy for a naturalist.'

'But what family does it belong to?'

'To the order of Ganoids, family of the Cephalaspides, genus . . .'

'Well?'

'Genus Pterychtis, I swear it is. But this fish displays a peculiarity, which is encountered in the fish of underground waters.'

'Which one?'

'It is blind.'

'Amazing!'

'Not only blind, but absolutely without organs of sight.'

I look. It really is true. This, however, may be an isolated instance. So the hook is baited again and thrown into the water. The ocean must be well stocked with fish, for in two hours we take a large number of Pterychtis, as well as fish belonging to another extinct family—the Dipterides,* though my uncle cannot classify it exactly. All are eyeless. This unexpected catch fortunately renews our stock of provisions.

It now seems very probable that this sea contains only fossil species—in which both fish and reptiles alike are more perfect the longer ago they were created.

Perhaps we are going to find some of those saurians which science has succeeded in recreating from bits of bone or cartilage?

I take the telescope and examine the sea. It is deserted. Doubtless we are still too near the coast.

I look up. Why should not some of the birds reconstructed by the immortal Cuvier* be flapping their wings in the heavy strata of the atmosphere? The fish would provide quite sufficient food. I search the space above, but the airs are as uninhabited as the shores.

Nevertheless, my imagination carries me away into the fantastic hypotheses of palaeontology. I am in a waking dream. I fancy I can see on the surface of the water those enormous Chersites, those tortoises from before the flood, as big as floating islands. Along those darkened shores are passing the great mammals of the first days, the Leptotherium found in the caverns of Brazil, the Mericotherium, all the way from the glacial regions of Siberia. Further up, the pachydermatous Lophiodon, that gigantic tapir, is concealing itself behind the rocks, ready to do battle for its prey with the Anoplothere, a singular animal taking after the rhinoceros, the horse, the hippopotamus, and the camel, as if the Creator, in too much of a hurry in the first hours of the world, had put together several animals in one.* The giant mastodon, twisting and turning his trunk, uses his tusks to break up the rocks on the shore, whereas the Megatherium, buttressed on its enormous legs, is excavating the earth for food, all the while awaking the sonorous echoes of the granite with his roaring. Higher up, the Protopithecus,* the first monkey to appear on the face of the globe, is clambering up the steep slopes. Still higher, the pterodactyl, with its winged claws, glides like a huge bat on the compressed air. Above them all, in the topmost layers, are immense birds, more powerful than the cassowary, greater than the ostrich, spreading their vast wings, about to hit their heads against the roof of the granite vault.

This whole fossil world relives in my imagination. I am going back to the biblical ages of the Creation, long before man was born, when the incomplete Earth was not yet ready for him.* My dream then goes ahead of the appearance of the animate beings. The mammals disappear, then the birds, then the reptiles of the Secondary Period, and finally the fish, the crustaceans, the molluscs, and the articulata. The zoophytes of the Transition Period themselves return to nothingness. The whole of the world's life is summed up in myself, and mine is the only heart that beats in this depopulated world! There are no longer seasons; no longer climates; the internal heat of the globe is increasing unceasingly, and cancelling out the effect of the radiant orb. The vegetation is multiplying exaggeratedly. I pass like a shadow amongst arborescent ferns, treading uncertainly on the iridescent marls and rainbow-coloured sandstones underfoot; I lean against the trunks of giant conifers; I lie down in the shade of Sphenophyllas, Asterophyllites, and Lycopodia a hundred feet high.

The centuries are flowing past like days! I am working my way up the series of earthly transformations. The plants disappear; the granitic rocks lose their purity; the liquid state is about to replace the solid under the action of a greater heat; the waters are flowing over the surface of the globe; they boil; they evaporate; the vapour is covering up the entire Earth, which stage by stage becomes nothing but a gaseous mass, heated to red- and white-hot, as big as the sun and shining as bright!

In the centre of this nebula, 1.4 million times as big as the globe it will one day form, I am being carried off into planetary space! My body is being subtilized, subliming in turn and commingling like an imponderable atom with these immense clouds, which inscribe their fiery orbit on infinite space!

What a dream! Where is it taking me? My feverish hand jots down the strange details. I have forgotten everything: the professor, the guide, the raft. A hallucination has taken hold of my head . . .

'What is the matter?'

My eyes, wide open, fix on my uncle without seeing.

'Take care, Axel, you're going to fall overboard!'

At the same time, I feel myself seized by Hans's firm hand. Had it not been for him, under the sway of my dream, I would have thrown myself into the waves.

'Is he going mad?' cries the professor.

'What is it?' I say at last, coming to.

'Are you ill?'

'No; I had a hallucination for a moment, but it's past. Is all well on board?'

'Yes, a beautiful breeze, a splendid sea. We are flying along and unless my calculations are out, we shall soon land.'

At these words, I rise and scan the horizon. But the line of water is still indistinguishable from the line of clouds.

33

SATURDAY, 15 August. The sea retains its uniform monotony. No land in sight. The horizon appears a very long way away.

My head is still dull from the violent effects of my dream.

My uncle, who has certainly not dreamed, is, however, in one of his moods. He is scanning every point in space with his telescope and crossing his arms disappointedly.

I notice that Professor Lidenbrock has a tendency to revert to his impatient character of before, and I note this circumstance in my log-book. It required my danger and sufferings to extract a spark of kindness from him; but now that I am better, his nature has taken charge again. And yet why get annoyed? Isn't the journey proceeding under the most favourable circumstances? Isn't the raft rushing along?

'You seem uneasy, Uncle?' I say, seeing him often putting the telescope to his eye.

'Uneasy? No.'

'Impatient then.'

'With good reason!'

'And yet we are advancing at a rate . . .'

'I do not care! It is not our speed that is too small, but the sea that is too big!'

I remember then that the professor, before our departure, estimated the length of this subterranean ocean to be about 70 miles. We have already done at least three times that distance, but haven't discovered the slightest sign of the southern shores.

'We are not going down,' continued the professor. 'All this is lost time. I did not come so far for a boat-trip on a pond!'

He calls this voyage a boat-trip, and this ocean a pond!

'But', I argue, 'since we have been following the route indicated by Saknussemm . . .'

'That is the question. *Have* we been following the route? Did Saknussemm ever encounter this great stretch of water? Did he cross it? Did the rivulet we took as a guide lead us astray?'

'In any case, we can't regret coming this far. The spectacle is magnificent, and . . .'

'Seeing is not the question. I set myself an objective and I mean to attain it. So don't talk to me about admiring!'

He doesn't need to say it again; and I let the professor bite into his lips with impatience. At six in the evening, Hans asks for his pay, and the three rix-dollars are counted out to him.

Sunday, 16 August. Nothing new. Same weather. The wind has a slight tendency to freshen. When I wake up, the first thing I do is observe the intensity of the light. I live in fear that the electric phenomenon might dim and then go out. Nothing of the sort happens. The shadow of the raft is clearly outlined on the surface of the water.

This sea is truly infinite. It must be as wide as the Mediterranean—or even the Atlantic. Why not?

My uncle tries sounding several times. He ties one of our heaviest picks to the end of a rope, and allows it to run out for 200 fathoms. We have great difficulty in pulling our sounding line in again.

When the pick has finally been dragged on board, Hans

calls my attention to some deep marks on its surface. The piece of iron looks as though it has been firmly gripped between two hard objects.

I look at the hunter.

'Tänder.'

I do not understand. I turn to my uncle, entirely absorbed in his reflections. I have little wish to disturb him, and come back to the Icelander. He opens and closes his mouth several times, and so conveys his meaning to me.

'Teeth!' I cry with stupefaction, examining the iron bar more closely.

Yes, the indentations on the metal are the marks of teeth! The jaws they adorn must have a prodigious strength! Is some monster of a lost species tossing under the deep strata of the waters, hungrier than the dogfish shark, more formidable than the whale? I am unable to detach my eyes from the gnawed bar. Is my dream of last night about to become reality?

These thoughts upset me all day, and my imagination scarcely calms down in a sleep of a few hours.

Monday, 17 August. I have been trying to remember the particular instincts of these antediluvian animals from the Secondary Period, which, following on from the molluscs, the crustaceans, and the fish, emerged before the mammals appeared on the globe. The reptiles then reigned supreme upon the Earth. These hideous monsters held absolute sway over the Jurassic seas.[1] Nature endowed them with the most complete structures. What gigantic organisms! What exceptional strength! The present-day saurians, even the largest and most formidable crocodiles and alligators, are but feeble reductions of their fathers of the first ages.*

I shudder at my own evocation of these monsters. No human eye has ever seen them alive. They appeared on the Earth a thousand centuries before man, but their fossil

[1] Seas of the Secondary Period which formed the terrains of which the Jura Mountains are composed.

bones, discovered in the clayey limestone that the British call lias, have allowed us to reconstruct them anatomically, and thus know about their colossal structures.

In the Natural History Museum of Hamburg I have seen the skeleton of one of these saurians measuring 30 feet from head to tail. Am I, then—an inhabitant of the Earth—going to find myself face to face with representatives of this antediluvian family? No, it is impossible. And yet marks of powerful teeth are engraved on the iron bar! I notice that they are conical like the crocodile's.

My eyes stare with terror at the sea. I am afraid that one of these inhabitants of the sub-marine caverns will suddenly emerge.

I imagine that Professor Lidenbrock shares my ideas, if not my fears, for after an examination of the pick, he casts his eyes over the ocean.

What could have possessed him to sound the ocean? He has disturbed some creature in its lair, and if we're attacked on the way . . .

I glance at our firearms, and check that they are in a state of readiness. My uncle sees me doing this and nods approvingly. Already wide disturbances on the surface of the water indicate the troubling of the greatest depths. Danger is near. We must keep a look-out.

Tuesday, 18 August. Night comes, or rather the hour when sleep closes our eyelids, for there is no night on this ocean, and the implacable light constantly tires our eyes, as if we were navigating in the sunlight on the Arctic seas. Hans is at the helm. During his watch I fall asleep.

Two hours later, I am awakened by an awful shock. The raft has been lifted right out of the water with indescribable force, and thrown down more than 100 feet away.

'Eh, what is it?' cries my uncle. 'Have we hit?'

Hans points at a massive blackish object, about a quarter of a mile away, which is moving steadily up and down. I look, then cry:

'But it's a colossal porpoise!'

'Yes, and over there is a sea lizard of a most unusual size.'

'And further on a prodigious crocodile. Look at its huge jaws, and its rows of aggressive teeth. Oh, it's disappeared!'

'A whale, a whale!' shouts the professor, 'I can see its enormous tail. Look, it's expelling air and water through its blowholes!'

Two liquid columns rise to a considerable height above the waves. We remain surprised, stupefied, horrified at the sight of this herd of sea-monsters. They have supernatural dimensions—the smallest of them could crush the raft with a single bite. Hans seizes the helm so as to run before the wind and flee this danger zone. But he notices more enemies on the other side, just as formidable: a tortoise about forty feet across, and a serpent, about thirty, thrusting an enormous head above the waters.

Impossible to flee. These reptiles advance upon us; then move round the raft with a speed that could not be equalled by trains flying at top speed. They swim about it in concentric circles. I pick up my rifle. But what effect could a bullet have on the scales covering the bodies of these animals?

We remain speechless with horror. They are now coming at us, the crocodile on one side, the sea-serpent on the other. The rest of the marine herd have disappeared. I am about to fire. Hans stops me with a sign. The two monsters pass within 100 yards of the raft, then make a rush at each other: their fury prevents them from seeing us.

The combat starts 200 yards from the raft. We distinctly see the two monsters seizing hold of each other.

But now the other animals also seem to be taking part in the struggle—the porpoise, the whale, the lizard, and the tortoise. I catch sight of them at every moment. I point them out to the Icelander. But he shakes his head.

'Tva,' he says.

'What, two? He claims there are only two animals . . .'

'He is right,' says my uncle, whose telescope has not left his eye.

'It's incredible!'

'No. The first of these monsters has the snout of a porpoise, the head of a lizard, and the teeth of a crocodile: hence our mistake. It is the most frightful of all the antediluvian reptiles: the ichthyosaurus.'*

'And the other?'

'A serpent, concealed under the hard shell of the turtle, and a mortal enemy of the first, the plesiosaurus.'*

Hans is quite right. Only two monsters are disturbing the surface of the sea. I have before me two reptiles from the Primitive oceans. I can see the bloody eye of the ichthyosaurus, as big as a man's head. Nature has given it an extremely powerful optical apparatus, able to resist the pressure of the water in the depths where it lives. It has been called the saurian whale, for it is just as big and just as quick. This one is not less than 100 feet long, and I can get some idea of its girth when it lifts its vertical tailfins out of the water. Its jaws are enormous and according to the naturalists contain as many as 182 teeth.

The plesiosaurus, a serpent with a cylindrical trunk and a short tail, has legs shaped into paddles. Its whole body is covered with a hard shell, and its neck, as flexible as a swan's, rises more than 30 feet above the waves.

These animals attack one another with indescribable fury. They raise mountains of water, which surge as far as the raft. Twenty times we are on the point of capsizing. Hisses of a frightening volume reach our ears. The two animals are tightly embraced. I cannot distinguish one from the other. Everything is to be feared from the rage of the victor.

One hour, two hours pass. The struggle continues unabated. The two foes now approach the raft, now move away from it. We remain motionless, ready to fire.

Suddenly the ichthyosaurus and plesiosaurus disappear, hollowing out a veritable maelstrom in the open sea. Several minutes go by. Will this combat finish in the ocean depths?

Suddenly, an enormous head surges out—the head of the great plesiosaurus. The monster is mortally wounded.

I can no longer see his enormous shell. Only his long neck stands up, beats down, rises, bends over again, lashes at the waters like a gigantic whip, writhes like a worm cut in two. The water spurts to a great distance. It blinds us. But soon the reptile's death-throes are nearly at their end, its movements diminish, its contortions calm down, and finally the long section of snake stretches out like an inert mass on the waters, now quiet again.

As for the ichthyosaurus, has it gone down to rest in its mighty underwater cavern; or will it reappear on the surface of the sea?

34

WEDNESDAY, *19 August.* Fortunately the wind, blowing with force, has allowed us to flee the scene of the struggle. Hans is still at the helm. My uncle, drawn from his absorbing ideas by the incidents of the battle, now retreats again into his impatient contemplation of the sea.

Our voyage becomes monotonous and uniform once more. But I have no desire to see it change, if it is at the cost of yesterday's dangers.

Thursday, 20 August. Light wind, NNE, variable. Temperature high. We are moving at a rate of 8 knots.

At about twelve o'clock a very distant sound is heard. I make a note here of the fact without being able to give an explanation for it. It is like a continuous roar.

'Far off', says the professor, 'is some rock or small island against which the sea is breaking.'

Hans hoists himself to the top of the mast, but does not signal a reef. The ocean is calm as far as the line of the horizon.

Three hours go by. The roaring seems to come from a distant cataract.

I mention this to my uncle, who shakes his head. I, however, am convinced that I am right. Are we heading for some mighty waterfall which will drop us into the abyss? This method of travel will probably please the professor, as it approaches the vertical, but for my part . . .

In any case, not many leagues to windward there must be some very noisy phenomenon, for now the sound of the roaring is extremely loud. Is it coming from the sea or the sky?

I look up at the water-vapour suspended in the atmosphere, and I try to penetrate its depths. But the sky is serene. The clouds, carried up to the very top of the vault, seem motionless, and are completely invisible in the intense glare of the light. We must therefore look elsewhere for the cause of the phenomenon.

I scrutinize the horizon, pure and free from all haze. Its appearance is unchanged. But if this noise is coming from a waterfall, from a cataract, if the ocean is being precipitated into a lower cavity, if these roars are being produced by masses of falling waters, there would be a current, and its increasing speed would show me the extent of the danger to which we are exposed. I check the current. There isn't one. An empty bottle we drop in the water simply remains to windward.

At about four o'clock Hans stands up, takes hold of the mast and climbs to the top. From there his eye scans the arc of the ocean's circle in front of the raft and stops at a particular point. His face expresses no astonishment, but his eyes do not move.

'He has seen something,' says my uncle.

'So it would seem.'

Hans climbs down, and stretches his arm out towards the south:

'Der nere!'

'Over there,' says my uncle.

And seizing the telescope, he gazes with great attention for about a minute, which to me appears an age.

'Yes. *Yes!*'

'What can you see?'

'A tremendous sheaf of water rising above the waves.'

'Another sea-monster?'

'Perhaps.'

'Then let us head more to the west, for we know what to expect from the dangers of meeting up with these antediluvian creatures.'

'Straight ahead,'* replies my uncle.

I turn towards Hans. He maintains course with an inflexible rigour.

Nevertheless, given the distance separating us from this creature, which cannot be less than 30 miles, and given that the column of water from its blowhole is clearly visible, its dimensions must be quite preternatural. To flee is therefore the course suggested by basic common sense. To run away would be to obey the most vulgar caution. But we are not here to be prudent.

We accordingly press on. The nearer we get, the taller the shaft of water becomes. What monster can fill itself with such volumes of water and shoot it out so continuously?

At 8 p.m., we are not more than five miles away. A black, enormous, mountainous body lies on the water like an island. Is it an illusion or is it our fear? It appears not less than a mile long. What, then, is this cetaceous monster which Cuvier and Blumenbach* never dreamed of? It is motionless as if asleep. The sea seems unable to shift it; it is the waves instead that lap at its side. The water-column, rising to a height of 500 feet, breaks into spray with a dull, sullen roar. We advance like lunatics towards that mighty hulk which a hundred whales could not feed for a single day.

I am terrified. I don't want to go any further. I will cut the halyard if need be! I mutiny openly against the professor: he makes no answer.

Suddenly Hans gets up and points with his finger at the menacing spot:

'Holme.'

'An island!' cries my uncle.

'An island?' I reply, raising my shoulders.

'Of course!' exclaims my uncle, bursting into loud laughter.

'But what about the water column?'

'Geyser,' says Hans.

'Yes, obviously a geyser,' responds my uncle, 'like those in Iceland.'[1]

At first I cannot admit that I am so totally wrong. To have taken an island for a sea-monster!* But one must give in to the evidence, and finally I have to accept my mistake. There is nothing here but a natural phenomenon.

As we get nearer, the dimensions of the sheaf become truly stupendous. It is difficult to tell the difference between the island and an enormous whale, with its head rising 60 feet above the swell. The geyser, a word the Icelanders pronounce 'gay-seer' and which means 'fury', emerges majestically at one end of the island. Dull detonations are heard every now and then, and the enormous jet, subject to violent furies, shakes off its plume of vapour and spurts up as far as the first stratum of cloud. It is alone. Neither exhalations nor hot springs surround it, and all the volcanic power is concentrated in it. Rays of electric light come and mix with this dazzling sheaf, with each drop taking on all the colours of the prism.

'Let's go alongside,' says the professor.

We have to take precautions, however, to avoid the water column, which would sink the raft in an instant. Hans, steering skilfully, takes us to the other end of the island.

I leap on to the rock. My uncle nimbly follows, while the hunter remains at his post, like a man beyond such wonders.

We walk over granite mixed with siliceous tuff; the soil shivers under our feet like the sides of boilers writhing with superheated steam: it feels burning-hot. We come in view of the little central hollow from which the geyser rises. I plunge an overflow thermometer* into the water bubbling from the centre: it registers a temperature of 163°!

This water, therefore, comes from a burning source of

---

[1] A very famous spring that gushes up, situated at the foot of Mount Hekla.*

heat. This is singularly in contradiction with Professor Lidenbrock's theories. I cannot resist pointing it out.

'Well,' says he, 'what does that prove against my theory?'

'Nothing,' I reply drily, seeing that I am up against an implacable stubbornness.

Nevertheless, I am forced to confess that we have been remarkably fortunate up until now, and that, for a reason which still escapes me, our journey is taking place in unusual conditions of temperature. But it appears evident, nay certain, that sooner or later we shall arrive at one of those regions where the central heat reaches its utmost limits and goes far beyond the gradations on the thermometers.

We shall see. That is now the professor's favourite phrase. Having baptized the volcanic island with the name of his nephew, he gives the signal to embark.

I stand still for a few minutes more, staring at the geyser. I notice that the jet of water is irregular in its outbursts: it diminishes in intensity, then regains new vigour, which I attribute to variations in the pressure of the vapour built up in its reservoir.

At last we leave, avoiding the sheer rocks of the southern side. Hans has taken advantage of this brief halt to reorganize the raft.

Before we put off, however, I make a few observations to calculate the distance covered, and note them in my log-book. Since Port Gräuben, we have covered 680 miles. We are now 1,550 miles from Iceland, and underneath Britain.*

35

FRIDAY, 21 *August.* The following day the magnificent geyser has disappeared. The wind has freshened, and quickly takes us away from Axel Island. The roaring sound gradually dies down.

The weather, if such a term may be used here, is about to change. The atmosphere is gradually being loaded with water-vapour, which carries with it the electricity generated when the salt waters evaporate. The clouds are lowering perceptibly and taking on a uniform olive hue; the electric rays can scarcely pierce this opaque curtain which has fallen on a stage where a stormy drama is going to be enacted.

I feel peculiarly influenced, like all creatures on Earth when a catastrophe is about to happen. The cumuli,[1] piled up in the south, present a sinister appearance: they have the 'pitiless' look I have often noticed at the beginning of a storm. The air is heavy, the sea calm.

In the distance, the clouds look like enormous bales of cotton, piled up in picturesque confusion. They gradually swell up, and gain in size what they lose in number: they are so heavy that they are unable to hoist themselves from the horizon. But in the breath from the upper streams of the air, they gradually melt together, become darker and soon present a single layer of a formidable appearance; now and then a ball of misty cloud, still lit up, collides with the grey carpet, and is soon swallowed up by the impenetrable mass.

There can be no doubt that the entire atmosphere is saturated with fluid; I am impregnated with it; my hair stands on end as if beside an electric machine. It occurs to me that if one of my companions touched me now, he would probably get a violent shock.

At 10 a.m., the symptoms of the storm become more pronounced; the wind seems to soften in order to draw breath again, as if in preparation; the cloud resembles a goatskin bottle inside which terrible storms are accumulating.

I do not want to accept the evidence of the sky's menacing signs, and yet I cannot stop myself saying:

'It looks as though we are going to have some bad weather.'

The professor does not answer. He is in an atrocious

---

[1] Clouds with round shapes.

mood at the sight of the ocean stretching interminably before his eyes. At my words he shrugs his shoulders.

'We're going to have a storm,' I continue, pointing towards the horizon. 'These clouds are lowering upon the sea, as if to crush it.'

A great silence. The wind falls. Nature lies as if dead, ceasing to breathe. Upon the mast, where I can already see a slight Saint Elmo's fire, the sail hangs in loose, heavy folds. The raft is motionless in the midst of that sticky sea, without swell. But since we are not moving, what is the point of keeping the canvas up, for it may be our downfall when the tempest first hits us?

'Let's lower the sail, let's bring down the mast! That would be the sensible thing to do.'

'No, for God's sake,' cries my uncle, 'a hundred times, no. May the wind take hold of us, may the storm sweep us away. Let me only see the rocks of some shore, even if the raft must break into smithereens on it.'

These words are scarcely out of his mouth, than the appearance of the southern horizon is transformed. The accumulated moisture resolves itself into water, and the air, violently sucked in to fill the vacuum produced by the condensation, becomes a raging storm. It comes from the most distant corners of the cavern. The darkness increases. I can only just take a few incomplete notes.

The raft rises, it leaps. My uncle is cast down. I drag myself over to him. He is holding on to the end of a rope with all his might, apparently gazing with pleasure at the spectacle of the unchained elements.

Hans does not move a muscle. His long hair, pushed down over his motionless face by the tempest, gives him a strange appearance, for the end of each hair is illuminated by a tiny, feather-like radiation. His frightening mask is that of an antediluvian man, living at the time of the ichthyosauruses and megatheres.

The mast still holds. The sail stretches like a bubble about to burst. The raft hurtles on at a velocity that I cannot estimate, but is still slower than the drops of water displaced below it, which the speed turns into clean straight lines.

'The sail, the sail!' I cry, beckoning that it should be brought down.

'No!'

'Nej,' says Hans, gently shaking his head.

By now, the rain forms a roaring cataract in front of this horizon towards which we race like madmen. But before we reach it, the veil of cloud is torn apart; the sea begins to boil; and the electricity, produced by some great chemical action in the upper layers, is brought into play. Dazzling streaks of lightning combine with fearful claps of thunder; flashes without number criss-cross amongst the crashes. The mass of water-vapour becomes white-hot; the hailstones striking the metal of our tools and firearms become luminous; each of the waves surging up resembles a fire-breathing breast, in which seethes an internal radiance, with each peak surmounted by plumes of flames.

My eyes are dazzled by the intensity of the light, my ears deafened by the din of the thunder. I am forced to hold on to the mast, which bends like a reed before the violence of the storm!

. . . .

[Here my travel notes became very incomplete. I have only found one or two fugitive observations, jotted down automatically so to speak. But even in their brevity, their incoherence, they are imprinted with the feelings which governed me and thus, better than my memory, portray my mood at the time.]

. . . .

Sunday, 23 August. Where are we? Being carried away with immeasurable speed.

The night has been awful. The storm is not calming down. We are living in the midst of an uproar, a constant detonation. Our ears are bleeding. We are unable to exchange a single word.

The lightning never stops striking. I see the retrograde zigzags flashing rapidly and then working their way back up to crash into the arch of the granite roof. What if it collapsed? Other flashes of lightning fork or become globes of fire and explode like bombshells. The general level of noise does not seem to be increased by this; it has already gone beyond the order of magnitude that the human ear can detect. If all the powder magazines in the world were to explode at the same time, it would not make any difference.

There is a constant production of light from the surface of the clouds; their molecules incessantly give off electrical matter; the gaseous principles of the air have been changed; innumerable columns of water leap up into the air and then fall down foaming.

Where are we going? My uncle is still flat out on the edge of the raft.

The heat increases even further. I look at the thermometer, it read ??°. [The figure is illegible.]

Monday, 24 August. Will this terrible storm ever end? Why should this state of the hyper-dense atmosphere, once it has been modified, not remain as it is indefinitely?

We are broken with fatigue. Hans the same as ever. The raft heads endlessly southeast. We have already done 500 miles since Axel Island.

At twelve the tempest becomes a hurricane. We are forced to lash down every item in the cargo. Each of us ties himself down as well. The waves pass over our heads.

Impossible to say a single word to each other for the last three days. We open our mouths, we move our lips; no audible sound is produced. Even speaking directly into the ear does not work.

My uncle comes close. He pronounces some words. I think he says: 'We are lost.' I am not certain.

I make up my mind, and write a few words to him: 'Let's take in the sail.'

He nods to indicate his consent.

His head has not had time to resume its original position, when a disc of fire appears on the edge of the raft. The mast and sail are carried off in a single movement, and I see them fly away to a tremendous height like a pterodactyl, that fantastic bird of the earliest centuries.

We are frozen with terror. The ball is half white, half electric blue, of the size of a ten-inch bombshell. It moves around leisurely, while turning with an astonishing speed under the lash of the storm. It runs about here and there, it clambers on to one of the cross-beams of the raft, jumps on the food bag, gives a little leap, then lightly touches our powder keg. Horror, we are about to explode. But no—the blinding disc moves to one side, it goes up to Hans, who stares at it without blinking; then to my uncle, who throws himself on his knees to avoid it; it comes towards me, as I stand pale and shivering in the dazzling heat and light; it pirouettes near my feet, which I try to pull back. I can't.

A smell of laughing-gas fills the air; it penetrates our throats and lungs. We choke on it.

Why can't I move my foot? Is it riveted to the spot? Then I understand: the arrival of the electric globe has magnetized all the iron on board.* The instruments, the tools, the firearms are crashing together with a keen jangling noise; the nails in my boot are violently attracted to a plate of iron encrusted in the wood. I can't shift my foot.

At last, by a violent effort, I tear my foot away, just as the rotational movements of the ball are about to seize hold of it and drag me away too, if . . .

Oh what intense light! The globe bursts—we are being covered in torrents of flames!

Then everything goes out. I just have time to see my uncle lying on the floor, Hans still at the helm, 'spitting fire' under the influence of the electricity; he is saturated with it.

Where will we end up, oh where?

. . . .

Tuesday, 25 August. I have just come out of a very long faint. The storm is still continuing; the lightning is unleashed like a swarm of snakes released into the air.

Are we still on the sea? Yes, being carried along with

incalculable speed. We have passed under Britain, under the Channel, under France, possibly under the whole of Europe!*

A new noise can be heard. Clearly the sea breaking on rocks. But then . . .

36

HERE ends what I have called the 'ship's log', fortunately saved from the shipwreck. I proceed with my narrative as before.

What happened when the raft hit the reefs on the shore, I cannot say. I felt myself being thrown into the waves, and if I escaped death, if my body was not torn to pieces by the sharp rocks, it was because Hans's strong arm pulled me from the abyss.

The fearless Icelander carried me out of reach of the waves and on to a burning sand, where I found myself lying side by side with my uncle.

Then he returned to the rocks, against which the furious waves were beating, in order to save a few stray pieces from the wreckage. I could not speak; I was broken with fear and fatigue; it took me more than an hour to recover.

The rain continued to fall, however, a positive deluge, but with that very violence which heralds the end of the storm. Some piled-up rocks gave us protection from the torrents from the heavens. Hans prepared some food which I was unable to touch; exhausted by the three nights keeping watch, I fell into a disturbing sleep.

Next day, the weather was magnificent. Sea and sky, as if by agreement, had regained their serenity. Every trace of the storm had disappeared. Cheerful words from the professor greeted me when I woke up. His gaiety was terrible.

'Well, my lad! Did you sleep soundly?'

Might one not have thought that we were in the old house in Königstrasse, that I was quietly coming down for breakfast, and that my wedding with poor Gräuben was to take place that very day?

Alas, if only the tempest had driven the raft eastwards, we would have passed under Germany, under my beloved city of Hamburg, under that street which contained all I loved in the world. At that point hardly 100 miles would have separated me from her. But 100 vertical miles of granite wall: in reality, more than 2,500 miles to cover!

All these unhappy ideas passed through my mind before I answered my uncle's question.

'What?' he repeated. 'Can you not say how you slept?'

'Perfectly. But every bone in my body aches. I'll be all right.'

'I am sure you will be completely all right, a little tired, nothing more.'

'You appear very gay this morning.'

'Delighted, my boy, delighted! We have arrived.'

'At the end of our expedition?'

'No; at the edge of that sea which seemed endless. We will now resume our journey by land, and really plunge into the vitals of the Earth.'

'Uncle, can I ask you a question?'

'Certainly, Axel.'

'How are we going to get back?'

'Get back? You are thinking about the return before we have even arrived!'

'Not really: all I want to know is how it will be done?'

'In the simplest way possible. Once we have reached the centre of our spheroid, either we shall find a new path to climb up to the surface, or we shall quite boringly turn round and go back the way we came. I do not imagine that the route will close up behind us.'

'Then we will have to think about repairing the raft.'

'Obviously.'

'But what about the food, have we got enough left to do all these great things?'

'Yes, certainly. Hans is a clever fellow, and I am sure he

has saved most of the cargo. But let's go and see for ourselves.'

We left this grotto, open to all the winds. I had a hope that was also a fear; it didn't seem possible to me that anything of what it had been carrying had survived the terrible landing of the raft. I was wrong. When I reached the shore, I found Hans in the middle of a large number of objects, all laid out in order. My uncle wrung the hunter's hands with deep gratitude. This man, of a super-human devotion, one that would perhaps never be equalled, had worked while we slept, saving the most precious articles at the risk of his life.

Nevertheless, we had experienced important losses: our firearms for example—but after all we could manage without them. The supply of powder had remained intact, after narrowly escaping being blown up in the storm.

'Well,' said the professor, 'as we have no guns, we will simply have to give up hunting.'

'Yes, but what about the instruments?'

'Here is the manometer, the most useful of all, and for which I would have given all the rest. With it I can calculate the depth and know when we have reached the centre. Without it, we might go too far and come out at the antipodes!'

His good mood was ferocious.

'But the compass?'

'Here it is on this rock, safe and sound, as well as the chronometer and thermometers. The hunter is a genius!'

One had to agree. Amongst the instruments, nothing was missing. As for the tools and implements, I spotted ladders, cords, pickaxes, picks, etc., scattered over the sand.

There was still the question of provisions to sort out.

'But what about the food?'

'Let us see about it.'

The boxes were lined up along the shore in a perfect state of preservation; most of their contents were un-harmed by the sea, and we could thus still count on a total of four months' supply of biscuits, salt meat, gin, and dried fish.

'Four months!' cried the professor. 'We have time to go there and come back, and with what is left I plan to give a huge dinner to my colleagues at the Johanneum!'

By this time I should have been used to my uncle's character, and yet this man still amazed me.

'Now,' said he, 'we must renew our stock of fresh water, using the rain that the storm has poured into the hollows in the granite. There is no danger of suffering from thirst. As for the raft, I shall ask Hans to repair it as best he can, although I do not believe we shall be requiring it again.'

'Why not?'

'Just one of my ideas, my boy. I do not believe we shall go out the way we came in.'

I looked at my uncle with suspicion. I wondered whether he had gone mad. And yet 'little did he know how right he was'.

'And now for breakfast,' he concluded.

I followed him on to a high promontory, after he had given instructions to the hunter. There, with dried meat, biscuits, and tea, we had an excellent meal: one of the best in my life, I must say. Hunger, the open air, the peace and quiet after the excitement, all combined to give me an excellent appetite.

During breakfast, I asked my uncle if he knew where we now were.

'It may be rather difficult to calculate,' I added.

'To calculate exactly, yes, even impossible, for I could keep no account of the speed or direction of the raft during the three days of the tempest. Still, we can estimate our approximate position.'

'Well, our last observation was made at the geyser island.'

'"At Axel Island", my boy! Do not decline the honour of giving your name to the first island discovered in the interior of the Earth.'

'All right. At Axel Island, we had done more than 670 nautical miles and were over 1,500 miles from Iceland.'

'Fine. Let us start then from that point, and count four

days of storm, during which our speed cannot have been less than 200 miles every 24 hours.'

'Very probably. That would make as much as 800 miles extra.'

'Yes, and the Lidenbrock Sea would then be about 1,500 miles across! Do you realize, Axel, that it is about as big as the Mediterranean?'

'Yes, especially if we have only crossed it and not gone its whole length!'

'Which is very likely.'

'And what is strange,' said I, 'is that if our calculations are right, we have over our heads at this very moment the Mediterranean itself.'

'Do you think so?'

'Yes, for we are 2,500 miles from Reykjavik.'

'A good stretch of road we have travelled, my boy. But whether we are under the Mediterranean, Turkey, or the Atlantic can only be ascertained if our direction has remained constant.'

'The wind appears steady to me. My view is that this shore must be southeast of Port Gräuben.'

'Well, it is easy to check by consulting the compass. Let us therefore go and check this compass!'

The professor headed for the rock on which Hans had placed the instruments. My uncle was gay and light-hearted; he rubbed his hands, he struck poses. A young man in truth! I followed him, rather curious to know whether I was right in my estimation.

As soon as we had reached the rock, my uncle took the compass, laid it flat and looked at the needle, which oscillated and then, under the magnetic influence, stopped in a fixed position.

My uncle looked, rubbed his eyes, then looked again. Finally he turned to me, flabbergasted.

'But what's the matter?'

He pointed at the instrument. I examined it and a loud cry of surprise escaped from my lips. The needle marked north where we expected south! It pointed at the shore rather than the high seas!

I shook the compass, then examined it again. It was in perfect condition. Whatever position we made the needle take, it returned obstinately to the same surprising direction.

There could be no doubt about it: during the tempest, there had been a sudden change of wind, one we had not noticed, and which had brought the raft back to the shores my uncle thought he had left behind for ever.

37

IT would be altogether impossible for me to give any idea of the feelings that shook the professor: amazement, incredulity, and finally rage. Never in my life had I seen someone so crestfallen at first, and then so furious. The fatigues of our crossing, the dangers we had passed through, everything had to be started all over again. Instead of making progress, we had gone backwards.

But my uncle was on top again very soon.

'Fate plays me such tricks! The elements are conspiring against me. Air, fire, and water are combining to stop me getting through. Well, they are going to see what my willpower can do. I shall not yield, I shall not retreat a tenth of an inch. We shall see who wins: man or nature!'

Standing on a rock, irritated, threatening, Otto Lidenbrock, like wild Ajax,* seemed to be hurling defiance at the gods. I judged it sensible to intervene and put some sort of check upon this mad eagerness.

'Listen to me,' I said in a firm voice. 'There must be some limit to every ambition in this world. One must not fight against the impossible. We are ill-equipped for a sea voyage; one cannot cover 1,200 miles on a poor construction of beams, with a blanket as a sail and a stick for a mast, against an unleashed contrary wind. Since we are unable to steer, we will become the playthings of the storm, and it is to act like lunatics to attempt this impossible crossing a second time.'

I was allowed to go through these irrefutable reasons

for about ten minutes without interruption. But this was only because of the professor's inattention: he did not hear a single word of my arguments.

'To the raft!' he cried.

Such was his response. In vain did I implore him, did I lose my temper: I came up against a will harder than granite.

Hans was just finishing his repairs to the raft. It was almost as if this strange being had guessed my uncle's projects. By means of a few pieces of *surtarbrandur*, he had strengthened the vessel. A sail had already been hoisted, and the wind was playing over its floating folds.

The professor said a few words to the guide, who immediately loaded our luggage on board and prepared everything for departure. The atmosphere was now pure, and the northwest wind held steady.

What could I do? Resist, one against two? Impossible. If only Hans had supported me. But no, as far as I could see, the Icelander had set aside all volition of his own and taken a vow of self-denial. I could get nothing out of a servant so feudally subjugated to his master. All I could do was not rock the boat.

I moved* to take my usual place on the raft, but my uncle stopped me with his hand.

'We shall only start tomorrow.'

I made the gesture of a man resigned to everything.

'I must not neglect a single factor. As fate has cast me upon this stretch of shore, I shall not leave again until I have explored it.'

In order to understand his remark, I need to explain that though we had come back to the northern coastline, this was not at exactly the same spot as our first starting-point. Port Gräuben had to be to westward. Hence nothing was more sensible than carefully reconnoitring the area around our new landfall.

'Let's explore!' I cried.

And we set off, leaving Hans to his activities. The area between the high-water tidemark and the foot of the cliffs was very large. It would take about half an hour to get to the rock wall. Our feet crushed innumerable seashells of every shape and size, once the houses of animals of the first ages. I also noticed enormous shells with a diameter of more than 15 feet. They once belonged to those gigantic glyptodonts* of the Pliocene period, of which the modern tortoise is but a minute reduction. In addition, the soil was covered with a large amount of stony jetsam, a sort of shingle rounded by the waves, arranged in successive rows. I came to the conclusion that in past ages the sea must have covered this area. The waves had left evident signs of their passage on the scattered rocks, now lying beyond their reach.

This could to a certain extent explain the existence of such an ocean, 100 miles below the surface of the Earth. According to my theory, this liquid mass must have been gradually lost into the bowels of the Earth: it clearly came from the water of the oceans, reaching its destination through some sort of fissure. Nevertheless, it had to be assumed that this fissure was now blocked up for, if not, the cavern, or rather the immense reservoir, would have been completely filled up in a relatively short period. Perhaps some of the water had even had to contend with the subterranean fires, and so became vaporized. Hence an explanation for the clouds suspended above our heads, and the emission of the electricity which created the storms inside the Earth's mass.

Such a theory of the phenomena we had witnessed struck me as satisfactory, for however great the marvels of nature, they can always be explained with physical reasons.

We were thus walking over a kind of sedimentary soil formed by the subsidence of the waters, like the very many terrains of that period on the surface of the globe. The professor carefully examined every crack in the rocks. If an opening existed, it became vital for him to plumb its depths.*

We had been following the shores of the Lidenbrock Sea for about a mile, when suddenly the ground changed appearance. It seemed to have been upset, turned upside down by a violent upheaval of the lower strata. In many places, hollows and hillocks bore witness to great dislocations of the terrestrial mass.*

We advanced with difficulty over the broken granite mixed with flint, quartz, and alluvial deposits, when a field—more than a field, a plain of bones, appeared before our eyes. It looked like an immense cemetery, where the generations of 2,000 years mingled their eternal dust. Large bulges* of remains stretched out in the layered distance. They undulated away to the limits of the horizon and were lost in an out-of-focus mist. Within that area, of perhaps three square miles, was accumulated the whole history of animal life, writ too small in the recent ground of the inhabited world.

We were carried forward by an impetuous curiosity. With a dry sound our feet crushed the remains of these prehistoric animals, whose rare and valuable fragments are fought over by the museums of the great cities. A thousand Cuviers would not have been enough to reconstruct the skeletons of all the once-living creatures which now rested in that magnificent bone-graveyard.

I remained dumbfounded. My uncle had raised his long arms towards the impenetrable vault which was our sky. His mouth was gaping tremendously, his eyes were flaring behind the lenses of his glasses, his head was moving up and down, to the left and right—his whole expression indicated utter astonishment. He was presented with a priceless assortment of Leptotheria, Mericotheria, Lophiodia, Anoplotheres, Megatheres, Mastodons, Protopithecae, Pterodactyls—of every monster from before the Flood, all in a pile there just for his gratification. Imagine the famous library in Alexandria that Omar burned, suddenly and miraculously reborn from its ashes; and transport a fanatical book-collector into it. That was my uncle Professor Lidenbrock!

But his awe reached a climax when, racing across the organic dust, he seized a bare skull and screamed in a trembling voice:

'Axel, Axel! It's a human head!'

'A human head?' I replied, just as dazed.

'Yes, my boy. Oh, Milne-Edwards, oh, Quatrefages.* How I wish you could see me here, Otto Lidenbrock!'

38

To explain this reference to the two distinguished scientists, it should be recalled that a palaeontological event of great importance had taken place some months before our departure.

On 28 March 1863, French workmen under the direction of M. Boucher of Perthes* had unearthed a human jaw-bone at a depth of 14 feet below the soil, in a quarry at Moulin-Quignon, near Abbeville (Somme). It was the first fossil of the sort ever to see the light of day. Near it were stone axes and worked flints, which time had covered with a uniform coloured patina.

This discovery had a huge impact, not only in France but in Britain and Germany. Many scholars from the Institut Français, including Messrs Milne-Edwards and Quatrefages, took the affair very much to heart; demonstrated the incontestable authenticity of the bones in question; and hence became the most impassioned defence witnesses in the 'trial of the jaw-bone', as it was called in Britain.

In addition to the United Kingdom geologists who considered the fact as certain—Messrs Falconer, Busk, Carpenter* *et al.*—stood the German scholars. Amongst the most eminent, the most enthusiastic, the most carried away, was my uncle Lidenbrock.

The authenticity of a human fossil from the Quaternary Era seemed therefore proved and approved beyond all shadow of a doubt.

Such a view, it is true, was vigorously challenged by M. Élie de Beaumont.* This authoritative and respected scientist maintained that the terrain of Moulin-Quignon did not belong to the 'flood' period but was more recent. In agreement with Cuvier on this point, he contended that the human race could not have existed at the same time as the animals of the Quaternary Era. But my uncle Lidenbrock, in accordance with the great majority of geologists, had held his ground, had argued and discussed—and M. Élie de Beaumont had remained relatively isolated in his view.

My uncle and I were familiar with the successive ins and outs of this affair. But what we did not know was that, after we had left, it had undergone further developments. Additional jaw-bones of the same sort, although belonging to individuals of different types and different nations, were discovered in the loose grey soil of certain large caves in France, Switzerland, and Belgium—together with weapons, utensils, tools, and the bones of children, adolescents, adults, and old people. The existence of Quaternary man became therefore more and more certain with each passing day.

And this was not all. New fragments excavated in Pliocene terrain from the Tertiary Period had enabled scientists with even livelier imaginations to attribute a much greater age to the human race. These fragments, it is true, were not human bones, but merely the products of his industry: tibias and femurs of fossil animals, marked with regular grooves, carved so to speak, bearing the signs of man's handiwork.

Thus, in a single move, man had leaped many centuries up the ladder of time. He now came before the mastodon; he became a contemporary of the *elephas meridionalis*;* his existence dated back a hundred thousand years, since that was when the geologists said the Pliocene terrain was formed!

The above elements constituted the state of palaeontological science at that time, and what we knew of them was sufficient to explain our reaction to this ossuary beside the Lidenbrock Sea. My uncle's stupefaction and joy are easy to understand, especially when, twenty yards further on, he found himself in the presence of, or rather face to face with, an authentic specimen of Quaternary man.

It was a perfectly recognizable human body. Had some

particularity of the soil, as in the Saint-Michel Cemetery in Bordeaux, preserved it unchanged down through the centuries? It was difficult to say. But in any case this body was before our eyes exactly as it had lived—complete with stretched, parchment-like skin, limbs still fleshy and soft, apparently at least, teeth still preserved, a considerable head of hair, and finger- and toe-nails of a frightening length.

I was dumbstruck at this apparition from another age. My uncle, usually possessed of such a way with words, normally so eager to make speeches about anything, fell silent as well. We propped the body up against a rock. He looked at us from his hollow eye-sockets. We twanged his sonorous chest.

After a few moments of silence, my uncle reverted to Herr Professor Otto Lidenbrock, undoubtedly carried away by his personality and forgetting the circumstances of the journey, our immediate surroundings, and the tremendous cavern holding us. He must have thought he was lecturing to his students at the Johanneum, for he adopted a professorial tone and addressed an imaginary audience:

'Gentlemen, I have the pleasure of introducing you to a man from the Quaternary Era. Some eminent scholars have argued that he does not exist, while others, no less eminent, have maintained that he does. The doubting Thomases of palaeontology, if they were here, would be able to touch his body with their hands, and thus be forced to admit their error. I know full well that science must be constantly on its guard concerning discoveries of this sort. I am not unaware of the exploitation of fossil men by the Barnums* and other charlatans of this world. I am not unacquainted with the story of Ajax's kneecap, with what was claimed to be Orestes' body as found by the Spartans, or with Asterius' ten-cubit-long body as described by Pausanias.* I have read the reports on the Trápani skeleton discovered in the fourteenth century, which people wished to believe was Polyphemus', as well as the accounts of the giant dug up in the sixteenth century near Palermo. You are as aware as I, gentlemen, of the analysis carried out at Lucerne in 1577 of the enormous bones claimed by the illustrious doctor Félix Plater to belong to a giant 19 feet tall. I have devoured Cassanion's treatises, and all the monographs, pamphlets, presentations, and counter-presentations ever published on the skeleton of Teutobochus, King of the Cimbrians, who invaded Gaul and who was excavated from a sandpit in the Dauphiné in 1613. In the eighteenth century, I would have combated Peter Camper's affirmations regarding the existence of Scheuchzer's* pre-Adamites! I have held in my hands the publication entitled *Gi . . .*'

Here re-emerged my uncle's inherent impediment of not being able to pronounce complicated words in public.

'The book entitled *Gi-Gi-gans . . .*'

He couldn't go any further.

'*Gi-gan-teo . . .*'

Impossible, the wretched word just would not come out! There would have been much laughter at the Johanneum.

'*Gigantosteology*,' Professor Lidenbrock said, between two oaths.

Then, continuing all the better, and warming up:

'Yes, gentlemen, I am aware of all these matters. I also know that Cuvier and Blumenbach have identified the bones as simply those of mammoths and other animals of the Quaternary Period. But to doubt in the present case would be to insult science! The corpse is there! You can inspect it, touch it. It is not a mere skeleton, it is an entire body, preserved for exclusively anthropological purposes!'

I was careful not to contradict this assertion.

'If I could wash it in a solution of sulphuric acid, I would remove all the earth encrustations and splendid shells attached to it. But the precious solvent is unavailable at present. However, as it stands, this body will recount its own story.'

Here, the professor picked up the fossil corpse and handled it with all the dexterity of a showman at a fair.

'As you can see, it is less than six feet tall, and we are a long way from the so-called giants. As for the race it belongs to, it is incontestably Caucasian. It is of the white race, it is of our own race! The skull of this fossil is oval-shaped and regular, without developed cheekbones, without a projecting jaw. It presents no sign of prognathism modifying the facial angle.[1] Measure this angle, it is nearly 90 degrees. But I will proceed further along the path of deductions, and I will venture to say that this human specimen belongs to the Japhetic family, which extends from the Indian Subcontinent to the far limits of Western Europe. Pray do not smile, gentlemen!'

Nobody was smiling, but the professor was used to seeing faces broadening during his scholarly perorations.

'Yes,' he continued with renewed vigour, 'this is a fossil man, and a contemporary of the mastodons whose bones fill this auditorium. But by what route it arrived here, how the strata it was enclosed in slid down into this enormous cavity of the globe, I am unable to tell you. Undoubtedly, in the Quaternary Period, considerable up-heavals in the Earth's crust still occurred. The lengthy cooling of the globe produced fissures, cracks, and faults, into which part of the upper terrain must have dropped. I am not committing myself, but, after all, this man is here, surrounded by the handiwork he produced, his axes and worked flints which define the Stone Age. Unless he came here as a tourist, as a scientific pioneer, I cannot then question the authenticity of his ancient origin.'

The professor stopped speaking, and I broke into un-animous applause. My uncle was in fact right, and more learned people than his nephew would have found it very difficult to argue with him.

Another clue. This fossilized body was not the only one in the enormous ossuary. With each step we took in this dust, we came across other bodies: my uncle was able to

[1] The facial angle is formed by the intersection of two planes, one more or less vertical and forming a tangent to the forehead and the incisor teeth, the other horizontal, passing through the opening of the auditory passages and the lower nasal cavity. One defines *prognathism*, in anthropological language, as this projection of the jaw-bone modify-ing the facial angle.*

pick out the most wonderful specimens that would have convinced the most sceptical.

It was indeed an amazing sight, that of generations of men and animals mingling in this cemetery. But a puzzling mystery then arose, that we were not yet able to solve. Had these creatures slid down to the shores of the Lidenbrock Sea during some convulsion of the Earth, when they were already dead? Or had they instead passed their lives down here, in this underworld, under this unnatural sky, being born and dying here, just like the inhabitants of the Earth? Until now, only monsters of the deep and fish had appeared before us in living form. Was some man of the abyss also still wandering along these lonely shores?

39

FOR another half-hour we trampled over the layers of bones. We went straight ahead, forced on by a burning curiosity. What other wonders did this cavern hold, what treasures of science? My eyes expected every surprise, my mind every astonishment.

The sea-shore had long since disappeared behind the hills of the bone-graveyard. The foolhardy professor, heedless of losing the way, led us further and further on. We walked in silence, bathed in the waves of electric light. By a phenomenon I cannot explain, the light was uniformly diffused, so that it lit up all the sides of objects equally. It no longer came from any definite point in space, and consequently there was not the slightest shadow. It was like being under the vertical rays of the sun at midday in midsummer in the midst of the equatorial regions. All mist had disappeared. The rocks, the distant mountains, the blurry forms of a few far-away forests, all took on a strange appearance under the even distribution of the luminous fluid. We were like that fantastic character of Hoffmann's who lost his shadow.*

After about a mile, we saw the edge of an immense

forest, but not this time a grove of mushrooms like the one near Port Gräuben.

It displayed the vegetation of the Tertiary Period in all its splendour. Great palm-trees of species no longer existing and superb palmaceae, pines, yews, cypress, and thujas* represented the coniferous family, all joined together by an impenetrable network of creepers. The ground was carpeted with a springy covering of moss and hepaticas. Streams murmured under the shade—if this term can be used, for there was no shadow. On the banks flourished tree ferns, like those that flourish in the hot-houses of the inhabited globe. Colours, however, were absent from all the trees, shrubs, and plants, deprived as they were of the life-giving heat of the sun. Everything was dissolved into a uniform hue, brownish and faded as if past. The leaves were not their usual green, and the very flowers, so numerous in the Tertiary Age when they first appeared, were at that time without colour or perfume, as if made of a paper that had been yellowed by the effect of the atmosphere.

My uncle ventured into this gigantic thicket. I followed, not without a certain apprehension. Where nature had provided such vast stores of vegetable foodstuffs, might fearful mammals not be encountered? In the large clearings left by trees chopped down and gnawed by time, I noticed leguminous plants, acerinae, rubiaceae, and a thousand edible shrubs, much appreciated by the ruminants of all periods. Then there appeared, all intermixed and intertwined, trees from highly different countries on the surface of the globe, the oak growing beside the palm-tree, the Australian eucalyptus leaning on the Norwegian fir, the northern birch mingling its branches with the New Zealand kauri. It was enough to upset the sanity of the most ingenious classifiers of terrestrial botany.

Suddenly I stopped short. I held my uncle back.

The uniform light made it possible to see the smallest objects in the depths of the thicket. I thought I saw, no, I really *did* see, enormous shapes wandering around under the trees! They were in fact gigantic animals, a whole herd of mastodons, no longer fossil, but fully alive, and resembling the ones whose remains were discovered in the bogs of Ohio in 1801. I watched these great elephants with their trunks swarming about below the trees like a host of serpents. I heard the sound of their great tusks as the ivory tore at the bark of the ancient tree-trunks. The branches cracked, and the leaves, torn off in great clumps, disappeared into the monsters' massive maws.

So the dream where I had seen the rebirth of this complete world from prehistoric times, combining the Tertiary and Quaternary Periods, had finally become reality! And we were there, alone, in the bowels of the Earth, at the mercy of its fierce inhabitants!

My uncle was gazing.

Suddenly he seized me by the arm, crying: 'Come on! Forward, forward!'

'No, no! We are unarmed! What could we do amongst these giant quadrupeds? Come, Uncle, come! No human creature can brave the anger of these monsters unscathed!'

'No human creature?' said my uncle, lowering his voice. 'You are wrong, Axel! Look, look over there! It seems to me that I can see a living creature—a being like us—a man!'

I looked, shrugging my shoulders, determined to push incredulity to its furthest limits. But struggle as I might, I had to give in to the evidence.

There, less than a quarter of a mile away, leaning against the trunk of an enormous kauri tree, was a human being, a Proteus of these underground realms, a new son of Neptune,* shepherding that uncountable drove of mastodons!

*Immanis pecoris custos, immanior ipse!**

'*Immanior ipse*' indeed! This was no longer the fossil creature whose body we had propped up amongst the bones: this was a giant, able to command these monsters. He was more than twelve feet tall. His head, as big as a buffalo's, was half-hidden in the brush of his wild locks—a real mane, like that of the elephants of the first ages. He swung in his hand an enormous bough, an appropriately primeval crook for this shepherd from before the Flood.*

We remained motionless, in a daze. But we might be spotted. We had to retreat.

'Run for it!' I shouted, dragging my uncle with me, who for the first time in his life didn't resist.

A quarter of an hour later, we were out of sight of this redoubtable foe.

And now, when I consider it calmly, now that peace has returned to my mind, now that months have gone by since this strange, this supernatural, encounter—what am I to think, what to believe? No, it's just not possible! Our senses must have been mistaken, our eyes can't have seen what they saw! No human creature lives in that underground world. No race of men populates those deep caverns of the globe, unconcerned with the inhabitants of the surface, not communicating with them in any way! It's insane, deeply insane!

I would rather believe that some animal existed with a humanoid structure, some ape from the first geological eras, some Protopithecus, some Mesopitheca like the one discovered by M. Lartet* in the bone-laden bed of Sansan! But this one was far bigger than all the measurements known to modern palaeontology. Never mind, however unlikely, it was an ape! But a man, a living man, and with him a whole generation entombed in the innards of the Earth? Never!

Meanwhile we had left the clear, luminous forest, speechless with shock, weighed down by a stupefaction that came close to brutishness. We couldn't help running. It was a real flight, like those terrifying automatisms that one sometimes gets caught up in in nightmares. Instinctively we made our way towards the Lidenbrock Sea. I do not know what wild paths my mind would have taken me along, if a particular worry hadn't brought me back to more practical considerations.*

Although I was certain I was covering ground we hadn't been over before, I kept noticing groups of rocks whose shapes reminded me of Port Gräuben. This in fact confirmed what the compass had indicated—that we had unintentionally headed back towards the north of the Lidenbrock Sea. Sometimes it all seemed uncannily similar. Hundreds of streams and cascades fell from the rocky outcrops. I imagined I was back near the layer of *surtarbrandur*, near our faithful Hans-Bach and the grotto where I had come back to life. Then, a few yards further on, the shape of the cliffs, the appearance of a stream, the surprising outline of a rock made me start doubting again.

I mentioned my hesitation to my uncle. He was wondering like me. He was unable to find his way through this uniform vista.*

'We obviously didn't come back to the exact point we left from,' I said. 'But the storm must have brought us back to just below it, and by following the coast, we'll reach Port Gräuben again.'*

'If that is true, then there seems no point in carrying on with this exploration, and it is best to return to the raft. But are you absolutely sure, Axel?'

'It's difficult to be definite, Uncle, for all the rocks look so similar. But I think I remember the promontory where Hans built the raft. We must be near the little harbour. And it may even be here,' I added, examining a creek I thought I recognized.*

'But then we would at least have come across our own traces, and I see nothing . . .'

'But *I* do!' I cried, springing towards an object glimmering on the sand.

'What is it?'

'There!'

I showed my uncle the rust-covered knife I had picked up.

'Well, well!' he said. 'So you brought this weapon with you?'

'No, I didn't. But did you?'

'Not to my knowledge; I have never knowingly had this thing on me.'*

'It's all most peculiar.'*

'It is all quite simple. The Icelanders often carry

weapons like this, and Hans must be its owner, and have dropped it . . .'*

I shook my head. Hans had never had this knife on him.

'Is it then the weapon of some warrior from before the Flood,' I exclaimed, 'of a living human being, of a contemporary of that gigantic shepherd? But it can't be! It isn't from the Stone Age! Not even the Bronze Age! This blade is made of steel . . .'

My uncle stopped me dead on this track where a new diversion was leading me, saying in his cold tone:

'Calm down, Axel, and use your head.* This knife is from the sixteenth century: it is an authentic dagger, like the ones that nobles used to carry on their belts for giving the *coup de grâce*. It is of Spanish manufacture. It belongs neither to me, nor to you, nor to the hunter, nor even to the human beings that may live in these bowels of the Earth!'*

'Do you mean . . . ?'

'Look, this blade has not become so notched by sinking into people's throats; and it is covered in a layer of rust, more than a day thick, more than a year, more than a century even.'

The professor, as usual, was getting excited as his imagination ran away with him.

'Axel, we are on the path of a great discovery. This blade has been lying on the sand for one, two, three hundred years, and it is scored because it was used on the rocks of this subterranean sea!'

'But it couldn't have just arrived on its own. Somebody must have got here before us!'

'Yes, a man.'

'Who?'

'The man who used this knife to engrave his name. His aim was to put his mark once more on the route to the centre. Let's see if we can find it!'

We excitedly worked our way along the high cliffs, looking for the smallest clefts that might turn into a gallery.

We eventually came to a place where the shore got narrower. The sea came nearly to the foot of the cliffs, leaving us at most two yards to pass. Between two projecting rocks loomed the entrance of a dark tunnel.

There, on a slab of granite, two mysterious letters were carved, half worn away: the twin initials of the bold and fantastic traveller:

· ⅄ · ⅄ ·

'A. S.!' cried my uncle. 'Arne Saknussemm once again!'

40

SINCE the beginning of our journey I had been astonished many times; I would have thought that I was immune to surprise and blasé at any new wonder. Nevertheless, at the sight of the two letters engraved on this spot three centuries ago, I felt an amazement which came close to utter stupidity. Not only could the signature of the learned alchemist be read clearly on the rock, but I had in my hand the stylus with which he had traced it. Unless I was completely dishonest with myself, I could no longer doubt the existence of the traveller or the truth of his journey.

While these thoughts whirled through my brain, Professor Lidenbrock was indulging in a slightly excessive praise of Arne Saknussemm:

'O marvellous genius! You did everything to open up to other mortals the way into the crust of the Earth, and now your comrades can follow the traces your feet left in these dark underpasses three hundred years ago! You intended these marvels to be contemplated by eyes other than your own! Your name, engraved on the successive sections of the route, leads the traveller bold enough to follow you straight to his goal, and it will be found yet again at the very centre of our planet, once more carved by your hand! Well, I too intend to sign my name on this, the last of the granite pages. But henceforth let this cape, first seen by you on this sea first discovered by you, be known as Cape Saknussemm!'

This, or something like it, was what I heard, and I felt won over myself by the enthusiasm conveyed by such words. An inner fire rekindled in my breast. I forgot everything, even the dangers of the downward journey and the perils of the return. What another had done I wished to do too, and nothing that was human seemed impossible to me.

'Forward, forward!'

I was already making my headlong way towards the dark gallery, when I was stopped: the professor, the one who normally got carried away, was recommending calm and patience.

'Let's first go and find Hans, and then bring the raft over here.'

I obeyed, not with any great pleasure; and slipped back between the rocks on shore.

'Have you thought, Uncle?' I said as we walked. 'We've been very lucky so far, haven't we?'

'Oh, do you think so?'

'Yes, even the storm helped put us on the right track again. Thank God it happened! It brought us back to this coast—which wouldn't have happened if we'd had fine weather. Imagine for a moment that our prow (in so far as a raft can be said to have a prow) had touched the southern coastline of the Lidenbrock Sea, what would have become of us? We wouldn't have seen Saknussemm's name, and we would now be washed up on a shore that offered no way out!'

'Yes, Axel, there is something providential in the fact that, sailing southwards, we should have come north and returned to Cape Saknussemm. Indeed it seems to me more than astonishing, and there is something here that I can't begin to explain.'

'Well it doesn't really matter. What counts is to make use of the facts, not explain them!'

'No doubt, my boy, but . . .'

'But now we are about to head north again, passing under the countries of Northern Europe, under Sweden, even under Siberia for all I know! We're not going to plunge under the deserts of Africa or the breakers of the ocean. That's all I need to know!'

'Yes, you are right. Everything is for the best, since we are going to leave this horizontal sea which was taking us nowhere. Now we shall go down, then further down, and then down again! Do you realize that we have less than 3,900 miles left to cover?'

'Bah, hardly worth mentioning! Off we go, come on!'

This insane conversation was still continuing when we joined up again with the hunter. Everything was ready for leaving immediately. All the packages were on board the raft. We embarked, hoisted the sail, and Hans steered us along the coast towards Cape Saknussemm.

The wind direction was not very favourable for a kind of vessel unable to tack against it. As a result, quite often we had to use the iron-tipped staves to move forward. The rocks, lurking under the surface, often forced us into long detours. Finally, after three hours' navigation, at about 6 p.m., we reached a suitable spot for landing.

I sprang ashore, followed by my uncle and the Icelander. The crossing had not calmed me down. I even suggested 'burning our boats' so as to cut off all possibility of retreat. But my uncle disagreed. I found him singularly half-hearted.

'At least let's set off without wasting a moment.'

'Yes, my boy, but first we should have a look at this new gallery, to decide whether we need to get the ladders ready.'

My uncle switched on his Ruhmkorff lamp. The raft, moored on the shore, was left to its own devices. The mouth of the gallery was less than twenty yards away, and our little expedition, with myself as leader, headed for it without waiting a second.

The opening, more or less round, was about five feet in diameter; the dark tunnel was cut into the living rock, and had been carefully bored by the eruptive substance that had passed through it; its floor was just near the ground, so that you could get into it without problem.

We were following an almost horizontal path when, after only about twenty feet, our way forward was blocked by an enormous obstruction.

'Blasted rock!' I cried, seeing myself abruptly frustrated by an insuperable obstacle.

In vain did we search to left and right, above and below: there was no passage, no alternative path. I felt bitterly disappointed, and could not accept that the barrier existed. I stooped down, and looked under the massive block: not even a crack. On top of it. The same granite barrier. Hans shone the light from the lamp on every part of the wall-covering; but it was perfectly continuous everywhere. Any hope of getting through had to be given up.

I sat on the bare ground. My uncle was pacing up and down with great strides.

'But what about Saknussemm?' I cried.

'Yes, was he stopped by a stone door?'

'No! This piece of rock must be there because of some earthquake or other, or one of those magnetic phenomena that shake the Earth's crust. The passage must have been suddenly closed off. A good many years passed between Saknussemm's return and the fall of the rock. Isn't it obvious that this gallery was formerly the route the lava took, and that the eruption flowed freely along it? Look, there are recent cracks running along this granite ceiling. The roof is made of pieces swept along, of enormous boulders, as if the hand of some giant had laboured to build it. But one day, the vertical pressure became too strong, and this block, like the keystone of a vault, fell to the ground and blocked off the whole passage. This is a chance obstacle that Saknussemm didn't meet, and if we can't beat it, we don't deserve to get to the centre of the world!'

That was the way I spoke. The professor's entire soul had passed into me. The spirit of discovery was arousing me. I forgot about the past, I didn't care about the future.

I had submerged myself in the bosom of that spheroid, and nothing existed for me on its surface: not the towns or the countryside, not Hamburg or Königstrasse, not even my poor Gräuben, who must have thought that I was lost for ever in the bowels of the Earth!

'Come on,' said my uncle, 'using the pickaxes and ice-picks, let's force our route, let's knock down these walls!'

'It's too hard for the pickaxes.'

'An ice-pick then.'

'It's too deep for an ice-pick.'

'But . . .'

'Well then, the powder, an explosion! Let's mine the obstacle and blow it up!'

'Blow it up?'

'Yes, it's only a bit of rock to break up!'

'Hans, to work!' shouted my uncle.

The Icelander went back to the raft, and soon returned with one of the pickaxes, which he used to hollow out a cavity for the explosive. It was not an easy task. He had to make a hole big enough to hold fifty pounds of gun-cotton, whose explosive force is four times as great as gunpowder's.

I was in an extreme state of excitement. While Hans worked, I devotedly helped my uncle to prepare a long fuse made of damp gunpowder wrapped in a canvas tube.

'We'll get through!'

'We'll get through,' repeated my uncle.

At midnight, our work as miners was complete; the guncotton charge was crammed in the hole in the rock, and the fuse unwound through the gallery to the outside.

A spark was now enough to set off this imposing device.

'Till tomorrow then,' said the professor.

I had to resign myself to waiting for six long hours!

41

THE following day, Thursday 27 August, was an important one in our underground journey. Every time that I think about it now, terror makes my heart beat faster. From that moment on, our reason, our judgement, our ingenuity were to have no influence at all on events: we were to become the mere playthings of the Earth.

We were up by six. The time had come to use explosives to force a way through the granite crust.

I requested the honour of lighting the fuse. Afterwards I would rejoin my companions on the raft, which had not yet been unloaded; then we would head out for the open sea, so as to reduce the danger from the explosion, which could easily affect an area well beyond the outcrop. According to our calculations, the fuse would burn for ten minutes before setting off the powder chamber. So I had plenty of time to get back to the raft. But it was not without a certain trepidation that I got ready to play my part.

After a hurried breakfast, my uncle and the hunter embarked on the raft while I remained on shore. I was equipped with a lighted lantern for setting off the fuse.

'It's time to go, Axel,' said my uncle, 'but do make sure you come straight back afterwards.'

'Don't worry, I'm not going to hang around.'

I made straight for the mouth. I opened the lantern and picked up the end of the fuse. The professor had his chronometer in his hand.

'Ready?' he shouted.

'Ready.'

'Well fire away, my lad!'

I pushed the fuse quickly into the flame and it spluttered into life as I sprinted back to the shore.

'Get on,' said my uncle, 'and we'll head out.'

With a forceful shove, Hans pushed us off. The raft

moved forty yards out. It was a tense moment. The professor was watching the hand of the chronometer.

'Five more minutes . . . Four . . . Three . . .'

My heart beat every half-second.

'Two . . . One . . . Take that, O granite mountains!'

What happened next? I don't think I actually heard the noise of the explosion. But the shapes of the rocks suddenly changed before my eyes: they swung away like curtains. I glimpsed an unfathomable void hollowed out from the very shore. The sea, seized with dizziness, had become nothing but one immense wave—on whose back the raft rose straight up.

The three of us were thrown over. Within a second, light had given way to the most utter darkness. Then I felt the solid support disappearing, not beneath my feet but under the raft itself. I thought for a moment that it was sinking, but soon realized that it couldn't be. I tried to speak to my uncle; but the bellowing of the waters stopped him from hearing me. Despite the darkness, the noise, the surprise, and the excitement, I soon understood what had happened. On the other side of the exploded outcrop was an abyss. The explosion had set off a sort of earthquake in the already shattered ground, a chasm had opened up, and the sea, transformed into a great river, had carried us down into it. I thought we were lost.

One hour, two hours—how could I tell?—went by in this way. We linked arms, we held each other's hands so as not to be thrown off the raft. It jolted with great violence whenever it touched the side. Such collisions were infrequent, however, and so I deduced that the gallery was getting considerably larger. There could be no doubt that this was Saknussemm's route; but instead of following it on our own, our carelessness had brought down an entire sea with us.

It will be understood that these ideas crossed my mind in indistinct and murky form. All association of ideas was difficult during this dizzy descent, more like free-fall. To tell from the air whipping past my face, the speed must have been greater than the fastest trains. Lighting a torch would have been impossible in such conditions, and our last electrical apparatus had been broken during the explosion.

I was therefore quite surprised suddenly to see a light beside me. Hans's calm face appeared. The adroit hunter had managed to light the lantern and although the flame flickered and almost went out, it threw some rays into the awful blackness.

As I thought, the gallery was a wide one, for the light was not strong enough to reveal both walls at the same time. The slope of the water bearing us on was greater than that of the most unsurmountable rapids in America. Its surface was as if made up of sheafs of liquid arrows let loose with total power: I cannot describe what I felt with any more precise comparison. When the raft got caught up in eddies, it was swept on while turning slowly round. When it went near the walls of the gallery, I shone the lantern on them, and got some idea of our speed from seeing the projections of the rocks as continuous lines, so that we were hemmed in by a network of moving streaks. I estimated our speed to be as much as 55 miles an hour.

My uncle and I looked at each other with wild eyes, leaning back on the stump of the mast which had broken in half during the catastrophe. We faced away from the air so as to avoid being suffocated by the speed of a motion that no human force could influence.

Meanwhile the hours went by. The basic situation remained the same, even if an incident came to complicate it. While trying to put some order to our cargo, I discovered that most of the possessions on board had disappeared when the sea had attacked us so violently during the explosion. I wished to know the exact position of our resources, so began a search while holding up the lantern. Of our instruments only the compass and chronometer remained. Of the ladders and ropes, a mere end coiled around the stump of the mast. Not a single pickaxe, not an ice-pick, not a hammer and, worse still, food for only one more day!

I searched amongst the cracks in the raft, in the smallest

gaps between the beams and the cross-beams. Nothing! Our provisions amounted to one piece of dried meat and a few dried biscuits.

I looked at them blankly, not wanting to understand. And yet what was the danger I was worrying about? Even had the victuals been enough for months or years, how could we get back out of the chasm that this inexorable river was carrying us into? What was the point of worrying about hunger-pains, when death was possible in so many other ways? Would we not have plenty of time to die of inanition?

Nevertheless, by a mysterious trick of the mind, I forgot about the immediate danger; for those of the future appeared to me in all their horror. In any case, perhaps we could escape the river's fury and get back to the globe's surface. How, I did not know. Where, didn't make any difference. A chance in a thousand is still a chance, while death through starvation left us no possibility of hope, not the least prospect.

I thought of telling my uncle everything, of showing him how few things we had left, of calculating exactly how much time we still had to live. But I had the strength to remain silent. I wanted him to retain all his self-control.

At this moment the lantern slowly dimmed, and then went out altogether. The wick had burned through, and total blackness ensued. There was no point in trying to reduce this impenetrable inkiness. We still had one torch left, but it wouldn't have stayed alight. So, like a child, I closed my eyes to shut out all the darkness.

After quite a long time, our speed got much faster, as I realized from the battering of air on my face. The angle of the water got worse. We no longer seemed to be sliding, but falling. I had the clear sensation of a near-vertical drop. My uncle's and Hans's hands, clamped on my arms, held firmly on to me.

After an indeterminate time, something like a sudden shock happened; the raft hadn't collided with a hard object, but it had abruptly stopped falling. A water-spout, a huge liquid column, crashed down over the raft. I was suffocating. I was drowning . . .

However, this flood did not last long. After a few seconds, I found myself gulping air down again. My uncle and Hans were gripping my arms as if to break them; and the raft was still bearing the three of us on.

42

IT must have been about 10 p.m. The first of my senses to start working after this last attack was that of hearing. Almost straightaway I heard—and this was a definite event—I heard silence falling in the gallery, replacing the roaring which had been filling my ears for so many hours. Words from my uncle finally reached me like a murmur:

'We're going up!'

'What do you mean?' I shouted.

'We're climbing! We're actually climbing!'

I stretched out my arm; I touched the wall; my hand got blood on it. We were rising very fast.

'The torch, the torch!'

Hans finally managed to light it and the flame, burning upwards despite our movement, spread enough light to reveal the scene.

'Exactly as I thought. We are in a narrow shaft, only 30 feet wide. When the water reached the bottom of the chasm, it started coming back up, taking us with it.'

'Where to?'

'I do not know, but we will have to be ready for any eventuality. I estimate our speed to be 13 feet per second, 780 feet per minute, or more than 14 miles per hour. At that rate, one can go places!'

'Yes, if nothing stops us and if this shaft has a way out. But if it's blocked, if the air gets more and more compressed by the pressure from the water-column, if we are doomed to be crushed to death!'

'Axel,' replied the professor very calmly. 'The situation

is virtually hopeless, but there exists a possibility of salvation, and it is that possibility which I am examining. If we may die at any moment, we may also at any moment be saved. Let us accordingly be ready to seize the slightest opportunity.'

'But what can be done?'

'Husband our forces by eating.'

At these words I looked at my uncle distraught. I had not been able to confess before, but now it had to be done:

'Eating?'

'Yes, without delay.'

The professor said a few words in Danish. Hans shook his head.

'What!' shouted my uncle. 'Has something happened to our food?'

'Yes, this is what is left: one piece of dried meat for the three of us!'

My uncle looked at me as if trying to understand my words.

'Well,' I said, 'do you still think we might be saved?'

My question received no answer. An hour passed. I began to feel a violent hunger. My companions were suffering as well, but not one of us dared touch the pathetic remains of the food. We were still rising very fast. Sometimes the air stopped us breathing properly, as it does with aeronauts who ascend too quickly. But whilst aeronauts are subject to cold proportional to their height amongst the layers of the atmosphere, we were undergoing the diametrically opposite effect. The temperature was rising worryingly and had easily reached 40°C.

What did such a change mean? Until now Lidenbrock and Davy's theory had been confirmed by the evidence; until now special conditions of refracting rocks, of electricity, or of magnetism had modified the general laws of nature, making the heat stay moderate. Given that the theory of a central fire remained in my view the only correct one, the only justifiable one, were we going to come back to an environment where this phenomenon held true, where the heat completely melted the rocks? I was afraid so, and said to the professor:

'If we aren't drowned or torn to pieces, if we don't starve to death, there's still the chance we might be burned alive.'

He merely shrugged his shoulders and returned to his thoughts.

An hour passed without anything happening apart from a slight increase in the temperature. At last my uncle said something.

'Look,' he said, 'we must decide.'

'Decide?'

'Yes. We must keep up our strength. If we try to extend our lives for a few more hours by eking out what is left of the food, then we will remain weak until the end.'

'Yes, till the end, which isn't far off.'

'Well then! Should a chance of salvation occur, should action become necessary, where will we find the strength to act if we reduce our forces by inanition?'

'But, Uncle, when we've eaten this piece of meat, what will we have left?'

'Nothing, Axel, nothing. But will devouring it with your eyes give you any more nourishment? Your arguments are those of a man with no will, a being without energy!'

'Then you've still not given up?' I shouted irritably.

'No!' he replied firmly.

'What! You still think we have a chance of being saved?'

'Yes, most certainly! And while his heart still beats, while his flesh still moves, I cannot accept that a being endowed with will-power can give in to despair.'

What words! The man who pronounced them in such circumstances was clearly of no ordinary mettle.

'But what do you suggest?'

'We eat every last scrap of food and get our strength back. All right, so this meal will be our last. But at least, instead of being exhausted, we will be men again.'

'Well what are we waiting for!'

My uncle took the piece of meat and the few biscuits

that had survived the shipwreck, divided them into three equal parts and handed them out. This produced about a pound of food each. The professor ate hungrily, with a sort of feverish abandon; myself without pleasure despite my hunger, almost with disgust; Hans quietly, moderately, soundlessly chewing small mouthfuls, savouring them with the calm of a man the problems of the future cannot worry. By looking everywhere, he had found half a flask of gin; he passed it over, and this beneficial liquid revived me slightly.

'Förtrafflig!' said Hans, drinking in turn.

'Excellent!' replied my uncle.

I had found some hope again. But we had just finished our last meal. It was five in the morning.

Man is made in such a way that his health has a purely negative effect; once his need to eat has been satisfied, he finds it difficult to imagine the horrors of hunger; to understand them he has to experience them. Consequently, after a long period without food, a few mouthfuls of meat and biscuits overcame our previous gloom.

Afterwards, each of us was lost in his thoughts. What was Hans dreaming about, this man from the extreme West, but ruled by the fatalistic resignation of the East? For my part all my thoughts were memories, bringing me back to that surface of the globe which I should never have left. The house in Königstrasse, my poor Gräuben, Martha the maid, passed before my eyes like visions; and in the sad rumblings coming through the rocks, I thought I could hear the towns of this Earth.

As for my uncle, always the professional, he was holding up the torch and carefully studying the nature of the terrain; he was trying to discover where we were from the successive strata. This calculation, or rather estimation, could at best be highly approximative; but a scholar remains a scholar, at least when he manages to retain his self-control—and Professor Lidenbrock certainly possessed this last quality to an extraordinary degree.

I heard him murmuring words from the science of geology; I understood them and could not help being interested in this final piece of work.

'Eruptive granite,' he was saying. 'We're still in the Primitive Period; but we're climbing, we're climbing! Who knows?'

Who knows? He had not given up hope. He touched the walls and a few moments later continued:

'Gneiss, mica schists. Good! We will soon be in the Transition Period, and then . . .'

What did the professor mean? Could he measure the thickness of the Earth's crust above our heads? Did he have a single justification for this calculation? No; he had no manometer and no estimation could take its place.

Meanwhile the temperature was increasing tremendously and I could feel myself bathing in a burning atmosphere. I could only compare it to the heat given off by the furnaces of a foundry when the metal is pouring out. By degrees Hans, my uncle, and I had taken off our jackets and waistcoats; the least garment caused us discomfort, even pain.

'Are we moving towards a fiery furnace?' I called out at a moment when the heat was getting much worse.

'No,' replied my uncle, 'it is not possible! It is not possible!'

'All the same,' I said testing the wall, 'it feels burning hot!'

As I said these words, my hand touched the surface of the water but I had to draw it back quickly.

'The water is boiling!' I shouted.

This time the professor replied only with an angry gesture.

An invincible terror then took hold of my mind and would not let go. I felt that a catastrophe was soon going to happen, one that the most daring of imaginations could not conceive. An idea that was at first vague and doubtful slowly became a certainty in my mind. I rejected it, but it came obstinately back, again and again.

I did not dare put it into words. But a number of involuntary observations convinced me. In the flickering light from the torch, I noticed convulsions in the granite strata; a phenomenon was clearly going to happen in which electricity had a role; but this terrible heat, the boiling water . . . I decided to look at the compass.

It had gone mad!

43

YES, mad! The needle was swinging round from direction to direction with sharp jerks, working its way through every successive point of the compass, as if completely dizzy.

I knew that, according to the generally accepted theories, the Earth's mineral crust is never in a complete state of rest. The changes caused by the decomposition of internal substances, the vibrations produced by the larger sea currents, and the actions of the magnetic forces all tend to shake it around constantly, although the creatures living on the surface have no idea that it is moving. This phenomenon on its own, therefore, would not specially have frightened me—or at least would not normally have produced a terrible suspicion.

But further phenomena, sending clues unlike any others, could no longer be ignored. Explosions were occurring with an increasing and alarming intensity. I could only compare them with the sound of dozens of carts being driven hard over cobblestones. Their thundering was continuous.

The compass, shaken madly around by the electrical phenomena, also helped me make up my mind. The mineral crust was threatening to break up, the granite masses to come together, the chasm to be plugged, the void filled in—and we, poor molecules, were going to be crushed in the harrowing embrace that resulted!

'Uncle, Uncle! We've had it!'

'What is this new panic?' he answered surprisingly calmly. 'What *is* the matter with you?'

'The matter? Look at the walls moving, this rock which is falling apart, this scorching heat, this boiling water, this thickening steam, this crazy needle: all signs of an impending earthquake!'

My uncle gently shook his head: 'An earthquake?'

'Yes.'

'I think, my boy, that you are mistaken.'

'What? Don't you realize that these symptoms . . .'

'. . . of an earthquake? No, I am expecting something better than that!'

'What do you mean?'

'I'm hoping for an eruption, Axel.'

'An eruption! We can't possibly be in the vent of an active volcano, can we?'

'I think we are,' said the professor, smiling. 'It is the best thing that could have happened to us.'

The best thing? Had my uncle gone quite mad? What did his words mean? How could he be so calm and happy?

'What?' I cried. 'We're in the middle of an eruption! Fate has placed us in the path of red-hot lava, fiery rocks, boiling water, of all the substances that are thrown up in eruptions! We are to be expelled, thrown out, rejected, regurgitated, spat out into the air, in a whirlwind of flame, along with huge amounts of rock and showers of ash and scoria! And that's the best thing that could happen to us!'

'Yes,' said the professor, looking at me over the top of his glasses. 'For it is the only chance we have of getting back to the surface of the Earth!'

I will skip the myriad ideas that intersected in my brain in that single moment. My uncle was right, absolutely right; and never had he seemed more fearless or more self-assured than at this moment, when calmly waiting, calculating the chances of an eruption.

Meanwhile, we had continued rising; the night went by without any change; only the noise all around became louder and louder. I was almost suffocating, I thought my last hour had come—and yet, imagination being such a strange thing, I gave in to truly childish thoughts. But I couldn't help my ideas: I had no control over them!

It was clear that we were being pushed upwards by the force of an eruption; under the raft there was turbulent, boiling water, and under that a whole sticky mass of lava, a huge conglomeration of rocks. When they got to the top of the crater, they would be thrown out in all directions. We were in the vent of a volcano. Of that there could be no doubt.

But this time, instead of the extinct Snæfells, we were dealing with a volcano in full activity. I was wondering therefore what mountain it could possibly be, and which part of the world we were going to be thrown out on to.

Some northern region, of course. Before it had gone insane, the compass had been consistently pointing in that direction. Since leaving Cape Saknussemm, we had been swept due north for hundreds and hundreds of miles. Were we underneath Iceland once more? Were we to be ejected from the crater of Mount Hekla or one of the seven other volcanoes on the island? Otherwise, within a radius of 1,200 miles and at that latitude, I could only think of the little-known volcanoes on the northwest coast of America. To the east, there was only one at less than 80° N: Esk, in Jan Mayen, not far from Spitzbergen.* On the other hand, there was no general lack of craters, and they all had plenty of room to spew out a whole army. I tried to guess which one would serve as our exit.

Towards morning our ascent became still faster. The heat was increasing rather than decreasing as we approached the surface of the globe: this had to be a local effect, due to the influence of some volcano. No longer could there be any doubt at all as to our means of transport. An enormous force, a pressure of several hundred atmospheres produced by the steam built up in the Earth's breast was irresistibly thrusting up at us. But how many terrible dangers would it expose us to?

Soon wild glowing lights shone in the walls of the vertical chimney, which was now widening out. On either side I could see deep corridors, like immense tunnels, sending forth thick steam and smoke, while tongues of flame crackled and licked at the walls.

'Look, Uncle!'

'Yes, sulphur flames. Nothing could be more normal during an eruption.'

'But what if they come and attack us?'

'They won't.'

'And what if we suffocate?'

'We shan't. The shaft is getting wider. If necessary we can get off the raft and take shelter in some fissure.'

'But the water, the water! Rising all the time!'

'There is no water left, Axel, just a viscous lava-stream which is lifting us up on its way to the mouth of the crater.'

It was true that the water had disappeared, replaced by relatively dense eruptive matter, which was boiling, however. The temperature was becoming unbearable. A thermometer would have indicated more than 70°. I was bathed in sweat. But for the speed of the climb, we would certainly have been suffocated.

The professor did not pursue his suggestion of leaving the raft, which was perhaps just as well. Those few beams, roughly joined together, gave us a solid base, which we wouldn't have had anywhere else.

Towards eight in the morning a new incident happened for the first time. The upward movement stopped all of a sudden, with the raft remaining absolutely motionless.

'What's happening?' I asked, shaken by this abrupt halt as if the raft had hit something.

'An intermission.'

'Is the eruption slowing down?'

'I sincerely hope not.'

I stood up. I tried to look around. Perhaps the raft had caught against a sticking-out rock and was momentarily holding back the flow of the eruptive material. If so, it ought to be freed at once.

But this wasn't the case. The column of ashes, scoria, rocks, and debris had itself stopped rising.

'Is the eruption stopping?'

'Ah!' said my uncle through clenched teeth. 'So that's what you are worrying about, my boy. But don't fret, this can only be a temporary lull; it has already lasted five minutes, and in a short while we shall be heading towards the mouth of the crater once again.'

While speaking, the professor consulted his chronometer; and he was soon proved right in this prediction as well. The raft was once more caught up in a rapid, disorderly flux, which lasted for about two minutes—then stopped again.

'Good,' said my uncle, noting the time. 'It will re-start in ten minutes.'

'Ten minutes?'

'Yes. We are dealing with a volcano whose eruption is periodic. It lets us breathe when it does.'

He was absolutely right. At the allotted time we were shot upwards again with great speed: we had to cling on to the beams or we would have been thrown off the raft. Then the thrust stopped once more.

Since that time, I have often thought about this remarkable phenomenon, but without being able to find a satisfactory explanation for it. Nevertheless, it seems clear to me that we can't have been in the principal chimney of the volcano, but rather a side-passage, where there was some sort of counter-effect.

How many times the process took place, I cannot say. All I can be certain of is that each time the movement began again, we were hurled forward with increasing force, as if lifted by an actual projectile. During the pauses, we suffocated; when we were moving, the burning air took my breath away. For a moment I thought of the ecstasy of suddenly finding myself in the Polar regions, at a temperature of −30°. In my over-stimulated imagination I wandered over the snowy plains of the Arctic ice-cap, and longed for the moment when I could roll on the frozen carpet of the Pole! But gradually my head, confused by the repeated shocks, gave up working altogether. If it had not been for Hans's arms, my skull would have been flung against the granite wall on more than one occasion.

As a consequence I have no clear memory of what

happened during the next few hours. I have a confused memory of endless blasts, of Earth movements, of a swirling motion which grabbed hold of the raft. Our vessel rose and fell on the waves of lava, amidst a rain of ashes. It was besieged by roaring flames. An eager gale, as if coming from some immense fan, added to the subterranean fires. One last time, Hans's face appeared to me in the light from the blaze. My last thought was the horrifying tragedy of the criminal fastened to the mouth of a cannon, at the moment that the shot goes off and sends his arms and legs flying into the air.

44

WHEN I opened my eyes again, I felt the strong hand of the guide clutching my belt. With the other he was holding on to my uncle. I was not seriously injured, merely bruised and aching all over. I saw that I was lying on the slope of a mountain, only a few feet away from a precipice which I would have fallen into at the slightest movement. Hans had clearly saved me from certain death while I was rolling down the flanks of the crater.

'Where are we?' asked my uncle, who looked highly annoyed to be back on Earth again.

The guide shrugged his shoulders as if to show he didn't know.

'In Iceland,' I ventured.

'Nej,' answered Hans.

'What does he mean, "no"?' cried the professor.

'He must be wrong,' I said, getting up.

After the many surprises of the journey, another was waiting for us. I expected to see a cone covered with eternal snows, in the midst of the arid deserts of the north, under the pale rays of the Polar heavens, beyond the furthest latitudes. But contrary to what I had expected, my uncle, the Icelander, and I were stretched out halfway up a mountain baked by the heat of the sun, scorching us with its rays.

I wasn't prepared to believe my eyes; but the indisputable burning my body was receiving brooked no reply. We had come out of the crater half-naked, and the radiant orb, of which we had asked nothing for two months, was now bestowing on us floods of heat and light, was pouring on to us waves of a splendid irradiation.

When my eyes had adjusted to this unaccustomed dazzle, I used them to make up for the failure of my imagination. At the very least, I was determined to be in Spitzbergen—I was not in the mood for giving up easily.

The professor found his voice first: 'It certainly doesn't look very much like Iceland.'

'Jan Mayen?' I tried.

'Hardly, my boy. This is not a northern volcano with granite peaks and a crown of snow.'

'And yet . . .'

'Just look, Axel, *look!*'

Above our heads, not more than 500 feet away, was the crater of the volcano. Every quarter of an hour there came flying from it a tall column of flames mixed with pumice-stone, ashes, and lava, together with a deafening explosion. I felt the whole mountain heave every time it breathed, sending out, like a whale, fire and air through its enormous blowholes. Below, on a steep slope, layers of eruptive material could be seen extending 700 or 800 feet down, meaning that the volcano couldn't be more than 2,000 feet high. Its base was hidden by a real basket of green trees, amongst which I distinguished olive and fig trees, plus vines laden with purple grapes.

It didn't look much like the Arctic, I had to admit.

When one's gaze passed beyond the ring of greenery, it soon went astray on the waters of an exquisite sea or lake, which made this enchanted land into an island only a few miles wide. On the eastern side appeared a little port, with a few houses grouped round it and boats of an unusual type rocking on the gentle swell of the turquoise ripples. Beyond, clusters of small islets rose from the liquid plain, in such great numbers as to resemble a huge ant-heap. In the west, rounded shores appeared on the distant horizon; on some lay blue mountains of exquisite contours, on others, still further away, appeared measureless cones, above whose high summits floated plumes of smoke. To the north, a broad expanse of water sparkled in the sun's rays, revealing here and there the top of a mast or a convex sail swelling in the wind.

That such a panorama was totally unexpected made it infinitely more wonderful and beautiful.

'Where can we be, oh where?' I murmured.

Hans shut his eyes in indifference, and my uncle stared uncomprehendingly.

'Whatever this mountain is,' he said at last, 'it is rather hot. The explosions are still continuing, and it would really not be worth coming out of an eruption, only to have one's head crushed by a hurtling rock. So let's go down and discover where we stand. Besides, I am dying of hunger and thirst.'

The professor was certainly not a contemplative. For my part, I could have stayed hours longer on that spot, forgetting all needs and fatigues—but was obliged to follow my companions down.

The slopes of the volcano proved very steep; we slipped into veritable quicksands of ashes, avoiding the lava-streams winding down the sides like fiery serpents. While we worked our way down, I talked a great deal, for my imagination was too full not to go off in words.

'We're in Asia, on the coast of India, in the Malay Archipelago, or in the middle of the South Seas! We have gone right across the Earth, and come out at the antipodes!'

'And the compass?' asked my uncle.

'Oh, the compass,' I said with embarrassment. 'If we listened to what it said, we would think we'd headed north all the time.'

'So it lied?'

'Lied? Not exactly.'

'Then this is the North Pole?'

'No, not actually the Pole, but . . .'

There was something that was indeed difficult to explain. I no longer knew what to think.

Meanwhile we were getting near the greenery which had looked so inviting. I was tormented by thirst and hunger. Fortunately, after two hours' march, a beautiful countryside came into view, completely covered with olive trees, pomegranates, and vines which seemed to belong to no-one in particular. Besides, in our beggarly state, we were not inclined to be choosers. What ecstasy we felt pressing these delicious fruits to our lips, and biting whole clusters off the purple vines! Not far off, amongst the grass under the delicious shade of the trees, I found a spring of fresh water. It was bliss to plunge our hands and faces into it.

While we were still enjoying a well-earned rest, a child appeared between two clumps of olives.

'So!' I cried. 'An inhabitant of this blessed country!'

He was a poor little creature, very badly clothed, rather sickly, and apparently much alarmed by our appearance. Indeed, half-naked as we were, with our untidy beards, we must certainly have presented a bizarre spectacle: unless this was a country of robbers, we were likely to frighten the natives.

Just as the urchin was about to run away, Hans darted after him and brought him back, ignoring the kicks and screams.

My uncle began by calming him down as well as he could, and then enquired in good German:

'What is the name of this mountain, my little friend?'

The child did not answer.

'Good,' said my uncle. 'We are not in Germany.'

He then asked the same question in English.

Still no answer. I followed the proceedings with great interest.

'Is he dumb?' cried the professor, who—very proud of his multilingualism—then tried the same question in French.

Continuing silence.

'Let's try Italian then. Dove siamo?'*

'Yes, where are we?' I repeated, slightly impatiently.

The boy said nothing.

'Humph! Will you answer!' cried my uncle, who was getting annoyed and shaking the urchin by the ears. 'Come si noma questa isola?'

'Stromboli,'* answered the little shepherd-boy, escaping from Hans's grasp and running through the olive trees towards the plain.

We weren't bothered about him! Stromboli! What an effect this unforeseen name produced on my mind! We were in the middle of the Mediterranean, surrounded by that Aeolian Archipelago of mythological memory, in that ancient Strongyle where Aeolus* held the winds and tempests on a chain! And those rounded blue hills to the east were the mountains of Calabria! And that volcano on the southern horizon was Etna, terrible Etna itself!

'Stromboli, Stromboli!' I repeated.

My uncle accompanied me with words and gestures. We were like a choir singing in unison.

Oh, what a journey, what an amazing journey! We had gone in by one volcano and out by another, and this other was nearly 3,000 miles from Snæfells, from the barren shores of Iceland and the outermost limits of the world! The hazards of our expedition had brought us to the heart of the most fortunate country on the globe! We had exchanged the lands of eternal snows for those of infinite greenery; and the greyish fogs of the freezing wastes above our heads had become the azure skies of Sicily!

After a delightful meal of fruit and cool water, we set off again towards the port of Stromboli. It did not seem advisable to say how we had arrived on the island; with their superstitious mentality, the Italians would certainly have thought us devils thrown up from the fires of Hell. We accordingly resigned ourselves to being mere victims of shipwreck. It was less glamorous, but safer.

On the way I heard my uncle murmuring:

'But what about the compass: it *did* point to the north! What can the reason be?'

'Really,' I said, with an air of great disdain. 'It's much simpler not to have to explain it!'

'What! A professor at the Johanneum would be disgraced if unable to discover the reason for a phenomenon of the physical world!'

Thus speaking, my uncle, half-naked, with his leather purse around his waist and settling his glasses on his nose, became once more the terrible professor of mineralogy.

An hour after leaving the olive-grove we arrived at the port of San Vincenzo, where Hans asked for his thirteenth week's wages. These were duly given him, together with heartfelt handshakes.

At that moment, even if he did not share our very natural feelings, he at least gave in to a most unusual display of emotion.

He touched our hands lightly with the tips of his fingers, and he smiled.

45

WE have now come to the end of a tale which many people, however determined to be surprised at nothing, will refuse to believe. But I am armed in advance against human scepticism.

The Stromboli fishermen received us with the kindness due to those who have undergone shipwreck. They provided food and clothing. On 31 August, after a wait of 48 hours, we were conveyed by a little *speronara** to Messina, where a few days' rest helped us recover from our fatigue.

On Friday, 4 September, we boarded the *Volturne*, one of the French Imperial Postal Packet-Boats,* and landed three days later in Marseilles, our minds submerged in only one problem, that of the wretched compass. This inexplicable fact continued to seriously bother me. On the evening of 9 September we arrived in Hamburg.

I will not attempt to describe Martha's amazement and Gräuben's joy at our return.

'Now that you're a hero, Axel,' said my dear fiancée, 'you will never need to leave me again.'

I looked at her. She was weeping and smiling at the same time.

I leave to the imagination whether Professor Lidenbrock's homecoming produced a sensation in Hamburg. Thanks to Martha's indiscretions, the news of his departure for the centre of the Earth had spread throughout the whole world. People had refused to believe it, and when he returned, they still refused.

However, the presence of Hans and a few items of news from Iceland slowly modified public opinion.

Eventually my uncle became a great man, and myself the nephew of a great man, already something to be. Hamburg gave a civic banquet in our honour. There was a public meeting held at the Johanneum, where the professor told the story of our expedition, omitting only the episodes involving the compass. The same day, he deposited Saknussemm's document in the municipal archives, and expressed his deep regret that circumstances stronger than his will had not allowed him to follow the footsteps of the Icelandic explorer down to the very centre of the Earth. He was modest in his glory, and it did his reputation a great deal of good.

So many honours made people jealous, of course. The professor received his share of envy, and since his theories, based on facts that were certain, contradicted the scientific doctrines of the fire in the centre, he engaged in some remarkable debates with scientists of every country, both in writing and in the flesh.

As for myself, I personally cannot accept the theory of the cooling of the Earth. Despite what I have seen, I believe, and always will do, in the heat at the centre. But I admit that circumstances which are still not properly explained can sometimes modify this law under the effect of certain natural phenomena.

At a moment when these questions were still being hotly discussed, my uncle experienced a real sadness. In spite of his entreaties, Hans decided to leave Hamburg; the man to whom we owed everything would not let us repay our debt. He was suffering from homesickness for Iceland.

'Farväl,' he said one day, and with this simple goodbye, he left for Reykjavik, where he arrived safely.

We were singularly attached to the excellent eider-hunter; although he is no longer with us, he will never be forgotten by those whose lives he saved, and I will certainly see him one last time before I die.

As a conclusion, I should perhaps say that this *Journey to the Centre of the Earth* created a sensation in the whole world. It was translated and published in every language: the most important newspapers competed for the main episodes, which were reviewed, discussed, attacked, and defended with equal fervour in the camps of both believers and unbelievers. Unusually, my uncle enjoyed during his lifetime all the fame he had won, and everyone, up to and including Mr Barnum himself, offered to 'exhibit' him in the entire United States, 'very much making it worth his while'.

But a worry, which might almost be called a torment, slipped into this fame. A single fact remained unfathomable: that of the compass. Now for a scientist an unexplained fact is mental torture. But Heaven intended my uncle to be completely happy.

One day, while arranging a collection of minerals in his study, I noticed the much-discussed compass, and began to examine it again.

It had been in its corner for six months, without suspecting the fuss it was causing.

Suddenly I was flabbergasted! I shouted out. The professor came running.

'What is it?'

'The compass ...'

'We-ell?'

'The needle points south not north!'

'What are you trying to say?'

'See, the poles are reversed!'

'Reversed?'

My uncle took a look, did a quick comparison, and

then made the whole house shake with a superb aerial leap.

What a light shone in his mind and in mine!

'So,' he cried when he could speak again, 'when we arrived at Cape Saknussemm, the needle of this accursed compass showed south instead of north?'

'Obviously.'

'Then our mistake is explained. But what could have caused this reversal of the poles?'

'Nothing simpler.'

'Explain yourself clearly, my boy.'

'During the storm on the Lidenbrock Sea, the fireball magnetized the iron on the raft and so quite simply disorientated our compass!'

'Oh!' exclaimed the professor, then burst out laughing. 'So it was all a trick done by electricity?'

From that day onwards, my uncle was the happiest of scientists. I was the happiest of men, for my pretty Virland girl, giving up her position as ward, took on responsibilities in the house in Königstrasse as both wife and niece. There is little need to add that her uncle was the illustrious Professor Otto Lidenbrock, a corresponding member of every scientific, geographical, and mineralogical society in the six continents.

THE END

EXPLANATORY NOTES

3 *Lidenbrock*: *Lid* is German for 'eye-lid', *brocken*, 'crumb, lump (of coal), or scrap' or 'to pluck'.

Axel: perhaps from *axe* ('axis'); also *lexa* ('words') backwards.

4 *the Johanneum*: a famous classical grammar school, founded in Hamburg in 1529 and still in existence.

ghelenites, fangasites: neither word seems to be in the dictionaries. The first may even mean 'gelignites' ('gélinites' is a variant spelling in French).

5 *Davy*: see note in ch. 6; *Humboldt*: Baron von Friedrich H. A. (1769–1859), German naturalist and traveller, also worked in Paris, author notably of *Kosmos* (1845), an essay on the physical constitution of the globe; *Franklin*: Sir John (1786–1847), British Arctic explorer, died after discovering Northwest Passage—as proved by an expedition later organized by his wife; *Sabine*: (later General) Sir Edward (1788–1883), British astronomer, accompanied Ross and Parry to Arctic 1818–20, specialist in terrestrial magnetism.

Becquerel: either Antoine César (1788–1878), used electrolysis to isolate metals from their ores, or possibly his son and assistant Alexander Edmond (1820–91), researched into solar radiation and diamagnetism; *Ebelmen*: (Verne: 'Ebelman') Jacques Joseph (1814–52), French chemist who synthesized precious stones; *Brewster*: probably Sir David (1781–1868), Scottish physicist, invented the kaleidoscope; *Dumas*: Jean-Baptiste André (1800–84), French chemist, noted for his research on vapour density and atomic weight; *Milne-Edwards*: see note in ch. 37; *Sainte-Claire Deville*: Charles (1814–76), French geologist, wrote *Éruptions actuelles du volcan de Stromboli*.

6 *Tugendbund*: 'League of Virtue' (1808–16).

Gräuben: Verne wrote 'Graüben' throughout, but, in line with normal German practice, this has been changed to 'Gräuben': *graben*, 'to dig (out), excavate, mine, burrow';

Grauen, 'horror, dread'; *üben*, 'to drill or exercise'; *from Virland*: ('Virlandaise') not a recognizable German word: undoubtedly one of Verne's mystifications based on 'ViRlaNdaisE' and on 'Vinland' (the Scandinavian colony in N. America, *c*.1000, settled from Iceland) + *vir* (Latin for 'man'; cf. 'virile'—it is Gräuben who wears the trousers).

8 *Bozérian*: (Verne: 'Bozerian') two brothers who produced luxurious bindings in Paris at the time of Napoleon.

Snorre Turleson: Snorri Sturluson (1179–1241), politician and historian, wrote a saga of St Olaf, rejecting some of the grosser hagiographical elements in his sources: this work forms the central part of his *Heimskringla*, chronicling Norse mythology and early history. At this time, books in Iceland were entirely made out of vellum, not just the covers.

runic: Verne saw runic characters on stone inscriptions near Oslo in 1861. In 1875, he said that he based his runes on those of an illustration in *L'Univers pittoresque*. The characters here resemble only approximately the runes used in Scandinavia from about 450 to the 1200s (and in Anglo-Saxon Britain between 650 and 1100). They were known to few people, hence were thought to have occult powers.

10 *loin of veal with plum sauce . . . prawns in sugar*: this would seem to be poking fun at the tendency of some northern nations to eat sweet things with meat. But it may also be a sign of the diabetes that Verne was later to contract.

12 *double m*: the corresponding rune is ᚸ which, as Lidenbrock says, is intended to equal a double *m*, given that the other *m*'s in the message are ᛘ . The French edition, nevertheless, gives 'm.rnlls': this has been corrected to 'mm.rnlls', in the light of Verne's own transcription of ᚸ on the next page, namely *mm*.

stain: there is an anecdote, reported by Maurice Métral in *Sur les pas de Jules Verne* (Neuchâtel, Nouvelle Bibliothèque, 1963), that Verne found the faded log-book of a frigate captain called Pierre Leguerte; it had a bloodstain on the last page, and he is meant to have often speculated what had happened to the author. But Métral is often unreliable, and there is no supporting evidence for this story.

13 *Arne Saknussemm*: loosely based on Professor Árni Magnússon (1663–1730), an Icelandic scholar who travelled on behalf of the King of Denmark to collect the manuscripts of the Sagas—and who always wrote in Latin. Some of his material was destroyed during a fire at the University of Copenhagen in 1728.

Avicenna: or Ibn Sina (980–1037), Islamic scientist and author of nearly 200 works; *Bacon*: Roger (1220–92), English philosopher and scientist, studied optics and gunpowder, accused of dealing in black magic; *Lull*: Raymond Lully (or Lull) (*c*.1232–1315), Spanish theologian and philosopher, author of the 'Lullian method' towards systematic knowledge; *Paracelsus*: (1493–1541), Swiss healer, advocated 'folk' and 'chemical' remedies to illness, also investigated mining and minerals in the Tyrol.

14 *Altona*: Sartre's *Les Séquestrés d'Altona* (1959) was set here, and the stage directions indicate a 19th-century room; in the autobiographical *Les Mots* (1963), Sartre repeatedly emphasizes his early passion for Verne.

15 *the Alster*: joins the Elbe in Hamburg.

18 *that word-puzzle ... solved*: part of Oedipus's quest was to solve a riddle set him by the Sphinx.

19 *in the third line*: in fact, in the second and third lines.

20 *A mere 'nothing'*: (French: *rien*) 'nothing' in medieval Latin is *rem*, which is not only the ending of *craterem*, but also the previously quoted *mer* ('sea') backwards.

22 *20 letters ... 133 digits*: the figure for 20 letters (20 factorial) is correct, provided that all 20 letters are different; but 132 factorial has in fact 125 digits.

25 *from ... first*: Verne probably derived this method of constructing a cryptogram from Poe's 'The Gold Bug', which he quotes extensively in his 'Edgar Poe et ses œuvres' (1864).

calends: the first day of the month in the Roman calendar.

Leyden jar: a kind of electrical condenser with a glass jar as a dielectric between sheets of tin foil, invented in 1745 at Leyden University.

27 *August Petermann of Leipzig*: (Verne: 'Augustus Peterman') (1822–78), cartographer and geographer, in fact from Hamburg and Gotha.

30 *4,000 miles*: ('quinze cents lieues') in ch. 39, the same
'quinze cents lieues' is given as the distance *still* to go. In
ch. 25, the radius at the latitude of Iceland is given more
exactly as 'quinze cent quatre-vingt-trois lieues et un tiers'
(3,936 miles, if a French league is taken to be exactly
4 km—the modern figure for the equatorial radius is 3,963
miles).

Fourier: Jean Baptiste Joseph (1768–1830). Known today
as a mathematician for the Fourier series, his work was
carried out on heat diffusion, which led him to invent the
idea of partial differential equations.

31 *Poisson*: Siméon Denis (1781–1840), applied mathematician at the Sorbonne. Known today for the Poisson
distribution in statistics.

Sir Humphry Davy: (1778–1829). Chemist, notably discovered laughing-gas, invented miners' safety-lamp and
proved that diamond was a form of carbon; *1825*: Lidenbrock is 'about 50' in 1863 (ch. 1)—which makes him
about 12 in 1825!

32 *the first days of the world*: a hangover from biblical
language.

41 *Valkyrie*: in Norse mythology, one of the maidens who
served Odin and rode over the battlefields to select dead
heroes and take them back to Valhalla; also an allusion to
Wagner, whom Verne refers to in several works.

42 *Thorvaldsen*: Bertel (1770–1844), of Icelandic descent.

43 *southeastern*: Verne: 'sudouest'.

45 *Hamlet's shadow stalking along the legendary terrace*: even
Hamlet seems to be a source for the decidedly all-englobing
Verne: including the theme of madness, the cemetery, the
skull, and the quotation 'That is the question' (ch. 33).
Hamlet was drawn from ancient Scandinavian legend, and
ultimately from Iceland, where the story features in many
different Sagas.

46 *Mykiness, the westernmost of the Faroes*: Verne: 'Mygan-
ness, la plus orientale [des Féroë]'.

47 *Point Skagen*: no trace of this point seems to exist: Verne
may have taken the name from Cape Skagen in Denmark,
mentioned two pages previously.

49 *danger of the congregation*: as early as 1810, travellers reported on the faulty state of the roof tiles in this church.

50 *'vadmel'*: literally 'homespun'.

53 *Olafsen*: Eggert Ólafsson, who carried out a comprehensive field survey of the country and people of Iceland (published in Danish in 1772); *Povelsen*: pseudonym of Bjarni Pálsson (1719–79), author of *Des vice-lavmands . . . Island* (Copenhagen, 1774–5), translated as *Voyage en Islande . . . (1802)*; *Troil's studies*: (Verne: 'Troïl') Uno von Troil, Bishop of Linköping then Archbishop of Uppsala, author of *Bref rörarde en resa til Island MDCCLXXII*, Uppsala, 1777 (translated as *Letters on Iceland*, 1780); *Gaimard*: Joseph Paul (1790–1858), French naturalist, directed scientific expeditions to Northern Europe (1835–6, 1838–40), author of *Voyage en Islande et au Groënland, exécuté pendant les années 1835 et 1836 sur la corvette 'La Recherche' . . . dans le but de découvrir les traces de 'La Lilloise'*; *Robert*: (Louis) Eugène (1806–79), collaborated on Gaimard's book; *Duperré*: Victor Guy (1775–1846), government minister; *Blosseville*: Jules A. R. P. (1802–33), French navigator, disappeared off east coast of Greenland; *Reine Hortense*: Verne is here indirectly alluding to one of his major sources, Charles Edmond (pseudonym of Edmund Chojecki—collaborated with Adolphe d'Ennery on many plays, who himself collaborated very extensively with Verne), *Voyage dans les mers du Nord à bord de la corvette la 'Reine Hortense'* (which contains a map of the journey and a geological chart of Iceland) (1857).

57 *'Efter'*: Icelandic: 'eftir', Danish: 'efter', Swedish: 'efter'. Hans's 'Danish' is in fact mostly Swedish—unlike the rest of the Danish in the book, which is more or less authentic.

58 *Ruhmkorff*: Heinrich Daniel (1803–77), born in Hanover, worked in Paris, invented miners' safety-lamp. According to one authority, it was in fact in 1858 that he was awarded the 50,000-franc prize for the most important discovery in the application of electricity (the induction coil in 1851).

60 *Et quacumque viam dederit fortuna sequamur*: 'And whatever route fortune gives, we shall follow' (*The Aeneid*, bk 11, v. 128).

61 *It covers 1,400 square 'miles'*: Verne wrote *milles* (without inverted commas), but since the area of Iceland is 39,738 square miles, these must be Icelandic 'miles'.

   trachytic: volcanic rocks with a rough or gritty surface.

63 *tuff*: produced by the consolidation of volcanic ash.

64 *Saurböer*: modern Saurbær.

   '*Färja*': Danish: 'farvel', Swedish: 'färja'; '*Der*': Danish and Swedish: 'där'; '*Tidvatten*' and '*förbida*' ('wait'):
65 Swedish; '*Ja*': Danish and Swedish.

68 '*Spetelsk*': Danish: 'spedalsk', Swedish: 'spetälsk'.

69 *the Alfa and Heta*: the Alfta and Hitard. 'Alfa' and 'Heta' are homophones in French of the Greek letters alpha and eta.

73 *1229*: cf. '1219' in ch. 6.

74 *pyroxenic rocks*: any of a large group of dark-coloured minerals containing silicates of magnesium, iron, and calcium.

80 '*hastigt*': Danish: 'hastig', Swedish: 'hastigt'.

82 *90 miles away*: the shortest distance from Iceland to Greenland is in fact about 180 miles.

83 *Pluto*: the Greek god of the Underworld.

86 '*Forüt*': 'förut' is Swedish for 'before, formerly'.

91 *Monday, 1 July*: this should logically be 'Monday, 29 June'.

92 *facilis descensus Averni*: 'an easy descent into the Avernus [Hades]' (*The Aeneid*, bk 6).

94 *Wuttemberg in Bohemia*: probably Württemberg, S. Germany.

95 *aisles of a Gothic cathedral*: Verne's 'contre-nefs' is apparently not in the dictionaries.

98 *the outlines of seaweeds and club-mosses*: seaweeds and club-mosses occurred in radically different environments, and at different times: is Verne here deliberately mixing opposites?

102 *Sigillarias*: fossil trees, leaving impressions in coal deposits; *Asterophyllites*: fossil plants, with leaves arranged in whorls, found in coal formations.

103 *smell ... disasters*: fire-damp has no smell: hence the danger!

108 *folia*: (Latin: 'leaves') laminae or thin layers.

113 *Spa*: in Belgium; *Tœplitz*: German name for Topliţa in modern Romania.

114 *Bach*: German for 'brook'.

115 *'the man of the perpendiculars'*: Hetzel referred to Verne's 'sense of the perpendicular'—meaning his ability to extrapolate from fact to fiction.

119 *east-a-quarter-southeast*: $101\frac{1}{2}°$ in absolute bearing.

120 *1,474.4°*: sic.

40: Verne: 'douze [lieues]'.

126 *a sign of madness*: a precursor of the self-cancelling logic of Catch-22: if one is sane enough to reason, then, given the circumstances, one must be mad; and if one is mad . . .

139 *Proserpina*: the Roman goddess of the Underworld.

grotto of Guachara: either Guácharo (after name of birds who live there), near Caripe, Venezuela, or Guácharos Caves, near Pitalito, Colombia; *Mammoth Cave in Kentucky*: *A Journey to the Centre of the Earth* (London, 1872; New York, 1874; and Boston, 1874) may have been a source for *The Adventures of Tom Sawyer* (written in 1875–6). The most striking scene of Twain's book is perhaps ch. 31 where Tom and Becky are lost in an underground labyrinth near the Mississippi. It bears many similarities to Verne within the space of a page and a half: '. . . aisles . . . names [on the] rock walls . . . a little stream of water . . . carrying a limestone sediment . . . steep natural stairway . . . branched off . . . spacious cavern . . . stalactites . . . numerous passages that opened into it . . . crystals . . . subterranean lake, which stretched its dim length away until its shape was lost in the shadows. He wanted to explore its borders . . . "All is lost"': there is also the same following of the stream, the same method of getting lost, the same panic flight 'at random', and the same protracted description of the last gleam of light going out.

141 *Bulliard*: Jean-Baptiste François, called Pierre (1752–93), published notably *Histoire des champignons de la France* (1784).

146 *Sir James Ross*: 1800–62, British naval officer, explorer of the Arctic and Antarctic; located the North Magnetic Pole in 1831.

146 *opposite shore*: Verne here quickly skips over the fact that there is little reason to cross the sea.

149 *from the northwest*: Verne's 'nord-est' has been corrected, as the subsequent calculations of distance require a constant wind-direction.

151 *Dipterides*: a genus of fish with only two fins.

152 *Cuvier*: Georges (1769–1832), French naturalist, founder of comparative anatomy and of palaeontology, researched on fossil bones, author notably of *Discours sur les révolutions du globe* (1821).

Leptotherium: 'Lepto': 'long and thin', 'therion': 'wild beast'; *Mericotherium*: 'meri': 'part'; *Lophiodon*: large, horse-like fossil mammal from the Eocene Period; *Anoplothere*: extinct pachydermatous quadruped; *the Creator... in one*: an example of Verne's sacrilegious humour (which was cut from the standard American translation (the 'Hardwigg' one), together with many other references to biblical Creation).

Megatherium: herbivorous edentate up to 18 feet tall, resembling the sloth, found in S. America; *Protopithecus*: extinct genus of monkeys, related to the modern howlers, found in the great caverns of Brazil.

153 *not yet ready for him*: this is the clearest indication of Verne's (and the mid-19th century's) last-ditch attempt to reconcile science and the literal truth of Genesis: by admitting that the Earth existed long before man, but with each of the six 'days' of Creation being in fact an 'age'.

156 *but feeble reductions of their fathers of the first ages*: this remark follows on from the idea that 'fish and reptiles alike are more perfect the longer ago they were created' (ch. 32). The creationist view held that positive evolution was not possible, only comparatively minor degradations or regressions: psychologically, this may be interpreted as consonant with a pre-Freudian inferiority complex with respect to one's forefathers.

159 *ichthyosaurus*: 'ichthy': 'fish', 'saur': 'lizard'.

plesiosaurus: 'plesi': 'near'. It is possible that one source of this battle between the two sea-monsters is Thomas Hawkins, *Great Sea Dragons* (1840).

162 '*Straight ahead*': previously the object had been 'to windward'.

Blumenbach: Johann Friedrich (1752–1840), German zoologist and anthropologist, pioneer in craniology.

163 *Mount Hekla*: near Mýrdals-jökull, S. Iceland; famous throughout the Middle Ages as a gateway to Hell. Major eruption in 1104.

To have taken an island for a sea-monster!: this section announces *Vingt mille lieues sous les mers*, which begins with evidence of a supernatural-seeming sea-monster.

an overflow thermometer: the first cousin of the escapement clock which generates 'Maître Zacharius' (1854), with clear Freudian overtones.

164 *underneath Britain*: in fact central France.

169 *magnetized . . . board*: *Le Sphinx des glaces* (1897), which culminates at an immense magnetic centre near the North Pole, is foreshadowed in this scene.

170 *passed . . . Europe*: in 'L'Éternel Adam' (1910), this scene is paralleled when the protagonists sail in search of land *over* the successive countries of a flooded Europe.

175 *wild Ajax*: in Greek mythology, a hero of the Trojan War, who killed himself when Achilles's armour was given to Odysseus.

176 *I moved*: ('j'allai'); 1864 edition: 'I was going to' ('j'allais'). The difference of a single letter, phonologically minimal and without much significance for the primary meaning, has nevertheless an important consequence on conceptions of tense in the novel: in particular, it marks a distinction between action and intention, between objective movement and internal reflection.

177 *glyptodonts*: extinct mammals in S. America, resembling giant armadillos.

its depths: the text from here until 'Although I was certain I was covering ground we hadn't been over before . . .' (ch. 39) was added in the seventh edition (1867).

178 *great dislocations of the terrestrial mass*: the text here bears witness to its own irruption into the previous edition.

large bulges: Verne's 'extumescences' is not in the dictionaries: perhaps one of his puns ('ex-tumescences').

179 *Milne-Edwards*: Henri (1800–85), French zoologist, worked especially on molluscs and crustaceans; *Quatrefages*: Jean-Louis-Armand de Quatrefages de Bréau (1810–92), French naturalist and anthropologist, opponent of Darwinism, author of *Histoire de l'homme* (1867).

Boucher of Perthes: (1788–1868), discovered flint tools near Abbeville in 1837 and 1844; and argued from 1846 onwards that man had existed in prehistoric times. Only following their recognition in Britain in 1860 were his arguments really debated in France in 1865 (hence the extra chapters in 1867). The theme of the undiscovered genius is an important one in Verne.

Falconer: Hugh (1808–65), British palaeontologist and botanist; *Busk*: George (1807–86), British specialist in the fossil marine polyzoa, author of several scientific works, including *Description of the Remains of Three Extinct Species of Elephant* (1865); *Carpenter*: William Benjamin (1813–85), British physiologist and author of *A Popular Cyclopaedia of Natural Science* (1841–4) and *Zoology . . . and Chief Forms of Fossil Remains* (1857, reissued 1866); also an expert on dredging the ocean depths; also author of *The Unconscious Action of the Brain* (1866–71).

Élie de Beaumont: (1798–1874), French geologist, argued that not all mountains are the same age.

180 *elephas meridionalis*: ('southern elephant') lived in Eurasia in the Quaternary Era.

181 *Barnums*: Phineas Taylor Barnum (1810–91), famous American showman; also prominent in Verne's 'Le Humbug'.

Orestes' body: Orestes, mythological son of Agamemnon and Clytemnestra; *Asterius*: or Asterion, a son of Minos II, King of Crete, perhaps descended from Aeolus; killed by Theseus, and so believed by some to be the Minotaur; *Pausanias*: Greek traveller, topographer, and author (*c.*100 BC): his best-known work was translated as *Pausanias; ou voyage historique de la Grèce. Nouvelle édition augmentée du 'Voyage autour du monde', par Scylax* (1797).

Trápani and *Palermo*: in Sicily; *Polyphemus*: son of Poseidon (Greek god of the sea and of earthquakes), and one of the Cyclopes; *Félix Plater*: Félix Platter or Platerus (in

Latin), the Elder and the Younger, German physiologists, studied in Montpellier in 16th century; *Cassanion*: Jean Chassanion or Joannes Cassanio, author of *De gigantibus, eorúmque reliquijs, atque ijs, quæ ante annos aliquot nostra ætate in Gallia repertę, sunt...*, Basle, 1580; *Cimbrians*: or Cimbri, German tribe originally from N. Jutland, but retreated northwards in 3rd century, and thus probably introduced the runic alphabet into Norway and Sweden; *Peter Camper*: (1722–89), Dutch anatomist, author of works on mammalian anatomy; *Scheuchzer*: Johann Jacob, Swiss author of selections from the Bible dealing with natural history, published with a commentary in 1731, translated from Latin as *Physique sacrée ou histoire naturelle de la Bible* (1732).

183 *the facial angle*: in the racist theories current at the time, it was the facial angle that helped determine the race.

184 *Hoffmann's ... shadow*: E. T. A. Hoffmann (1776–1822), German writer; the character is Peter Schlemihl, referred to in Hoffmann's *New Year's Eve* as drawn from *The Shadowless Man; or the Wonderful History of Peter Schlemihl* (published in German in 1839, English translation in 1843), by Louis de Boncourt Chamisso. But the essential idea here is undoubtedly the traditional one that a person who loses his shadow is in the land of the dead.

185 *cypress and thujas*: the cypress traditionally represents mourning, and the thuja is also known as the arbor vitae ('tree of life'). The juxtaposition of opposites is a favourite topos of Verne's.

186 *Proteus*: a minor sea-god, herdsman of the flocks of the sea, also had the power to take on many shapes; *Neptune*: Roman god of the sea; part of the ritual of his festival was the building of shady arbours (*umbrae*) made of boughs. Verne is here also hinting at a parallel evolutionary tree.

Immanis pecoris custos, immanior ipse!: 'Guardian of a monstrous herd, and more monstrous himself!': Verne is borrowing this quotation from Victor Hugo, *Notre-Dame de Paris* (pt 4, ch. 3), which adapts Virgil (*Bucolica*, v. 44), 'formosi pecoris custos formosior ipse' ('Guardian of a fine herd, finer still himself').

187 *bough ... shepherd from before the Flood*: cf. books 11 and 12 of *The Odyssey*, where Odysseus in Hades sees a giant pursuing wild animals with a club in his hand.

187 *Lartet*: Édouard-A.-I.-H. (1801–71), French archaeologist, one of the founders of palaeontology. In 1864 he discovered an ivory blade depicting a mammoth in the Dordogne area.

considerations.: this is the end of the main section of text added in the 1867 edition.

188 *I . . . vista.*: 1864 edition: 'The professor shared my hesitation; he was unable to find his way through this uniform vista. I realized this from the occasional words that he uttered.'

'But . . . again.': 1864 edition: ' "But certainly, by working our way along the coast, we'll get near Port Gräuben again." '

'It's . . . recognized.': this paragraph contains three very minor changes from the 1864 edition.

'But then . . . me.': five minor changes from the 1864 edition in these eight paragraphs, including the addition of the word 'rust-covered'.

'It's all most peculiar.': in the 1864 edition this paragraph was preceded by the words: ' "And me still less, Uncle." '

189 *'It . . . dropped it . . .'*: this paragraph was ascribed to Axel rather than Lidenbrock in the 1864 edition; and has also undergone four minor textual changes.

I shook . . . head.: these three-and-a-half paragraphs are new in the 1867 edition. In their place, the 1864 edition read: ' "Hans," said my uncle, shaking his head.¶ Then he examined the weapon attentively.¶ "Axel," he said to me in a serious tone, "this knife . . ." '

nor even . . . the Earth!': these words were added in the 1867 edition. From this point onwards, the two editions are identical, with the exception of one punctuation mark changed in the sixth paragraph following.

206 *Esk, in Jan Mayen, not far from Spitzbergen*: in fact several hundred miles away. The volcano on this island, which is extinct, does not seem to be called Esk (whereas there is an Esk in Alaska).

212 *'Dove siamo?'*: Verne: 'Dove noi siamo?'

213 *Stromboli*: the 'Strombolian' type of eruption involves moderate, intermittent bursts of expanding gases.

Aeolian Archipelago: also known as the Eolie or Lipari Islands, off NE Sicily; *Strongyle*: ('cone') Latin name for Stromboli; *Aeolus*: king of storms and winds, and inventor of sails.

214 *speronara*: a small rowing-boat.

Volturne: French for Volturno, a river in S. Central Italy; site of a victory by Garibaldi in 1860; 'VoltuRNE' is also an anagram of 'Vern'; *French Imperial Postal Packet-Boats*: one of the rare allusions in Verne's works to contemporary political events: Napoleon III had been Emperor since 1852.

APPENDIX

Verne as Seen by the Critics

1. 'We have the good fortune to have to draw to our readers' attention a new and charming book by M. Jules Verne. The [sic] Journey to the Centre of the Earth, like Five Weeks in a Balloon and The British at the North Pole [original title of the first volume of Captain Hatteras], combines the most solid scientific qualities with the amusement and interest of a drama and a tale. Young people and people in society will not find a more agreeable and excellent guide than M. Verne to initiate them to geological discoveries and to the mysterious and so little known history of the Earth's massif on which we live' (Stahl [pseudonym of Hetzel]: publicity announcement in the Magasin d'éducation et de récréation, 1866).

2. 'This fictional journey has all the colours and movement of reality; and if the author had not taken the care to tell us himself, the illusion would be almost too complete. M. Jules Verne is a true scientist, a delightful story-teller, and a writer of the greatest merit' (Gustave Landol, 1864).

3. 'Journey to the Centre of the Earth is phantasmagoric; but the reader is so caught up in Axel's anguish ... that the improbability of the events takes on secondary importance ... Interior and exterior adventures are so closely interwoven that it is not until Axel has completed his final test that we emerge from the fiction and begin to wonder where the truth of the matter was ... One feels that the book was Verne's escape ... into the world of dream, one that he was never to undertake again on this scale' (Jean Jules-Verne, 1973, trans. by Roger Greaves).

4. 'Lidenbrock conveys a new vision of space. What distinguishes two points now is how close or how far they are from the centre ... The corresponding map is a half-line, where points situated at the same distance are indistinguishable. This accounts for Lidenbrock's behaviour, "the man of the perpendiculars", whose only wish is to "slide down the Earth's radius", and for whom the worst torture is to have to navigate on that interior sea that we find so magnificent' (Dominique Lacaze, 1979).

5. 'The particularity of the novel of initiation, when it is the work of a great writer, is to be both realistic and symbolic. It is the adventure novel, however, that best lends itself to this spiritual transformation, and I have observed with astonishment that, while the great Romantic novels have not been considered by the critics as initiatory works, those of Jules Verne have ... If Baudelaire is Poe's brother, Verne is his half-brother' (Léon Cellier, 1964).

6. '[Verne] recycles the literary ocean-depths: the Promethean challenge of the terrestrial forces, the quest for the father ... His scientists and explorers are nature's psychoanalysts. They unlock the ancient desires of the sleeping elements. Electricity liberates the earthly powers. And a scientific alchemy officiates at the perfect marriage between fire, water, earth, and air. The fantastic forms a bottomless pit. Verne gives lessons in chasms ... More poetic than scientific, he leaves his dreams a margin. His heroes don't land on the moon or reach the centre of the Earth. His conquerors of the impossible maintain that distance, allowing the mysteries to be seen but not touched. He doesn't destroy our myths' (J. Cabau, 1974).

7. 'The volcano participates doubly in Verne's binary topology of prominences and cavities: it is a hollow pyramid connecting the heavens with the underground inferno; and it is a two-way sliproad on to the dual carriageway of human traffic leading into and out of the Earth's core ... The Vernian law of reciprocity requires that not only should man urgently plumb the depths of the planet, but that the Earth's core should equally strain to escape from secrecy, burst through its fragile skin and so stand revealed in the sight of men ... The volcano is the entrance to an inverted universe; and it preserves an imprint of that inversion, comprising a portion of the subterranean world violently everted and solidified, the abyss turned inside out by an explosion. Conversely, the outer world appears to have slipped inwards ... in the shape of a gigantic cavern, equipped with its own Mediterranean and pseudo-firmament' (Andrew Martin, 1985).

8. 'There are these sparks. Science and suspense ... Say Ruhmkorff lamp, gutta percha, Snæfells, or guncotton, and something happens. In the nineteenth century, the scholar-travellers of the unknown left on a quest for the Holy Grail' (J.-F. Held).

9. 'But if this detour, this journey belongs to the imaginary, there is another, very real, trajectory: the thread of the tale. The

234 *Appendix*

novel becomes itself through the journey. The two advance together. One can even argue that the novel is the real aim: when he comes back, Axel publishes his story . . . The book is both an imaginary journey to the centre of the Earth and a real journey to the centre of the text' (Daniel Compère, 1977).

Some of these quotations were first cited by Simone Vierne in *Jules Verne* (Balland (Phares), 1986), to whom grateful acknowledgements are recorded here.